purity
reigns

LaureL shadrach series
1

purity reigns

stephanie perry moore

MOODY PUBLISHERS
CHICAGO

ISBN-10: 0-8024-4035-5
ISBN-13: 978-0-8024-4035-8

We hope you enjoy this book from Moody Publishers. Our goal is to provide high-quality, thought-provoking books and products that connect truth to your real needs and challenges. For more information on other books and products written and produced from a biblical perspective, go to www.moodypublishers.com or write to:

Moody Publishers
820 N. LaSalle Boulevard
Chicago, IL 60610

5 7 9 10 8 6

Printed in the United States of America

For Daddy

Dr. Franklin Dennis Perry Sr.

God used you to show me
the vision for this series.
I love you,
my friend, mentor, and dad.
Every girl desires to have a
wonderful father.
I'm blessed to have two:
you and God!

contents

acknowledgments

I've finished writing this novel at a difficult time in my life. Quite frankly, I want things that I just don't have. Not material stuff but position, power, and influence. I have big dreams, and not all have come true. This is frustrating because my thirty-second birthday is steadily approaching, and I want to do it all. So, for my readers who aren't satisfied with their teenage life, I understand.

However, I'm learning that God is good all the time and that His love can sustain in the midst of adversity. Give all your feelings of anxiety, despair, and stress to God. He can fix the tough stuff. For when you focus on Christ and possess a pure heart for Him, before you know it, He'll give you your heart's desire. I know, because this series was once just a dream. Now you are reading the first book. God is awesome!

To Franklin and Shirley Perry (my parents); my publishing company, Moody Press (particularly Greg Thornton);

my reading pool (Laurel Basso, Sarah Hunter, Carol Shadrach, Marrietta Shadrach, and Nyka Wiseman); my assistants, Nakia Austin and Rachel Splaine; my daughters, Sydni and Sheldyn; my husband, Derrick Moore; and last but not least, my Lord Jesus Christ . . . without you all, this novel would not have been written. Thanks!

ONE

keeping it together

"Picture this," my handsome boyfriend of two years, Branson Price, whispered in my ear. "The hottest guy in school and the cutest girl in school—seniors! A couple again, ready to rule Salem High School. Every guy wanting her, every girl wanting him, but everyone else is out of luck because they want each other. Do you know what I'm talking about, Laurel? Can you picture it?"

All I could do was smile. He was talking about us. Though he had been my boyfriend since we were sophomores at one of the top schools in the state of Georgia, we had an on-again, off-again relationship. We were as fragile as the wind at times. Everything seemed to blow us apart, but we had made a commitment over the summer and now it was August. It was a hot day in Georgia and we were at Six Flags enjoying one of our last days of freedom. However, we weren't really disappointed about the thought of going back to school. After all, it was our senior year, the moment we'd been waiting for since kindergarten.

We were standing in line for the Freefall, a ride that dropped hundreds of feet straight down. I could imagine my heart falling out of my chest. I was scared and didn't want to get on the ride.

"You're riding with me," Branson said. "Relax. I've got ya."

I relaxed.

Six Flags was packed. It was the Friday before we had to go back to school. Although it was scorching outside, we were having a blast. We didn't need friends to accompany us. Just the two of us—that was the way I liked it. All of his attention focused on me.

Branson had grown a lot in our junior year. He was more mature as well as a lot more physically fit. Muscles rippled in his chest and a cute, tailored haircut accented his blond hair. He'd worn glasses the year before but now, with his new contact lenses, those beautiful blue eyes were even more vivid. Every time I peered his way, I was mesmerized. He had me in the palm of his hand. Whatever he said, I wanted to do instantly. Even the most uncomfortable things seemed all right.

As we waited in the long line to get on that scary ride, Branson propped himself up on the black iron gate, pulling me to him and whispering sweet things in my ear. He cupped his hand against the back of my head, then slowly fluttered his fingers through my light-brown hair, which fell in layers down to the middle of my back.

I loved his attentions. But when I saw a little girl of about nine years old watching us, I felt uncomfortable. She reminded me of Little Orphan Annie, from the movie I'd seen with my brothers the week before. This wasn't a sight she should see: a couple practically making out in an amusement park.

I didn't really want to stop my boyfriend. Things had

been great between us in the last two months and I didn't want to rock the boat before school started. However, my instincts pulled me back.

"What are you doing?" Branson asked with subtle frustration. "You're beautiful and you're mine. Don't turn away."

I always melted when he called me beautiful. My three younger brothers called me exactly the opposite, especially when I took too long in the bathroom washing my hair, putting on makeup, and deciding what to wear.

I was always trying to do more to make myself look beautiful. But no matter what I did, I never felt like I measured up to the other girls.

My best friend, Brittany Cox, was drop-dead gorgeous. She had blonde hair like Christina Aguilera. She dressed, talked, and even walked like some of the hottest pop-music stars. I didn't want to be like her, but I did admire her natural beauty. If she woke up and went to school without even combing her hair or putting on any makeup, she would still be beautiful . . . and she knew it. Her attitude made me lay into her quite often, but I guess that's what best friends are for—telling each other the real deal. Besides, I wouldn't have traded her for anything. I knew she would always be there for me.

My other good friend, Meagan Munson, was a cute redhead who was extremely shy.

I came across as shy to some people, but I wasn't. I was just not really confident, except on the balance beam in gymnastics. You can't step on the balance beam and do flips without being totally confident that you're going to make your next move.

I'd been competing in gymnastics since I was in the fourth grade. Salem High School didn't have an official gymnastics team, which was a huge disappointment to me. But Mom signed me up at Rockdale County Gym, which had lessons three evenings a week and every Saturday during gymnastics season, which started the same week school did.

Rockdale Gym always competed in a big state meet right after Christmas. This year I really wanted to qualify and compete in the National Championship. All the scouts would be there, and I desperately wanted to go to UCLA or the University of Georgia on a gymnastics scholarship.

The previous year, however, had not been a good one for me. My coach, Mr. Milligent, who had the build and face of a professional wrestler, was really hard on me. I guess that was good in a way. He always got me to do my best.

As much as I wanted to go to college on a scholarship, I also wanted to quit gymnastics altogether so I could spend more time with my friends. That was part of the reason Branson and I broke up so many times. He kept saying, "Gymnastics is coming before me again."

I always tried to make him feel like that wasn't the case, but one day I lost it and said, "Yeah, just like football comes before me every single time. And what are you gonna do about it?"

He shocked me when he said, "I wanna break up."

I thought back to the disheartening moments of being apart from him all that May, not even being able to go near his locker in the hall for fear he might be with another girl.

I didn't want to go through all that again. I wanted this to be the picture-perfect senior year. I could see us being the happiest, hottest senior couple around. As we got off the ride, which I had survived thanks to Branson holding hands with me, I knew we would make it.

My father, Rev. Dave Shadrach, was the pastor of our church in Conyers, Georgia, where we lived. We'd moved there from Conway, Arkansas, four years before. Conway and Conyers were both small country towns, and I had grown comfortable in the growing city of Conyers.

Being a preacher's daughter had never been difficult for me . . . until that year. I started to feel emotions for my boyfriend that went totally against the things my dad preached about every Sunday and in our Saturday Bible study and at our Friday-night youth meetings. Abstinence was one of his big messages to us teens, and as adamant as he was about it to the church congregation, he was even stronger on the issues with his own children. He always said he knew how tough it was for us kids, but I knew he wouldn't understand or want to hear about my inner struggles. I could never walk up to him and say, "Dad, I just want to put my hands all over Branson, and when he gives me a peck on the cheek I want the kiss to last for days."

There is so much I didn't dare say. Partly because I knew my dad didn't really want to hear it, and also because I knew I shouldn't feel that way.

Branson and I walked hand in hand to the next ride. Since we were both sweating, we decided it should be Splash Waterfalls.

As we walked I thought, *Most precious God, I thank You for answering my prayers and putting me back with my boyfriend. Only You know how much I care for Branson and what a big place he holds in my heart. Now You have given him back to me and I know I need to honor that. But whenever I walk with his strong, tanned hand in mine, like now, I feel a little dizzy inside. I know those feelings are a sign of trouble. Help me stay focused in this relationship. In Jesus' name, Amen.*

"Earth to Laurel." Branson's voice broke into my thoughts. "Hey, where did you go?"

"I'm sorry," I said, tearing my gaze from the beautiful, cloudless sky. "I was just looking above. It's such a pretty day."

All of a sudden, with thousands of people walking all around us, he stopped me dead in my tracks and kissed me. After about six seconds, we pulled apart.

"I really dig it that you appreciate the little things," Branson whispered. "And that kiss should show you how much I appreciate you." His voice grew husky and seductive. "I want to appreciate every part of you. Why don't we leave Six Flags and go cruisin'?"

"Aw, c'mon," I said, pulling his hand. "Let's go on the log ride."

I really had been looking forward to Splash Waterfalls. But the main reason I put him off was that I didn't trust myself to leave with him, even though I had just prayed for strength.

The Lord knew I needed to stay in a public place. After some convincing, Branson finally conceded and we enjoyed the rest of the afternoon in the park.

We got home too late to make it to the Friday-night youth meeting, so we skipped it. As Branson drove me home in his blue Camaro, with my head buried in his chest, I was deep in thought. I wondered how I would be able to fight these feelings that Branson was having trouble holding in. I could tell he wanted to take our relationship further, but I couldn't agree to that. A strong voice in my heart and my spirit said no. But my flesh was speaking a language altogether different. And with a guy as hot and handsome as the 6'1", 210-pound stud beside me, I didn't know what might happen if I wasn't careful.

"I can't believe you don't have a boyfriend," I said to my best friend, Brittany, as she helped me prepare for my date that Saturday evening.

"Boyfriends tie you down," Britt replied. "I prefer the freedom of being able to go out with a different guy every weekend if I want to. That's why I never let a guy think I'm his. Besides, if I had a boyfriend, I wouldn't be able to take care of you and Branson like I do."

"Oh, and I thank you so much," I said sincerely, wrapping my arms around her neck. "We wouldn't be back together if it wasn't for you. I don't know what you told him, Brittany, but it saved us."

She hugged me back. "Don't mention it. It was my pleasure. Do you like my nail polish?" She held up her square, bright-red nails.

"It's a pretty color," I conceded, "but it is totally not you." Brittany was into French manicures, cotton-candy nail polish, and natural colors that go with anything. She got her fingernails and toenails done at a salon every Saturday while I was at Bible study. We were opposites, but for some weird reason, we had a connection.

My family wasn't at all like hers either. When her parents got divorced, she and her brother, Gabriel, went to live with their father. Now that Gabe was off at the University of South Carolina, Brittany was practically an only child. Her father gave her everything she ever wanted.

Meagan was spoiled too. Her parents were still together, but they worked all the time. Meagan was practically raising her younger sister, Elise, who was entering the ninth grade. Their parents always left before Meagan and Elise got up for school, and they didn't return until ten or eleven at night. They were both lawyers—her dad was with the district attorney's office and her mom was in private practice. Meagan always said she was proud of her parents for their accomplishments, but I knew she wished they spent more time at home.

My mom was always around. She'd been a stay-at-home mom all my life, even after all four of us kids were in high school. I was about to start the twelfth grade. My oldest brother, Liam, the creative one, was going into eleventh grade. My middle brother, Lance, the athletic one, was starting tenth grade, and my youngest brother, Luke, the brain, would be in ninth. Luke was the smartest of my brothers because he'd been around older kids all his life. My father's first priority was always home and family, even though he was the pastor of an always growing church. That was definitely a good thing, but sometimes he could be a little overbearing.

"What should I wear for my date with Branson tonight?" I asked Brittany, holding up two shirts. One was a pale-blue blouse with spaghetti straps and pearly buttons that I begged my mom to let me get last year because "everyone" was wearing them. The other was a scoop-neck beige tank top that went with just about every skirt I owned.

"Ugh! I don't like either one of those," my friend ragged on me.

"But these are my favorites," I cried. I knew my closet wasn't a walk-in mall, but I thought I looked good in some of my stuff.

Brittany tilted her head. "I'm sorry, but both of those shirts are so . . . yesterday. You know what I'm saying? Hey, you asked my opinion, and that's it. You have got to get some new stuff already. Tell me you've gone shopping for new school clothes. You can't be wearing last year's stuff. You're a senior now!"

"My mom has picked me up a few pieces here and there," I said in a weak voice.

"Where are they? Pull them out," Brittany insisted, her hands on her curvaceous hips.

"Actually, I haven't even seen them yet. When I was at Six Flags with Branson yesterday, she took my brothers shopping and she said she bought me some stuff."

Brittany's big blue eyes opened as large as the dangly gold hoops hanging from her earlobes. "Girl, tell me I just heard you wrong! Do you mean to tell me you let your mother pick out clothes for you? And she just got you a few pieces two days before school is about to start?"

"So?"

"So do you want to look good for your date tonight or not?"

I wasn't sure how to answer that question. Sure, I wanted to look good for my boyfriend, but after being with Branson yesterday, I knew the surface stuff didn't matter anymore. Our relationship had gone deeper than that. After all, Branson said he wanted to take it to the next level, and that proved things were extremely serious between us. He loved me and I loved him, and if I wore a paper bag, then my Branson wouldn't care.

So, after talking myself into believing that Brittany's comments didn't make sense, I tossed the tank top on the nearest chair, pulled on the spaghetti-strap top and a modest-length skirt, and smiled at my friend and myself in the mirror.

Brittany sprawled across my bed. "What are you doing tomorrow?"

"It's Sunday; I'm going to church," I replied. It was a dumb question to ask. Brittany knew I went to church every week of my life.

She sat up and folded her shapely legs under her. "But you went to that Bible study thing at your church this morning. And tomorrow's the day before our first day of school!"

"So what's your point?" I asked, curling the ends of my long hair with a hot iron.

"How can you stand being cooped up in church all the time when there's so much stuff to be done? Aren't you sick of being a pastor's kid?"

"Are you sick of being a doctor's kid?" I teased.

"My dad is so tired after working all week that the last thing he thinks about on Sunday is getting up and going to a worship service. And that's just fine with me," Brittany bragged, as if sleeping in on Sundays was a good thing.

I turned away from the mirror, sat next to her on my bed, and looked her in the eye. "For me, going to church is a joy. I have so many insecurities and so many crazy thoughts, the house of the Lord is a safe haven for me. It's a place where I can thank God for all He has done in my life."

She didn't look convinced.

"Our church is different from a lot of other churches around."

"Oh yeah? How so?"

"Why don't you come with me and find out? We go everywhere else together. Why not church?"

Brittany stared at her fingernail polish. "I wonder why they call this 'waitress red.' I've never seen a waitress wear this color. It really is pretty, though, don't you think?"

I couldn't believe my friend was so set against learning more about God. Suddenly, for the first time in four years, it hit me that Brittany couldn't care less about the Lord. But I needed a friend who could keep me accountable, a friend who would help me follow the things of the Spirit, not the things of the flesh. If waitress-red fingernail polish and fashionable clothes were so important to Brittany, how in the world could she help me get closer to God?

"So," she said, grabbing a pillow, "tell me about Six Flags yesterday. Did you go straight home afterward or did you guys go . . . you know . . . parking?"

"What are you insinuating, Brittany?"

"Oh, don't play dumb with me. Remember our conversation two months ago when I spent the night over here? You told me everything that was inside that Christian brain of yours. You said you wanted to put your hands all over every inch of Branson's body."

I got up and looked under the bed for my shoes. "Do you have to remind me? You know I feel horrible about that. I'm trying to put those thoughts out of my mind."

Her eyes sparkled. "Why?"

"You know why," I said, slipping on my Converse All Stars.

"Yeah, yeah, yeah. That Bible stuff again. OK, I'll leave you alone for now. But I've got to tell you two things."

"What?" I asked, not sure I wanted to know.

"First of all, we're seniors now, and Branson is so hot he can have his pick of any girl at Salem High. So don't give him a reason to pick someone other than you. Get my drift?"

I nodded. "What's the second thing?"

Brittany looked at my tennis shoes. "You have got to get yourself some platform shoes, girl. Seriously!"

We had a good, long laugh. Then I noticed the time.

"Hey, Branson's going to be here any second. I'll call you after church tomorrow."

"No way," Brittany said, getting up off my bed. "Call me tonight. I want to hear the details."

As I walked her to her car, Branson's blue Camaro pulled up. "Hey, Britt," I said, "I've got to run inside real quick. I don't have my purse or keys, and I need to let my mom know I'm leaving. Can you tell Branson I'll be right back?"

"No problem," she said. "I'll be happy to talk to him for you."

"You're the greatest," I told her, giving her a hug. "I'll be right back." I raced up the sidewalk and barreled through the door.

"So, where are you two going?" my mom asked.

"Just a movie," I said, grabbing my purse and keys off the table in the hall.

"Which one?"

"I don't know yet," I said. Rolling my eyes, I added, "Something PG, Mom, I promise."

"Sweetheart, I know you're getting older and you don't think you should have to report to your parents about everything you do. But I need to know where you're going."

"Don't you trust me?" I asked.

Mom straightened a wisp of my bangs. "Sometimes it's better to be safe than sorry. Besides, you're a teenager, and it seems you really like this boy."

It scared me how perceptive my mom could be. But then, she was more than my mom; she was my friend. I'd always found it easy to talk to her when I was younger. But lately, with all the tough issues I was facing, things were different. It was like she could read my mind and knew what to say about stuff even before I brought it up. Maybe it was the Lord talking to me through her. Or maybe she just remembered her own adolescence and was giving me the same advice her mother gave her. That didn't mean I always liked what she had to say. Even when I knew she was telling me what I needed to hear, my spirit often rebelled against it.

"Look, Mom, I'll be in by eleven," I promised. "We plan to watch the movie, not make out the whole time."

"Don't get sassy with me, Laurel. I'm not joking."

"Sorry, Mom."

"Just be responsible and have a good time."

That's all I wanted to hear. I gave her a quick hug, then headed out the door. Brittany was doing a great job keeping Branson occupied. I was worried he wouldn't be entertained, but when I came out he was all smiles. The three of us talked for about five minutes, then said our good-byes and I hopped into Branson's car.

We drove for about ten miles, and Branson hadn't said a word to me.

"Why are you so quiet?" I asked.

He gave me a strange look but still didn't say anything.

"Talk to me, Branson."

"Britt told me you struggled with what to put on for our date tonight, that you didn't think I'd like any of your clothes because they're old or something. I hate it when you go through all that trouble for me. I thought our relationship was deeper than that."

"I just want to look good for you," I said.

"Baby, you always look gorgeous." Branson pulled into the parking lot of the movie theater. "As a matter of fact, I love that outfit you've got on." He reached over and easily unbuttoned the top button of my blouse.

"What are you doing?" I asked, staring down at my too-exposed chest.

"I just thought you needed to loosen up a little," he said, putting the car into park. "We're going to a movie, not prep school." He leaned over and nibbled on my ear. "I've been thinking about you all day."

"C'mon, we're gonna be late for the movie," I said, opening my door.

As Branson stood in line to buy tickets, I lingered near the theater entrance, replaying his words in my head. Why in the world would Brittany tell my boyfriend the opposite of what had happened in my room? She was the one saying my clothes were too old to wear. It made no sense. She had to have some reason to misrepresent the situation. Or maybe Branson got it all wrong. Whatever it was, something wasn't right and I was determined to find out what was going on.

Branson smiled at me from the ticket line. He was so cute! Two teenage girls behind him started giggling. Though I couldn't hear what they were saying, I could tell they were whispering about how attractive he was. It was clear that they would have loved to be out on a date with him.

What if Brittany was right about other girls giving him what I wouldn't? Could I let that happen? A wave of jealousy ran up my spine. I didn't want Branson to be with anyone besides me. I walked up to him and kissed him on the cheek. I wasn't trying to gloat, but I wanted those girls to know this man was taken.

Sitting in the back row of the theater was kind of romantic, I thought. We held hands until the movie started. Then Branson cupped his hand around my knee and started sliding it up my skirt.

"What are you doing?" I whispered.

"No one can see us," he whispered back. "And with the surround sound in here, no one can hear us either." He tilted my head toward his and kissed me passionately.

I melted in his arms. Then his hand went back to my leg and started moving to an area that was definitely off limits. Without interrupting the kiss, I grabbed his wrist and kept him from going any farther. Suddenly, he stopped kissing me. He sat up, crossed his arms over his chest, and stared at the movie screen.

I didn't know what to say. Couldn't he see how hard this

was for me? Sure, I wanted to give him what he desired. And to be perfectly honest, I had some of those same desires too. But part of me knew it was wrong, and that part had allowed me to stop the passion.

I reached over and started stroking his hand. I wanted to tell him, *"Look, I understand this is tough. It doesn't seem fair. But I love you and we're going to be OK."* But his eyes stayed focused on the screen, and his hand remained tightly clenched around his forearm.

"I'm sorry," I whispered, still rubbing his hand.

Without looking at me, Branson yanked his hand back, got up, and left the theater. Suddenly, without his warm body next to me, the place felt frigidly cold.

I waited for five minutes, rubbing my arms and trying to figure out what was going on in the movie. *OK, Branson,* I thought, *you can come back any time now.*

Five more minutes passed. I began to wonder if my boyfriend had gone home without me. If he was still at the theater, was he waiting for me to come out? I felt confused and fragile. We had just gotten things back on track, and with school starting in two days I had to do whatever it took to make sure things stayed right between us.

I exited the theater in a panic. I looked everywhere for Branson. I even asked the guy working the refreshments counter to check the men's room for my blond-haired boyfriend. When he came out alone, shaking his head, I realized that my man had bailed on me.

My stomach started churning. I headed for the door, briefly explaining to the manager that I had to check the parking lot for my boyfriend's car. I wished I had a cell phone like Britt and Meagan. I did have some money with me, so I could call home and ask my dad to pick me up if I had to.

Of course, I could never tell my father why my boyfriend had left the theater without me. Branson and his family were strong members of our church, and everyone in our congregation thought we were the perfect match. If my dad knew why he had to come and pick me up, Branson's name would end up on the "not good enough for my daughter" list for sure. Then I'd never be allowed to date him again.

Relief swept through me when I saw Branson's car still parked in the same place. I heard loud rock music coming from it, so I knew he was inside. I walked up and tried to open the passenger door. It was locked. I tapped on the tinted window. No response. I banged harder. *Why won't he let me in?*

The tears I'd been holding back refused to stay captive any longer. I leaned against the car, sobbing. Finally I heard the lock pop up. I quickly brushed the tears off my cheeks and crawled in.

Branson was leaning way back in his seat, not even looking my way.

"I'm so sorry," I whispered. Then, without thinking about it, I started unbuttoning my blouse. He turned to me and smiled. Then I seduced him as if it was the most natural thing in the world.

The windows in the Camaro fogged up. Somehow Branson got on top of me in the driver's seat. His hands mingled through my hair. Even though we were only seventeen, I felt like an adult. I didn't want his kisses to stop.

Then, without warning, my spirit prevailed and I pulled away.

"Laurel, what are you doing to me?" Branson asked with disgust. "You can't do this. Look at me, I'm excited."

Without even asking if I wanted to continue, he started kissing my neck. He was double my weight, but I prayed for God to give me the strength to push Branson off me. I shoved with so much force he bumped his head on the top of the car.

Rubbing his skull with one hand, he yanked me out of his seat with the other. "Get back to your side of the car. I'm taking you home now!" Before I could fasten my seat belt, he had the engine revving. "This is crazy," he grumbled as he shoved the car into gear. "I don't know why I thought things would work out for us. I thought you were ready for me."

"I'm sorry," I whimpered. "I'm sorry."

I hadn't been trying to lead him on. But I felt like I was two different people. One girl desired him; the other wanted to push him away.

Branson drove me home in silence. I could practically see the steam coming out of his ears. He pulled up to the curb but didn't turn off the engine.

"Branson, I . . ." I wanted to say something, anything, whatever would make things right between us. But I couldn't think of the right words, and I didn't think he'd hear me anyway. I got out of the car. The Camaro's tires started squealing the instant I shut the door.

I adjusted my clothes and ran my fingers through my hair to pull out the tangles. Then I trudged up to the front porch and let myself in. As soon as I opened the door, Mom came in from the kitchen.

"You're home early," she said. "How was the movie?"

I didn't want to be rude, but I really couldn't talk just then. So I just continued on up to my room without a word.

Mom followed me. "Laurel, honey, what's wrong?"

"Nothing, Mom." I flopped onto my bed and buried my face in the pillows.

"Sweetie, I know you," she said, standing next to my bed. "Something's up."

I lay still, ignoring her, pretending the world didn't exist.

"If you don't want to talk about it, then go ahead and get some rest," Mom said, then she slipped out of my room and gently closed the door.

The next morning my head was pounding from lying awake half the night waiting for Branson to call, and then crying the rest of the night. But after I cleaned up and got dressed, I started to feel a little better. My family went out for breakfast to our favorite place, the Cracker Barrel. Their butter-pecan pancakes made my day look almost bright.

Dad's church looked more like a theater than a sanctuary. Instead of a robed choir, we had a live band with drums and guitars. A group of teens and adults always put on skits and plays to coordinate with the message. We even had spotlights and a terrific sound system.

My brother Liam sang a solo with the band. By the time my father got up to deliver the sermon, the congregation was ready to hear what he had to say.

His message touched my heart in a powerful way. He talked about what a privilege it is to be part of the body of Christ. And with that privilege comes responsibility. God has high expectations of His children. The members of God's family should live godly, holy lives.

I knew I wasn't doing that. I didn't have a firm grip on my Christianity, and that needed to change. I had really been struggling between obeying God and giving in to my fleshly desires. I needed to trust God and believe that His way was best for me.

After the service, I headed up the aisle toward the door, where several people were standing around talking to my father. I saw Branson's parents there, and he was waiting beside them. I slipped out a side door and nearly bumped into Foster McDowell.

Foster was tall and handsome, with a tan to die for. He'd come to our school in the middle of last year, and he struck me as sort of quiet and mysterious. When baseball season came around, he ended up being the star of the team.

"Foster, right?" I asked, pretending I wasn't sure.

"Yeah." He flashed me an intriguing smile. "So, Laurel, how's your summer been?"

Before I could think of an answer, Branson came up and grabbed my hand. "Hey, Foster," he said, "I see you're back on the street. How was that Christian camp of yours?"

"FCA camp? It was great."

Branson sounded like he was trying to make a joke at

Foster's expense. But Foster didn't seem to care. He looked calm and collected. He also looked like he was eyeing me.

"Come on, Laurel," Branson said, tugging on my hand. "Your dad said he wants to talk to you."

"Hey, it was good to see you," Foster said as Branson pulled me away. "See you tomorrow at school."

I smiled back at Foster. Then I pulled my hand out of Branson's grip.

My dad came up to us before I could ask Branson what he thought he was doing. "I'm so happy that my daughter has found a good guy like you to date," he said, patting Branson on the back.

Branson put his arm around me and squeezed my waist, playing the part of the attentive boyfriend and making it seem like we were still the cute couple everyone thought we were. I still wanted us to be together. I just wasn't sure what it would take to make that happen. At the moment, it felt like we were barely keeping it together.

hoping
for sunshine

hurry up and get in!" Brittany yelled at me. Apparently I was taking too long to get into her car.

"I hope this drizzle doesn't turn into much more," I said, climbing into her brand-new, black Jetta. A twenty-thousand-dollar car seemed a little much for a high school senior. But Brittany was definitely spoiled, sometimes to the point of being a brat about it. She didn't mean to flaunt her wealth in my face. She just liked talking about her material possessions. As her best friend, I guess it was my job to listen.

"Close the door already! I don't want my car getting all wet."

"It's just sprinkling, Britt. Calm down."

"You should just be happy I'm picking you up," she said as she headed off toward school.

"Why do you say that?"

"Oh, come on," she replied. "We're seniors now. We can't have our moms dropping us off anymore. That would be way too corny. Besides, with me, you can ride in style. Much better than having Laura drop you off."

"My mom's name is Mrs. Shadrach to you."

"Yeah, right!" Brittany giggled. "Only when she's around. It's just you and me talking now."

"Whatever, Brittany." I really didn't want to get into this on the first day of senior year.

"Why does it bother you anyway?" Brittany persisted. "We are almost adults now, you know."

I tried to ignore her by staring out the window. The gray clouds mirrored my mood. This was supposed to be the happiest time of my life. The start of my last year in high school.

I remembered the first day I stepped foot in Salem High School four years ago. The walls seemed so big and the halls so long. I didn't know anyone from middle school because my family had just moved to Conyers. As the years passed I made friends, and the place that was once scary became as comfy and cozy as home.

Unfortunately, the one guy I most wanted to be cozy with was angry at me. He hadn't called since Saturday night. Oh, he'd put on a show in front of people we knew at church. But I wanted to talk through this whole thing. I wanted to see if we could work it out. I needed Branson to understand where I was coming from.

From the looks of that sky, it didn't seem like the sun was ever going to come out. I could only hope my day at school wouldn't be so dim.

"Hey, what's wrong with you?" Brittany's voice broke into my depressed thoughts. "We're supposed to be talking about the first day of school and it feels like I'm riding in the car alone."

"Sorry," I whispered.

"What you got to be sorry about, girl?" She glanced in my direction. "Your hair looks great. That blue eyeliner makes your brown eyes practically shine. You even have on a cute outfit."

Did Brittany really think that was all that mattered in life?

"OK," she said. "Maybe I'm not being sensitive enough. I'll put what's going on with me on the side and put you at the forefront of my thoughts. Now, talk to me. What's going on?"

"I don't know," I mumbled. "It's just that—"

"Trouble in paradise again, huh?"

"It's not at all paradise right now for Branson and me."

"Well, what exactly is the problem? You've got a hot guy who wants to be with you. So make it work. Don't rock the boat; don't shake the baby; don't jump off the bridge."

"What are you talking about?" I asked, totally confused.

"Let me put this into language you'll understand. You do whatever it takes to keep that boy. Got it? Whatever it takes, Laurel! That goody-goody act of yours is cute and all, but playing nice only *gets* the guy. It doesn't keep him."

I wanted to say, *"You're a fine one to be giving me advice."* I kept my mouth shut, but my eyes must have communicated the thought for me.

"Why are you looking at me like that?" she said. "You think I'm not telling the truth, that I don't know because I don't have a steady boyfriend? Look in my purse, and you'll find ten numbers from guys I could have right now with one cell-phone call. Hey!" Brittany hollered when another car almost crashed into us. "People sure don't know how to drive."

"Maybe you'd better slow down. It's raining kinda hard."

"I wish you didn't live way out in the sticks," she complained.

I never could understand why Brittany went out of her way to pick me up and take me to school. I told her she didn't have to, that my mom didn't mind driving since she had to take my brothers to school anyway. I guess she just wanted an entourage.

When we finally pulled into the school parking lot, Brittany looked at me with a pleading expression in her eyes. "Come around and get me," she begged.

"Why?"

"You've got that big umbrella."

"Are you making fun of my stuff? Where's your dainty little umbrella that curls up and fits in your purse?"

"I left it at home. I'm sorry for teasing you. Please don't make me walk in the rain." She was whining like a baby.

I shook my head. Brittany was one of those girls you either loved or hated. I loved her. Among other things, I found her extremely comical.

I did as my friend asked and we walked together, under my big umbrella, to the school building. As we stepped onto campus and went our separate ways, I held my breath. This was going to be the first day of my last high school year. I really wanted it to meet, or even surpass, all my high expectations.

Lord, I prayed, *go with me this year. Help me to please You in everything I do. I'm starting to become fearful of things unknown, but I know You've got my future in the palm of Your hand. Help me release it to You. Help me to be strong. And help me to have a good first day. Amen.*

Just then, I felt a strong, masculine hand grab hold of mine. Before I could look up, I got a kiss on my cheek. Then sweet words were whispered in my ear. "You look better today than you did in my dreams."

I smiled, still not looking up. My heart was warm because I knew who it was. And I knew I would be thinking about those words all night long!

Branson turned me toward him, put his hand under my chin, lifted my face to his, and planted a soft kiss on my lips. "We're OK," he mouthed.

We walked hand in hand down the hall. It was a feeling unlike any other. Girls were watching him and guys were watching me . . . some in awe and some just jealous. Even though we were surrounded by other people, I kinda felt like we were the only two in the school, because as long as I had Branson, no one else mattered. The rain was still pouring outside, but we were fine. Better than fine; we were great. The tough issues still hadn't been discussed, but I knew we could work through everything. Even though he hadn't called me the day before, at least he thought about me. Maybe at the same moment that I had wrapped my arms around my pillow and stared up at the ceiling pretending to see his face, he was envisioning mine too.

We decided to share a locker, and since mine was positioned better than his, that was the one we used. The first thing he did was pull a prom picture from last year out of his pocket and stick it to the locker. He must have planned ahead because there was already tape on the back of it. Then he took a marker, and even though we weren't supposed to mark up school property, he wrote, "Branson loves Laurel."

Just as I was about to kiss him, Meagan came up and grabbed my arm. "We're gonna be late," she hollered. "You're in my first-period class. Now, let's go. Come on."

Meagan tried to tug me away from my man. But Branson tugged back. They were pulling on me from opposite directions like I was the wishbone from a Thanksgiving turkey. Branson finally won, and I gave him a laugh, a hug, and a kiss.

Meagan started to leave without me.

"I've gotta go," I said. "But you . . . you really made my day!" I messed up his hair, then rushed to catch up with Meagan. This was not only going to be a great day but a great year. Branson had said we were fine, and that was the way my heart desperately wanted it to be.

"You're all smiles, I see," Meagan teased as we picked seats for our first-period class.

"Why shouldn't I be?" I said with a grin. "Things are great between Branson and me!"

"I'm glad you've got a steady boyfriend." She busied herself getting things out of her backpack.

"Meagan, you say that like you can't get somebody."

"Well, I don't have it like Brittany," she said, "with a different guy for every day of the week." She shook her head. "Still, there is this one guy . . ."

"Really?" I squealed. "That's great!"

"But I don't know what to say to him. Laurel," she pleaded, "you've got to help me. I mean, I don't want to just come out and reveal everything I've been thinking."

"So who is this guy?"

"I don't know his name. But he's really suave, you know? I mean, you can imagine him on a motorcycle poppin' wheelies, showing off like he was James Dean or something. Then again, he kind of looks like he could be a supermodel."

"OK, I get it. He's hot."

"Yeah, he's definitely a ten-plus."

As I tried to put my stuff on the desk without taking my attention away from Meagan, I misjudged the distance and my books and papers fell onto the floor. Meagan laughed. When I bent down to pick up my things, a kind gentleman bent down with me.

"Here, let me help you," a familiar voice volunteered.

"Thanks," I said. When I looked up I saw it was Foster McDowell who had come to my aid. "Thanks a lot."

After helping me pick up my mess, Foster asked, "So, how was your night?"

I was a bit taken back. I mean, why would he care how my night was? It seemed like a weird question. I answered anyway, not wanting to be rude. "It was great. And yours?"

"It was cool. I spent most of my time trying to imagine what the first day of school was going to be like."

"You too?"

"Since I've only been here less than one semester, I was tempted to call you and ask you to fill me in on everything. But I didn't have your number."

"Here," I said, grabbing a pen, "let me give it to you." I ripped out a corner of paper from my spiral notebook. "Call me anytime. I know everything there is to know about Conyers." I jotted down my number. "Not that I've been here all my life, but it is a small town. I can tell you all the places to go and hang out, where the library is, all that stuff."

"Thanks." After slipping my number into his pants pocket, he headed to the back of the class.

When I looked back at Meagan, she had a disturbed look on her face. "What's wrong with you?" I asked.

"That's the guy," she whispered, nodding toward Foster without looking his way. "He's the one I think is so hot. And you gave him your number! Laurel, you already have a boyfriend. Can't you think of anybody other than yourself?"

"What are you talking about?" I argued. "How was I supposed to know he's the guy you were talking about? You never said his name. I gave him my number because we're friends. He goes to my church, and he knows I have a boyfriend because he saw me with Branson yesterday."

Megan played with her pencil. "I could tell he likes you."

"Whatever!"

"You didn't even introduce me to him," she pouted. "I think you just want him for yourself."

"Oh, now you are really going off the deep end."

Fortunately, our teacher showed up at that moment. I wasn't excited about studying but getting into a book was much better than carrying on a hopeless conversation with Meagan.

She and Brittany were total opposites. I didn't agree with Brittany's style, but at least when she liked a guy she didn't make herself invisible. She fought for what she wanted, found ways around obstacles, and dealt head-on with competition. Meagan needed some of that spunkiness. I would never recommend going after a guy, but making yourself nonexistent to someone you want to notice you just doesn't make sense. A simple hello was all she had to say.

I wanted to be angry with her because she was blaming

me for Foster not noticing her. But then I remembered how immature I used to act when I wanted Branson to talk to me. I liked him way back in the ninth grade, and all that year, he never once looked my way. It bothered me when I saw him speaking to every girl in the hall except me. Then I realized that when he came my way I always turned around because I was too nervous to acknowledge him. When I finally mustered up the confidence to smile at him, he did notice me. And he had never forgotten!

When the teacher turned her back to write on the board, I wrote Meagan a note. "I'll introduce you to Foster after class. I'm sorry I didn't do it sooner. Great choice. He's a nice guy, and if I weren't with Branson . . . Just kidding!"

I passed the note to Meagan. She perked up after reading it, so I knew she had forgiven me.

True to my word, I introduced Meagan to Foster as soon as we got into the hallway after class. Then I made an excuse to leave so they could talk.

Halfway down the hall, I saw Brittany headed toward them. I cut her off. "Where do you think you're going?" I asked.

"I just want to find out who she's talking to. It seems to me that boy's got my name written all over him."

"I don't think so," I said. "Meg likes him."

"She can at least tell me his name. I want to log him into my address book." Brittany started toward them again, but I pulled on her shirt to stop her.

"Let go," she whined. "You're gonna ruin my blouse."

"I'll only let go if you promise to behave," I told her.

"Going over to introduce myself isn't against the rules."

"Oh, come on, who are you fooling? You just said you wanted to get with him. Meagan likes him, and it's her chance to—"

"What? Strike out?" Brittany replied.

I didn't like the mean, hateful way she was talking about

Meagan. But I let go of her shirt anyway. She stayed put but continued eyeing Meagan and Foster. I could tell she was planning something devious, plotting against Meagan, who was supposedly her friend. I was beginning to wonder just how much Brittany valued friendship.

Just then I remembered a promise I had made to the Lord about my senior year. I was determined to say what I thought and stop holding stuff in. In the past, I had always harbored my feelings inside and let them fester and grow. I knew I needed to deal with the tough issues and let people know my true feelings or one day they would explode.

I needed to start exercising my new resolve, so I said to Brittany, "You know, I see something wrong with this. Meagan is your friend, she likes this guy, and you just want to try and take him away from her."

"Take him away?" she asked, her thin eyebrows raised. "Those are pretty strong words. I can't take something away from Meagan that she never had in the first place. I mean, look at her. She's standing ten feet away from the guy and she isn't even trying to turn him on. This isn't elementary school, Laurel; this is high school. If she wants a guy to consider her as something more than a friend, she needs to do something."

I stood my ground without saying a word.

"OK, I won't give free advice," Brittany said, twirling her long blonde hair. "But anyone can see he's not interested in her." Brittany swung her hair over her shoulder and headed to her next class.

Meagan had asked me to watch from a distance so I could give her pointers on how she did. I wasn't an expert or anything, but I did have a boyfriend. And when I thought about that, I suddenly realized that I needed to tend to my own concerns and not sit there and baby-sit her. I hadn't seen Branson in almost an hour.

I tried to get Meagan's attention to let her know I had to go. But she wasn't looking my way, so I figured I was in the clear. After all, their conversation had already gone past the two-minute marker.

See, we had a thing around our school that if a guy talked to you for more than two minutes, at least he didn't think you were a geek. Knowing there were only a few more minutes until the bell rang, I left Meagan on her own and headed for my locker to meet with Branson.

"Where have you been?" he asked as I turned the corner. "I've been waiting for you."

"Do we have any classes together?" I asked, getting out my schedule.

Branson dug his schedule out of his book bag and checked. A big smile spread across my face when I noticed we had the same fourth-period math class. I would have loved to have had more than one class, but if I could only have one, fourth period was perfect. That was right before lunchtime, which meant an extra forty minutes each day that we could spend together. I guess it was a good thing he wasn't in all my classes, 'cause if he was, I wouldn't get any work done.

"Come on, Laurel," he said, gathering his stuff. "Walk with me to my class."

"But it's on the other end and mine is that way."

"I've been standing here waiting for you," Branson complained, "ever since I got out of class. I don't know what you were doing. I'm just asking you to walk me to my class. You know you'll get back to yours on time."

I felt like saying, *You should be walking me to mine.*

That's when I realized that my resolve to let people know what was on my mind could have very different results in various situations. I knew I had to express myself more often, but I had to do it wisely. I didn't want to become rude.

I reached for Branson's hand, but he reached around my waist instead. So I wrapped my arm around his waist too. The stares were intense as we walked toward his class. He was my guy and I was his girl, and I wanted everyone to know how much I loved him.

On the way down the hall, we ran into my brother Liam, who sometimes acted like he was my dad instead of my brother.

"Hey," Branson said to Liam.

Liam lifted his head in the air like he thought he was cool. I could tell he wanted to speak to me, and I could guess about what. I knew he wouldn't like the physical display I was showing with my boyfriend.

I figured I should give him the chance to say what was on his mind. I could always let his words go in one ear and out the other. "I have to talk to Liam," I said to Branson. "Why don't you go on to class so you're not late."

"Go ahead," Branson replied, being the sweetheart that he is. "I'll wait."

I walked a few feet away with Liam. "So, what's the deal?" I asked.

"It looks really cheap walking down the hall like that so everyone can see. Don't you have any self-respect?"

"OK, OK," I said, not being able to ignore his comments after all. "But Liam, you're not being fair. He's my boyfriend and I was just walking him to his class. I don't know what your problem is."

"My problem is him," Liam said, pointing his thumb at Branson. "Every time you guys break up, he snags five or six girls, and then he brags about it to the whole football team."

"And how do you know that?" I asked. I could feel my face getting hot.

"Lance tells me everything he says. And you know what? One day we're both gonna tell Branson Price what we think of him."

"Oh, really?" I said, my hand on my hip. "And what's that?"

"That he's not as tough as he thinks. And that he shouldn't treat anyone the way he treats you."

My blood was really boiling now. "And what's wrong with the way he treats me?" I demanded.

"Whenever he decides he's ready to get together with you again, you go right back to him. And you two go walking down the hall hand in hand, or arm in arm, or whatever you call that thing you guys were doing."

"And what's wrong with that?" I asked.

"It makes people believe all those rumors Branson says about you."

I couldn't believe what my brother was saying. "Branson would never spread anything about me!" I threw up my hands in disgust. "Why am I listening to this? I'm gonna be late to class." I turned to leave, but my brother grabbed my elbow.

"Fine, Laurel, have it your way," he said. "But the next time you want someone's shoulder to cry on because that jerk walked all over you, don't come to me. Because when you get back together with him, it's not easy for me to forget what he's done to you." Liam walked away, shaking his head.

It wasn't the first time my brother had tried to tell me Branson was no good, or at least not good enough for me. I just had to figure out whether or not to believe him.

I looked back at Branson. He was laughing with a group of freshman girls, who were giggling at everything he said. Suddenly my brother's advice seemed way too real.

"Branson," I called, with a touch of anger in my voice, "let's go."

He said good-bye to the girls and sauntered up to me. But when he tried to put his arm around my waist again, I pulled away. Whether my brother was right or not, I didn't feel comfortable with that anymore.

Branson didn't seem bothered. He just chatted away, saying the silly, fun things that always made me really like him. At the end of the hallway, he grabbed my hand and took me under the stairs to a little corner I had never seen before. As the bell rang he kissed me passionately. It was so unexpected that all I could do was respond.

No freshman could handle this man, I assured myself, or make him feel appreciated the way I did. I was his girlfriend and that was enough.

We were still kissing when the bell stopped ringing. At that instant, I heard the voice of our principal, Dr. Wood.

"To my office, now!" she yelled.

Dr. Wood dragged me into her office, and the vice principal escorted Branson into his. When the door to the office closed, my heart skipped a beat. Dr. Wood was a friend of my mother's. They were in the same Bible study class. Explaining to my mom why I was in the principal's office on the very first day of school was not something I was looking forward to.

Even though they were friends, the principal and my mother were definitely opposites. Dr. Wood was unmarried, held a doctorate degree, and had a lot of power. My mother, on the other hand, stayed at home, had four children, and was only responsible for running the household. Although that's a really tough job, she didn't have a faculty and about two thousand students to control. I respected and loved my mom. She was always there for us. However, as I thought about my own life and where I wanted to go, Dr. Wood's career path seemed far more appealing. I thought it strange that they shared a common bond, but then again, Christ was the tie that bound their friendship together.

"Laurel," Dr. Wood asked as she sat in her chair, "do you want to explain yourself?"

My lips refused to move. I didn't think she would appreciate me telling her that I was in love and sometimes love makes you do crazy things.

"You're not talking to me, Laurel. You are one of the brightest students here. What's going on with you?"

She must not have checked my grades lately, because there was nothing marvelous about them. I had barely managed a 3.0 GPA last semester.

She must have noticed the look on my face. "Laurel, I know you're not an A student, but I do keep up with you. You're not a troublemaker. You have a positive attitude and you've got goals. A lot of kids here don't look forward to anything past the end of the day, but you're better than that. I don't want your vision to be clouded because of a man." She leaned back in her chair. "I know you and Branson were dating last year, but what I witnessed today was much more serious."

"I do apologize, Dr. Wood," I managed to say. "I know that's unacceptable behavior on school grounds."

"You're right about that. Physical affection should not be displayed in the Rockdale County School System. But Laurel, is that acceptable elsewhere? I know I'm not a teenager, but I do understand what guys think."

She straightened and looked me in the eye. "I don't want you to go down the road that leads to a dead end. Right now, I'm talking to you as your principal, so I'm limited as to what I can say. But if you need a friend, I want you to know that you can come and talk to me anytime. My door is always open."

Part of me was tempted. Maybe it would help to get an adult's view on things. It was possible Dr. Wood might have some interesting insights on my situation. But I knew there was no way.

"What's the problem, Laurel?" she asked.

I decided to be honest with her. "How can I talk to you when I know you'll just tell my mom everything I say?"

She smiled. "Well, maybe it's your mom that you need to go and talk to."

I let out a quick laugh. "Yeah, right. Like I could tell her some of the crazy things I've been thinking."

Dr. Wood leaned closer to me and spoke softly. "Laurel, have you prayed about your feelings? Have you released this to the Lord?"

"Yes, definitely," I said.

She said nothing, but her expression encouraged me to explain myself.

"God has stopped me many times from going too far with Branson. But there's a whole other side to it, Dr. Wood. It's hard to explain."

"It's called the flesh, Laurel," she told me, "and I understand. I'm forty-seven years old and not married. I struggle with the same issues you do. But every time those inappropriate thoughts and desires come into play, I just talk to the Lord and ask Him to help me. And He does. Do you know how He does it?"

I was hanging on her every word. "How?"

"He teaches me to love Him more than anything or anyone. To focus on His Word and what He has for my life. Laurel, you've got to quit thinking about pleasing yourself and pleasing Branson and focus on pleasing God. The strength you lack in that area will be restored. Trust me. God did it for me and He'll do it for you too."

The thought of being forty-seven, unmarried, and still struggling with this area was beyond my comprehension. Granted, I didn't know when I was getting married, but I sure hoped it would be way before Dr. Wood's age. Then again, if it was God's plan for my life that He was my only mate, would that be enough for me? I knew the answer had to be yes, that I was supposed to love God regardless of where He led me.

As Dr. Wood walked me out the door, I thanked her several times. She told me I wouldn't be getting any punishment for my actions. "This will just be between us," she said.

I thanked her again. "I won't ever let you down," I promised, "at least not in this area."

"I'm going to hold you to it," she said with a smile.

Branson was getting out of the vice principal's office at the same time. We walked down the hall together. But this time we didn't touch each other. If there were three people in the hallway, they could have walked between us.

"What did Mr. Racklin say?" I asked.

Branson got a smug look on his face.

"Come on, what did he say?"

"That we can't do that stuff here. But he told me about a couple of places I could take you if we wanted to continue what Dr. Wood saw going on." He gave me a seductive look. "Do you want to?"

"No way," I said, totally appalled.

"No way what? You don't want to continue, or you don't want to try those places?"

"I mean I can't believe the vice principal said that to you!"

"Well, he is a man, so he understands what I'm going through."

I felt like slapping him, but I restrained myself. "Look, don't make this about you, Branson. I thought this was about us."

He stopped walking and stared at me, his eyes cold. "I just can't seem to get on the same page with you. First you get me hot and then you go cold on me. Come on, Laurel, what's it gonna be? Football is the only game I want to play."

I couldn't think of anything to say. I wasn't playing games; I just wanted to do the right thing. I wanted what we had to be special.

"I'll see you later," he said, then he turned and strolled away.

I walked in late to my last class of the day, which was physics. I didn't see anyone I knew in the classroom, and there was only one empty seat, next to an African-American girl. I didn't know too many black students, although a lot of them had come into my school since my freshman year. I wasn't prejudiced or anything; I just hadn't made a point of making friends from different races.

Her fluffy haircut was really cute, and she had on an outfit I knew Brittany would love. She was a little shorter than I was, with caramel skin and a killer body. I figured she probably worked out.

"Hi, I'm Laurel," I whispered, trying not to draw the teacher's attention. "Is anyone sitting here?"

"I guess you're sitting there now," she said. She wasn't cold, but she didn't sound overly friendly either. I turned my attention to the teacher.

"You are going to be lab partners with whoever you are sitting next to," he said, "so take a few minutes to get to know that person."

I turned back toward the girl beside me, but I didn't know what to say to her. She seemed totally closed off. Why did I have to be the one to break the ice?

"I don't think I've seen you here before," I said, trying to sound friendly.

"That's because it's my first day in this school," she answered without even looking at me.

"Really?" I said, acting like I didn't notice her cool tone. "Where are you from? Let me guess. Michigan? Philadelphia? Illinois?"

She glared at me. "Now, why would you guess those places? Are you trying to say that all black people are from the north?"

"No, no," I said, "it's not a black thing at all. I was just playing a guessing game." *For crying out loud, girl, lighten up already,* I thought.

"I'm from Decatur," she finally said. "Do you know where that is?"

"Yeah, I do. It's about forty minutes from here, right?"

"More like twenty."

Picky, picky. "It must have been awful to have to change schools in your senior year and leave all your friends," I said, trying to show her a little compassion.

"You got that right," she said, folding her arms across her chest. "And I'm sure I won't be making many here." She scanned the classroom, and I realized for the first time that every student in there was white.

If the teacher hadn't told us to get to know our lab

partners, I would have just let this girl stay in her own little world and left her alone. But she wasn't making any effort to get to know me, so I didn't see that I had much choice. "Where did you go before you came here?" I asked.

"Southwest DeKalb High School," she said, "an all-black school."

I couldn't imagine how hard it would be for me to go from an all-white school to one that was predominantly black. No wonder this girl was so closed off. "What do your parents do?"

She leered at me. "Why are you all up in my business?"

"Did I do something to hurt you? If so, I want to apologize. The teacher said we have to be lab partners, so I was just trying to make conversation. Maybe I should ask the teacher if we could switch or something." I started to get up, but she nodded for me to sit back down, so I did.

"My name's Robyn," she said softly. "I'm sorry. It's been a long summer and I haven't had a very good first day of school." Her eyes became misty. "This place is so different from my world. I've been here all day, and I can count on one hand the number of people who have said hello to me." She quickly brushed the back of her hand across her cheek. "It's really frustrating, but I didn't mean to take it out on you."

"I never really thought about our school that way." I wasn't sure my words were helping any, but I did want to try to make Robyn feel a little better. "I kind of know how you feel, though. My parents decided to move here from Arkansas when I was in the ninth grade. I had to leave all my friends and I hardly ever see them anymore. At least you're only twenty minutes away from where you used to live." Robyn still wasn't saying anything, but her eyes had lost some of their hardness. "Hey, do you have your driver's license?"

"Yeah."

"Well, you're a step ahead of me on that one. Maybe you can visit your old neighborhood on the weekends." I thought about how I'd feel about only seeing my friends two days out of the week. "But hey, I'm sure you'll make some new friends here."

She smiled. Finally, I'd said the right thing!

Unfortunately, the bell rang just then and the first day of school was over. "I'll see you around, Robyn," I said, then took off to my locker to find Branson.

When I got within a few feet of it, I saw my boyfriend whispering into some girl's ear. I stopped in my tracks. Several people in the hall started saying, "Uh-oh" and "Ooh!"

I brushed right past Branson as if he wasn't even there.

When he saw me, he chased after me. "Laurel, wait! Wait!"

I spun around to face him. "Come on, Branson. Talk your way out of this one. What were you doing with that girl? Giving her your number for a homework assignment?"

"This jealousy stuff is ridiculous, Laurel. I know we're together, but you've got to give me some space."

"Oh, I'll give you plenty of space," I said, then I stomped down the hall and out of the building.

It was raining again outside, and now it was raining in my heart. I had just walked out on my boyfriend without even saying good-bye. What was going to happen? What did I want to happen?

I didn't care about the rain hitting my face. I only cared about what was going on in Branson's mind. And I was desperately hoping for sunshine.

partying too much

the end of the first week of school finally arrived. Having seven classes was definitely draining. To top it all off, I was taking Joint Enrollment classes, where college professors came to our school to teach college courses. If I passed, the classes would count as college credit.

Branson and I still shared a locker but that was pretty much it. Our conversations were minimal but cordial. We weren't at each other's throats, but we weren't all lovey-dovey either.

That Saturday night was the first Salem football game, and I sat in the stands with my family. Every time I watched Brittany and Meagan cheer, my heart longed to be with them, even though I knew I'd made the right choice to stay with my gymnastics lessons. Brittany was the cheerleading captain, and Meagan barely made the squad—again. Still, she did make it, and I was in the bleachers watching the two of them have fun. My parents came to the game to support my middle brother, Lance. But Lance was on the bench because he was the second-string quarterback. The starting QB was my guy, Branson Price. And he was playing great.

"Laurel, honey," my dad said, "what's wrong? Your boyfriend just scored a touchdown and you're sitting there with a somber look on your face."

I heard his words but didn't respond to them.

"Look," he said, "I know you don't want to share everything with your dad now that you're getting older, but I've always been here for you before and I want you to know I'm here for you now too."

I couldn't even look up at him. I was crying on the inside. Branson and I had avoided our problems all week. But we were at a crossroads, a point where a decision would have to be made soon. I knew it wouldn't be an easy choice to make.

"I'm fine, Dad," I finally told him, hoping he would watch the game instead of trying to figure me out.

"No, I don't believe you are," Dad said, "but clearly you don't want to talk, so I won't pry." He put his arm around me. "Like I said, you know I'm here. I'm not a teenager anymore, but I remember what it's like. I know it can be really hard when troubles arise with someone you care about. Working through conflict is never easy."

"Dad, I'm OK. Really. I never said there was any conflict."

"All right," Dad said, although I knew I hadn't convinced him. "Tell you what. Just in case you ever do have conflict, let me offer you some advice. When two people care about each other but feel different on serious issues, it's often best to try to find a compromise."

"Yeah, but what if your beliefs are so different that there isn't any common ground?" I asked, staring at my hands. "What if there's no way to make both people happy?" I didn't really want to talk to my dad, but the words just spilled out. I guess I needed more help than I was willing to admit.

"If that's the case, then maybe the people involved aren't equal to each other."

"Huh?" I looked up at my dad, wondering what on earth he was talking about.

"When the common ground is Christ," he explained, "eventually anything can be worked out. But when two people don't have the Lord in common, disaster and chaos can easily enter."

I turned my eyes back to the game, pretending that a play had caught my attention. Truth was, I'd heard what my father said and I knew what he meant. I just didn't want to deal with the reality of what he was telling me. "I'm gonna get a hot dog," I said. "Does anybody want anything?"

Luke said he would go to the snack bar with me. Though he was my youngest brother, he was a lot of fun to hang out with. A real comedian, every minute telling a joke, and most of the time they were hilarious.

"Laurel," he said as we waited in line, "our football team usually loses every game they play. This is our first game of the season, and so far we're ahead. It looks like we might even win. So why are you so sad?" Luke was not only funny, he was pretty observant too.

"I'm not sad," I said, "just quiet."

"Want to talk about it?" he offered.

"Why does everybody keep giving me grief about this?" I spouted. "Dad said the same thing!"

"Well, excuse me," he complained. My brother was obviously not going to be as patient with me as Dad. "Just keep being sad all you want. I'm going back to the game." Luke started walking away.

"Fine," I hollered after him. "I'll stay here in line." *Maybe I won't get him a hot dog after all.*

"Hey," I heard a voice behind me say. "I thought you weren't coming to the game tonight."

Darn. It was my new friend, Robyn. She and I had been talking all week about whether I wanted to go to the football game with her, but I told her a million times I wasn't going. It wasn't a lie. I hadn't planned on coming, but my parents insisted I had to support my brother. I thought that was stupid, seeing that he wasn't getting any playing time. His uniform always stayed as clean as when he put it on.

"Robyn," I said, turning around, trying to tell if she looked mad. "I wasn't planning on being here. My parents forced me to come."

"Yeah, right," she said with one hand on her hip. "All you had to do was tell me that you didn't want to come with me. You didn't have to lie. I'm a big girl. If you don't want to go to a game with me, just tell me. I can understand that we can be friends only when your other friends don't see us together."

"Robyn, no! That's not it at all."

"Save it for someone who wants to hear it." Robyn walked away, obviously angry and hurt.

When I got back to my seat, I handed my brother his hot dog and told him I was going to go hang out with my new friend, Robyn, even though I had no idea where she was sitting. I wandered around the stadium for a while. When I finally spotted her in a corner, I went over and plopped down next to her.

"So," I said, trying to make light conversation, "my boyfriend's out there tonight. That's the real reason I'm here. He's the quarterback."

"Branson Price is your boyfriend?" she said, noticeably impressed.

"Yeah," I said. "We've been having some problems, so I wasn't going to come to the game tonight. I mean, I'm really into his world, but he's barely into mine at all."

Robyn turned her attention back to the game.

"My brother is the backup quarterback," I continued. "My parents made me come to see him. I told them I didn't want to go."

She took a sip of her soda.

"Look," I said, "the reason I told you I wasn't going to the game had nothing to do with not wanting to hang out with you. I know you don't really know me and I don't know you. I admit I have a lot of flaws, but I think I'm a good, fair person. And I believe that friendships are precious. Now, I don't know what we're developing here, but . . ."

"We've got a nice vibe going," she finished for me.

"Yeah, that's a good way of putting it. And I really want to build on that. Look, there are still two quarters left in the game, and my dad has been talking my ear off. Mind if I stay here with you?"

She gave me a big, bright smile. "That'd be cool."

Robyn made the game a lot more fun. We talked about her issues, thoughts, and problems, so I didn't have to focus on mine. It always seemed a lot easier to solve other people's problems than my own.

Her situation was similar to Meagan's. Robyn had her eye on our number-one defensive player, Jackson Reid. She didn't admit to me that she dug him, but I could tell. Every time he stepped on the field, she cheered a little too much. And the two times he caught an interception she about fell out of the bleachers. A girl knows when her friend is interested in a guy. And this girl definitely had it bad.

"Are you guys dating?" I asked her.

"Who?" she asked, trying to act like she had no clue what I was talking about.

"You know," I said. "Jackson."

"Jackson?" she asked, still putting on the front. "Oh, you mean Jackson Reid?" She shook the ice in her soda glass. "No, uh . . . of course not."

"Then why are you stuttering all over your words, girl? Look at you. You like him!"

"I don't even know him."

"Well, I do. I've known him for four years."

She suddenly lost all interest in her glass of ice. "Does he have a girlfriend?"

"Let's see," I said. "Only about twenty."

I could tell from the look in her eyes that I'd burst her bubble.

"So I guess he just hasn't found the right one yet."

Her smile returned. "Good way of looking at it, Laurel. You know, I didn't think there would be any guy around here that would turn my head. But when I saw him walking down the hall yesterday . . . Mmmm-mmmm!"

"Oh, listen to you. You sound like you just polished off a Snickers bar!"

"You know it," she replied.

"So," I said, leaning closer, "do you think you really like him? Or just his body?"

"Well, that's why I want to get to know him. If everything else is half as good as his physique, then we might have something."

We both laughed.

Amazingly, the Salem High Seminoles ended up winning the game. Maroon-and-gold pom-poms twisted high in the air. I watched Branson shake hands with the other team and then congratulate his teammates on the field. Cheerleaders were jumping on his back like he was a hero.

I started feeling bad about giving him such a hard time. He had led his team to victory, and I understood how difficult sports can be. I was proud of him and wanted to go out and celebrate the victory with him.

"Is the team going anywhere special?" Robyn asked. "You know, a party somewhere after the game? Do you guys party all together, or does each grade go somewhere separately?"

"We all usually go to the Waffle House or sometimes to somebody's house. I guess it might be a little different this year, though, since we're seniors now. We don't really have a set tradition yet."

"So, are you gonna hang out with everybody, or are you going back home?" As I thought about it, she said, "Oh, come on. Have some fun. Your boyfriend just had a big night. You shouldn't even be thinking about going home! I don't know much about your relationship with that quarterback guy, but he'll surely want to go celebrate with somebody. And if you're not around . . ."

"Then he should be thinking about me," I argued.

"Yeah, he should," she said. "But you and I both know boys are stupid."

I laughed.

"So why give him a reason to start trouble?"

"I guess you have a point."

"Darn right I do! Look, I can tell you're not sure if you want to go or not. So just come and introduce me to Jackson and then you can leave."

"Sure," I said, grateful for the excuse. "No problem."

Robyn and I made our way down to the field, where all sorts of action was going on. I bumped into Brittany and Meagan on the sidelines, so I introduced my old friends to my new one.

"Hey," Brittany said, barely acknowledging Robyn, "we're going out tonight. Can you come?"

"Brittany, I'm introducing you to my friend. Why are you being so rude?"

"I said hello," Brittany replied, sounding a bit touchy. "What else do you want me to say? Now, did you see Branson?"

"We're talking about Robyn," I said, getting touchy right back.

"Come on, Laurel," she said, grabbing my arm, "you've got to say hi to your boyfriend."

I looked at Meagan, hoping to get some support. Instead she just grabbed my other arm and my two friends dragged me over toward the sidelines where Branson was still hugging his teammates. I looked back and saw Robyn standing there all by herself. I hadn't even introduced her to Jackson yet. I felt horrible, but what could I do? I was being kidnapped! And there was so much action on the field that when I turned around again to try and find Robyn, I couldn't see her anywhere.

Branson picked me up and twirled me around. "Laurel, we won! We won! We won! So are you coming with me to celebrate?" Before I could answer, he said, "We're gonna have a great time. We won!" He twisted me around again.

All through the postgame party, the players were so into congratulating each other that Branson forgot all about me. But I was totally OK with that because it gave me more time before I had to deal with the uncomfortable task of facing my boyfriend.

Brittany gave me a ride home from the party. I wasn't sure Branson even noticed I left.

The next day after church, while Branson was at practice, I went over to his house to help his mom prepare for his surprise birthday party.

"Laurel," she said as she frosted the cupcakes, "you've been such a help to me today." She licked a dab of frosting off her finger. "Are you sure he has no clue?"

"No, ma'am," I answered as I stood on a chair stringing maroon and gold crepe-paper streamers across the doorway. "He hasn't even mentioned his birthday. He's been so focused on the game all week, he hasn't been able to talk about anything else." Not even our relationship. "And after the game, he was too excited about the victory to even think about turning a year older."

"Laurel, did you invite your friend Brittany to the party?"

"Yes, Mrs. Price." I hopped down from the chair to admire my handiwork.

"And Meagan too?" she asked for the millionth time.

"Yes, ma'am."

Branson's mom was a college professor at Emory. She

was really nice and extremely articulate, but she was beginning to bug me. As a matter of fact, this party-planning stuff had been driving me crazy for days. But Mrs. Price's question after question after question was starting to make me wish I hadn't offered to come over early after all.

"Are you sure the captain of his football team is going to show up?"

Obviously, she didn't understand that anytime you said "party" to my friends, they were going to show up.

"Laurel, I'm sorry." Mrs. Price sighed. "I know I'm asking you the same questions over and over again. It's just that Branson is an only child, and he's never had a surprise party before, and I want it to be perfect. Next year he'll be off at college somewhere." She looked at me with a wistful look in her eyes. "You understand, don't you?"

"Yes, ma'am," I replied again.

Branson's birthday was August 31, so he was the first in our class to turn eighteen. His mom had told me that when he first started kindergarten, he seemed smaller than the other kids, so she let him stay back a year. I had just turned seventeen in July, so I had a long way to go.

As I started blowing up balloons, I thought about the day Branson first asked me out. I remembered his exact words. "Will you go out with me?" he'd said. "I really like you and I think you're special."

I knew a lot of girls at my school liked him, and I wasn't sure if I could trust him. So I said, "I don't know if that's such a good thing. I mean, how can I be sure you'll stay committed to me?"

"I'm not like my dad," he responded in an angry voice. "My feelings are too strong to ever let you down. Be my girlfriend and let me prove to you that one is more than enough for me."

For as long as I'd known him, Branson was always angry at his dad for not being there. Mr. Price always had some late meeting or business trip. One day Branson decided to play detective and he caught his dad with someone other than his mom. His parents worked everything out, but Branson never stopped being angry with his father.

In spite of his feelings about his dad, I had decided to give this fine boy a chance. I'd hugged him in our fifth-period P.E. class and happily accepted his offer to be his girl.

As I blew up the last balloon, I looked up from my memories. "Oh, Mrs. Price, the place looks great!" It really did.

"Do you think so?" she asked. "You don't think the maroon and gold balloons are too much?"

I laughed. "He's gonna love it."

"I'm so glad Branson won that game last night." Mrs. Price smiled.

"Defense is what did it," I said. "Not that your son didn't do good. He made some great passes. And he ran the ball too."

"I don't like it when he runs like that. He's not the running back." She shook her head. "He isn't supposed to get hit either. If a quarterback isn't blocked, he's going to get hit."

"You're right about that," I agreed. "Getting hit on those plays is definitely not good!" We both laughed.

She started talking about our defensive back, Jackson, and how he was really something special and a lot of colleges wanted to recruit him. That reminded me about Robyn. I'd wanted to invite her to the birthday party, but after we got separated at the game I didn't see her again. I had her number written down, but it was at home. I desperately wanted to apologize to her, but from what I'd seen of Robyn so far, she tended to take things personally. So she might be mad at me indefinitely. Still, I was determined to win her over despite the odds.

"Mrs. Price," I said, "if that's everything, I'd like to go home and change for the party."

She looked confused. "But you look fine, dear."

Yeah, right. I'd spent all afternoon blowing up balloons and climbing on chairs to hang streamers. I was dressed in faded denim shorts and an old beige tank top. My hair was pulled back in a ponytail. I wasn't even wearing any makeup.

"I understand," she said. "You go along. I'll finish things up here."

I thanked her and took off.

As I was trying to figure out what to wear, Brittany showed up. Somehow, she always seemed to know when I was picking out clothes, because she always came along to tell me how bad I looked.

"It's your boyfriend's party," she said, like it was the Academy Awards or something. "Why don't you go shopping?"

"I don't have the time or the money to go shopping." And she knew it too.

"Do you want to borrow something from one of my closets?" she offered.

I sighed as I stared at my hangers full of nothing. "Yeah, I guess," I said in a pitiful tone.

She grabbed her big tote bag and started pulling out clothes, dumping them onto my bed. "I might wear this one myself," she said, picking up a short, skintight, red knit dress. But you can pick any of the others." She looked up at me. "You should definitely do something with your hair. It looks awful!"

"I spent all afternoon decorating Branson's house," I said, yanking the scrunchie out of my hair. "Of course my hair's a mess."

"So," she said, picking up a cute coral top and holding it next to my face, "what's going on with you and Branson?"

"Quit being nosy," I grumbled, picking up a denim miniskirt that was slit halfway up the back.

"Why don't you want to tell me? What's your big secret? I mean, your guy won the first football game of the year, right?"

"Right."

"But you left the party after the game without even saying good-bye to him."

I checked myself out in the mirror, pretending to be interested in seeing how the denim skirt would look on me. "So?"

"So, did you guys get back together after the party to . . . you know . . . celebrate privately?" She winked at me.

I gave her a disgusted look. "Britt, get your mind out of the gutter."

"Well, that answers my question," she said, kicking off her platform shoes. "You are such a goody-goody, Laurel."

"And what's wrong with that?" I asked, staring at the coral top.

"Oh, nothing," she said, checking out her toenail polish. "Except that Branson told me he wants to do a little bit more than just hold hands."

"What?" I hollered.

She looked up at me with an expression of pity on her face.

"Now, why would my boyfriend be talking to you about that?" I asked.

"It's not a big deal." She shrugged. "I guess whenever he needs someone to talk to, I just happen to be there."

I couldn't believe what I was hearing. "Well, when he needs someone to talk to, tell him to come to me. I'm his girlfriend, whether you think I'm worthy or not."

"Hey," she said, walking to the mirror and holding the red knit dress in front of her, "don't get mad at me. Branson and I have been friends ever since—"

"Elementary school. I know. You always throw that up in my face." I glared at her reflection in the mirror. "Just because I've only been here for four years, you love talking about your history with these people. Well, I've got some history here now too. And having a past with people is great, but it's not everything. It's the quality of friendship that matters, not quantity."

Brittany turned to face me, the dress dangling from her fingers. "Look, I've known Branson for a long time, and if he needs to talk to me, I'm not going to turn him away." She walked to the bed. "Tell me what you're going to wear so I can take the rest home."

I grabbed the cute coral top. Brittany stuffed the rest of the clothes back into her bag and left.

When I heard the front door close, I got down on my knees beside the bed. "Lord, life is crazy. I've got a girlfriend I don't understand and a boyfriend who doesn't understand me. My parents want to understand too much, and there's a whole lot of stuff in between. Everything's so foggy. This is supposed to be the best year of my life, and I'm not at all excited about it. Show me Your will for my life. And Lord, give me a willing heart so I can see Your plan. I thank You for another year with Branson. Please make tonight special and help me focus on You. I do love You, Lord. Thanks for listening and always being there. Amen."

As I stood up, I decided to try to find Robyn's phone number. I searched for an hour before I finally found it. "Thank You, Lord!" I cried. I picked up the receiver. "I hope she's home, I hope she's home," I chanted as the phone rang three times.

Finally, a pleasant voice said, "Hello?"

"Is this Robyn's mom?" I asked.

"Yes, it is." Her voice was warm and inviting.

"Hi," I said. "My name is Laurel Shadrach. I'm a classmate of Robyn's."

"Yes, she told me about you. How are you, Laurel?"

"I'm doing good," I said. "And you?"

"Quite well, thank you. I just finished a novel."

"You like reading too?" I said. Though I'd never met her, Robyn's mom sounded like someone I had known all my life. "Which book was it? Maybe I've read it."

"Oh, I don't think so," she said. I could tell she was smiling. "You see, I just finished *writing* this one."

"You write books?" I asked, my mouth dropping open.

"Yes," she said. "I write Christian novels for teenagers. You'll have to come over sometime and give me your opinion of my work. I love doing research with girls your age, so maybe you can help me."

"I'd love to," I said. Suddenly remembering my reason for calling, I asked, "Is Robyn home?"

"Yes, she is. Hold on one second."

Wow. I'd never met a real author before. I couldn't wait to see what she'd written. And to think, she actually wanted my opinion on it!

"Laurel, I'm surprised you're calling me," Robyn said without even saying hello. "I thought you'd be at the mall with your friends. The way they tugged you away, I didn't think you had time for anybody."

"OK, I deserve that," I said. " I hope you know I didn't mean to abandon you. I really did look for you, but I couldn't find you. Where'd you go?"

"I didn't know anybody on the field, so I left. What did you think I'd do, hang around all night waiting for you to come back?"

"I'm sorry."

"Is that all you called to say?" she asked in a surly voice.

Man, this girl had a chip on her shoulder. I hoped I could help her peel it off. "Robyn, I called because I wanted to apologize, but I also wanted to see if you were free tonight."

"Why?" she asked casually. "What's up?"

"We're having a surprise birthday party for Branson tonight, and I think Jackson might be there. Do you want to come?"

"Maybe," Robyn said.

"If you're not doing anything else, I think you should go. Everybody's supposed to be there by 7:30, and I'm going to bring Branson at eight."

"I don't know," she hedged. "Your friends don't really seem like my type of crowd."

I didn't know what to say to make her change her mind, so I just said, "Well, the offer is open if you want to drop by." I gave her Branson's address. "I hope you make it."

When we hung up, I still had no clue whether she would come or not. At least she didn't seem to be mad at me anymore, and that was a good thing.

I slipped into Brittany's coral top, still trying to figure out a plan to get Branson home by 8:00.

He picked me up just as I finished getting ready. "So, what did you want to do for my birthday?" he asked as I hopped into his Camaro.

"Let's just drive around town for a while," I suggested.

He looked at me funny but took off down the road. "You know, my friends wanted me to hang out with them tonight," he said.

"Well, you're not supposed to be hanging out with the guys on your birthday. Wouldn't you rather be with your girlfriend tonight?"

He looked at me, trying to figure out what I had in mind. "Sure," he said.

I grinned at him. "I've got something really special planned."

"Really?" He grinned back at me. My guy looked so cute in his khaki shorts and his blue button-down Gap shirt. He looked totally preppy, but I knew he wasn't like that at all.

There was no doubt in my mind that I loved Branson Price, and if I had a million dollars I would have bought him whatever he wanted for his birthday. The problem was, the gift he really wanted from me was priceless. And because I loved God so much, I knew I couldn't afford to give him that. So I decided to take my dad's advice and find a compromise.

"Why don't you find someplace to park," I suggested, "so I can give you your birthday present."

His eyes lit up as they looked around for a good place to pull over. "And what are you going to give me?"

"You'll see," I said in my most romantic voice.

Branson quickly found a parking spot under a large oak tree. "OK," he said, "I'm ready for my present."

I scooted closer and gave him a long, passionate birthday kiss. "So," I said when I finally pulled away, "what do you think of your gift?"

"It was great. Now, let me thank you for it." He kissed me back.

"OK," I said when the kiss started to get heavy. "Why don't we go over to your house, since your parents aren't home, so I can give you the rest of your birthday present."

We got to Branson's place in record time.

"Do you really mean this, Laurel?" he asked as he pulled up to the curb.

I smiled.

He gently squeezed my knee. The serious look he gave me made me wonder what he was thinking. "I love you," he whispered. "Thank you so much for trusting me right now."

I suddenly realized that Branson honestly believed I'd brought him there so we could go all the way. I had no intention of carrying out what I had insinuated. I'd just been flirting and teasing, but he had taken me seriously. I could only hope the party would be so exciting that he'd forget about everything I'd done to get him there.

Branson ran his fingers through my long brown hair. I loved it. I closed my eyes and relaxed into his embrace.

"Don't go to sleep on me now," he whispered.

I didn't open my eyes, but I smiled to let him know I was still awake. I wished our relationship could always be like this. Why did he have to spoil it by pushing me to become more physical?

"If you think rubbing your head feels good," he murmured, "wait until I rub every inch of you."

"Branson . . ."

"There's no need to be shy. It's finally our time. And you know I care for you." He took his hand from my head and placed it in my hand. I glanced at his watch. It said the time was 8:10. Branson's house was dark, revealing no hint of the tons of people who were waiting inside to surprise him.

Branson squeezed my hand. "Being with you is definitely a great birthday present." He kissed my forehead.

"Well," I said, "what are we waiting for? Let's go inside."

He gave me a questioning look, then got out of the car, hopped around to my side, and let me out. The kissing started again, and I felt a little embarrassed. Although he didn't think anyone was home, I figured some of the people inside were probably watching us, so I grabbed his arm and said, "Come on, let's go."

"Yeah, yeah," he said. He kissed me again. He didn't seem to be in any hurry to get into the house, which really surprised me considering what he thought was going to happen in there.

"Come on," I said, trying to hurry him. I hoped he hadn't figured out what was really going on. "What's wrong?"

"I don't know," he said, pulling back a little. "You seem too . . . eager. You've been fighting me on this for the longest time, and now you're ready to jump right on in."

"Branson!" I didn't know what to say now. "Just give me the house key." I grabbed the key ring out of his hand and walked up the sidewalk, hoping he'd follow me.

He did. When we got to the porch, Branson took the keys from me and opened the door. For a moment, I didn't hear a sound. If I hadn't known better, I would have thought no one was home. But then the lights came on, confetti was thrown, and a large crowd of people yelled, "Surprise!" The music came on and our friends popped out from hiding places all over the room. They crowded around Branson, pushing us apart.

Branson loved it! He smiled and laughed and hugged his friends. And when everybody asked if we really had surprised him, he assured them that he didn't have a clue. Everything turned out great.

Since Branson's focus was no longer on me, I went into the kitchen to check on his mom. She was putting a tray of hot wings in the oven. "Can I do anything?" I asked.

She looked up as she closed the oven door. "Oh, honey, just getting him here was help enough. You two were a little late and I was beginning to worry, but it turned out great."

"He really was surprised," I said.

"Yes." She wiped her hands on a towel hanging from the oven door. "But I noticed Branson looked quite eager to bring you into the house, considering he thought no one was home." She looked right at me. "You kids aren't doing . . . that, are you?"

I gulped. "No, ma'am." I didn't feel comfortable telling her about everything that was going on with Branson and me.

She took my hand in both of hers. "I know you're not my daughter, Laurel, but if I had one, I would want her to be just like you. Don't let my son or anyone else pressure you into doing something you don't want to do."

She stood there looking at me, as if she was waiting for my response. So I said, "Yes, ma'am."

Just then, Robyn walked into the kitchen. Mrs. Price let go of my hand.

"Robyn!" I said, giving her a hug, "I'm so glad you came!"

"Thanks for inviting me," she said softly.

"This is Branson's mom," I said, turning to her. "Mrs. Price, this is a friend of mine, Robyn Williams. She's new at Salem."

"Nice to meet you, Robyn. Thanks for coming to my son's birthday party."

"Well," I said, thankful for an excuse to get out of there, "I'll see you later, Mrs. Price."

"You girls have fun," she responded.

I walked Robyn into the next room. "How long have you been here?" I asked.

"Just a little while."

"Have you seen anyone interesting?"

Robyn giggled. "Yeah, he's here."

I grabbed her arm. "Well, let's go introduce you to him."

"Wait," she said, pulling back. "Let me go to the bathroom and do some freshening up first."

I laughed. "Robyn, you are so cute!"

"Thanks, Laurel," she said. "But I want to make sure Jackson thinks so."

"All right, then. The bathroom's that way." I pointed down the hall. "I'll go find Jackson."

I searched all three levels of Branson's house but couldn't spot him or Jackson anywhere. I did find my friend Meagan, so I asked if she'd seen them.

"Last time I saw Branson, he was up in his room," she said. "But you might not want to go there."

"Why not?" I asked.

She lowered her voice. "I heard giggles coming from inside, and they were definitely female."

My heart started pounding. I'd been enjoying the party so much I hadn't really focused on my guy. Apparently, someone else was. I hoped I was wrong.

I scurried up the stairs and down the hall to Branson's room. Sure enough, I heard a girl's voice giggling! When I peeked in, I saw Brittany helping Branson pick out CDs for the party music. I was so happy to see it was her!

"Hey, you guys," I said.

"We were just talking about you," Brittany said.

Branson threw his arms around me. "Doesn't my girl look great tonight?"

"Yeah, my coral shirt looks terrific on her." Brittany grinned.

"Your shirt?" Branson asked, raising an eyebrow at her.

"Yeah," she said. "She wears a lot of my clothes. Especially when she doesn't think anything in her wardrobe looks good."

66

My happy smile turned into a dim frown. I didn't know if she realized she'd hurt my feelings, or even cared. But I didn't understand why the two of them were talking about it. I felt embarrassed. Before I could let it get to me, Robyn barged into the room.

"He's over there," she whispered, pointing. She grabbed my arm and walked saucily toward Jackson.

Even though I wasn't into anyone but Branson, I had to admit Jackson Reid was pretty hot. He reminded me of Will Smith.

I don't know what Robyn did with herself in the bathroom, because she looked the same to me. But whatever it was, it worked. Jackson noticed her right away.

"Laurel," he said in an interested voice, "who's this?"

I grinned. "Jackson, this is Robyn. She's new at our school. She went to Southwest DeKalb last year."

He beamed at Robyn. "Really? I know lots of people down there. We should talk." He put his hand on her back and they walked off. I knew she would be fine without me.

As I stood there in the hall, Branson came up and wrapped his arms around me. "You look beautiful no matter what you wear."

"I know." I rested my head against his chest. "I just feel bad sometimes because I don't have a car or new clothes or anything. All my friends get whatever they want. Sometimes it gets to me."

"You may not have what they have," he said, "but you have me. I hope that counts for something."

I looked up into his gorgeous blue eyes. "Sometimes you know just the right thing to say."

He squeezed my shoulder. "It's easy to say the right things when they come from the heart." He kissed the top of my head. "Dance with me, Laurel. I don't want to stay up here all night. I'd rather spend this birthday partying too much!"

jumping into tension

at the end of the third week of school, our team played Heritage High School. It was our second home game, and this time I accepted Robyn's invitation to go to the game with her. Afterward we were going to double-date with Branson and Jackson.

"So things are going well with you two?" I hinted as I nudged her.

"I like him a lot," Robyn admitted. "He calls me every night, and even though we're not boyfriend and girlfriend, he really turns me on."

"Robyn!" I said, a little bit shocked.

"Yeah, right," she jumped back. "Like Branson doesn't ruffle your innocent little feathers."

"I wouldn't quite put it like that."

"However you put it," Robyn said, "it's all the same."

Wanting to change the subject, I asked, "How does it feel to have a mom who's an author?"

"What do you mean?" she asked.

"She's practically a celebrity!" I gushed.

"I'm sure it's no different than your dad being the pastor of a big church."

"Yeah, but my dad is only important in Conyers. OK, maybe in Georgia, possibly even in the Southeast. Anyway, he's known here and there, but your mom has stuff in bookstores!"

"Well, excuse me," Robyn said defensively.

"Look, I wasn't trying to correct you to prove a point or anything."

"I know," she said, elbowing me in the ribs. "I was just kidding."

"Writing is my worst subject in school, but I love reading Christian fiction. My favorite author is—"

She cut me off. "Don't tell me. Robin Jones Gunn."

"Yeah," I said, thrilled that she had guessed. "She writes the Kristy Little books and the Sarah Jenson series."

"I know. She's a really good friend of my mom's. I was named after her."

"Are you serious?" I squealed. "Your mom knows her?"

"They met at a Christian booksellers conference like eighteen years ago. Ms. Gunn helped my mom learn the industry."

I felt goose-bumpy all over. "That's so neat! You know, she asked me to read some of her stuff. I told her I'd be honored. I have tons of info for her." A ruckus on the playing field caught my eye. "Oh, my goodness, they're fighting!"

Several of our football players were punching guys on the opposing team. Heritage High was our rival, and we were losing by thirty-one points.

"There are only about four minutes left in the game," I said. "What happened?"

"I don't know," Robyn said.

The guy sitting in front of us turned around. "One of the Heritage players jumped off the sidelines and ran straight into Price. They got a five-yard penalty for it, but our offensive players took it personally. They started fighting, and the next thing you know, defense starts running onto the field. That good defensive back—what's his name? Reid?"

"Jackson's out there?" Robyn said, staring intently at the players.

"Yeah, that's his name, Jackson Reid. He just got ejected from the game." The guy turned his attention back to the field.

Robyn leaned back against the bleachers. "Well, there goes our date," she moaned. "He's gonna be angry about this for sure."

"Maybe you can cheer him up," I suggested.

After the game Robyn and I went to Pizza Hut. She was right; the guys were extremely tense. I didn't know what to say to make them loosen up and apparently Robyn didn't either because her lips were sealed. The guys were just smacking on the pizza, and that seemed to be the only thing that gave them pleasure.

"Maybe next week will turn out better," I said.

"Next week!" Jackson glared at me. "We got kicked two weeks in a row. I can't even think about next week. The way I see it, we might as well stay home and tell the other team they've already won."

"We can't just give up and quit," Branson said.

"Why not?" Jackson grumbled.

"Look, you can't be on the team if you're not going to play."

"Fine by me."

Branson stared at his defensive back. "Is that how you really feel?"

Their voices were escalating, and everyone in the place starting looking at them. I was afraid they were going to get into a fight, and I knew I needed to say something. Our team would really be in trouble if our offensive captain and defensive captain started going at it.

I decided to try reasoning with Jackson. "Look, I compete on a high level, too, and I see Branson's point. No matter how tough things get, you've got to hang in there."

He sneered at me. "Girl, you don't know nothin' about football."

"She didn't mean it like that," Robyn said.

"How would you know?" Jackson hollered at her.

Robyn stared him down for a minute, then took his hand. "Come on," she said softly, leading him toward the door, "let's go outside for some fresh air."

I breathed a sigh of relief when they left the restaurant and Branson and I were alone at the table.

"He's got such a hot temper," Branson said, eyeing the last slice of sausage, mushroom, and pepperoni. "It was my battle today. But as soon as I got a little push, defense ran onto the field. I know Jackson started it."

"Well, I guess I'd better not say anything about football again," I teased, "because I obviously don't know anything about the sport."

"He didn't mean that," Branson said, looking up at me. "I'm sorry I'm being such a jerk tonight. I thought this year would be so much better for us."

He put his arm around me and gave me a kiss on the cheek. It wasn't that great a kiss because he left a smear of pizza sauce on my cheek. I discreetly picked up a napkin and blotted it off.

Robyn came back alone. "You guys, Jackson's ready to go. He doesn't even want to come back inside."

"I'll go talk to him," Branson said, taking off.

"Thanks." Robyn plopped down into the bench opposite me. "Our first official date, and it starts out like this. First he gets into a fight on the football field, and then he starts another fight here. What do you know about this guy, Laurel?"

"Well, I don't know much," I admitted. "But I do know that he lives with a white foster family."

Her eyebrows shot up. "Really?"

"I think he moved in with them when he was twelve."

"So why haven't they adopted him?"

I shrugged. "I don't know. From what I hear, every time the subject comes up, Jackson does something to make them think twice."

"Do you know anything about his birth parents?"

"Nope," I said, sipping on my soda. "He's been suspended from school a couple of times, though. He gets pretty angry sometimes, but he must be pretty smart. After all, he told me I didn't know anything."

"That was about football, Laurel."

"Yeah," I said. "So I guess I won't hold it against him."

Branson and Jackson came back laughing. Robyn and I smiled at each other.

"Laurel," Jackson said, "I owe you an apology. I was trippin' and I shouldn't have gone off on you like that. Are we cool?"

"Sure," I said, shrugging. "I appreciate your apology."

"So," he asked, sitting down next to Robyn, "what sports do you do?"

"I'm a gymnast."

"Oh, with the balance beam and stuff. You know how to stay up on those things?"

"That's my favorite part. I'm not that great of a vaulter, but Branson told me he was going to show me how to get more power." I gave my boyfriend a grateful look as he sat next to me in the booth.

"Wow!" Jackson seemed truly impressed. "I watched the Olympics gymnastics competition, and it was pretty cool."

"I've always wanted to compete on that level, but I don't think I'm that good."

"Don't say that," Branson said. "You can do whatever you want to." He picked up the last slice of pizza. "You guys will have to come to a meet sometime. They start in January," he said as he took a big mouthful.

"You bet," Jackson said.

"That'll be fun," Robyn added.

I looked at the two of them. They made a cute couple, but she seemed a bit more polished than he did. Not that it was a problem, but I could tell they were from two different worlds. They say opposites attract, and with the way he was whispering in her ear and making her fall all over him, there was definitely an attraction.

Branson wiped his fingers on a napkin, then placed his hand on my knee under the table. At first I thought he was just missing my attention, especially seeing how mushy Robyn and Jackson were acting. But then he started stroking my leg, and I wondered what he was thinking. He was saying quite a bit in that touch, quite a bit indeed.

I looked at my watch. "Hey, you guys," I said, "it's 10:30 already."

"So what do you want to do now?" Jackson asked.

"Well, I've got to get home pretty soon, but I think I could spare some time."

"Let's go driving," Jackson suggested. "I know the perfect spot. Follow me."

Jackson and Robyn took off in his red 1965 Mustang, and Branson and I followed in the Camaro. We drove into the parking lot of a shopping center that was under construction. There were no lights anywhere and no one around.

Branson pulled up beside the Mustang. Jackson came over to talk to Branson, so I started to get out to go talk to Robyn.

My boyfriend grabbed my hand. "Make it quick," he said. "I want us to spend some time together before I have to get you home."

"I want to be with you too," I told him.

I could tell that statement made his night. I quivered, wondering if I was setting myself up for trouble by telling Branson what he wanted to hear instead of what I really wanted to say.

"Hey," Robyn said as I hopped into Jackson's car, "what's wrong?"

"I'm nervous," I admitted. "Aren't you?"

"Well, it's our first date so I don't plan on doing anything tonight. But if it gets to that point, I'll be shaking just like you." We laughed. "Are you a virgin?" she whispered.

"Well, yeah. Are you?"

"I haven't done it a lot, but I did get physical with this guy I was dating for a while back at DeKalb."

I stared at my friend. "You talk about it like it's no big deal. But you're a Christian. Doesn't it bother you that—"

"That what?" she cut me off. "That I've gone against God's will for my life?"

"Yeah," I replied, ignoring her sarcasm.

"Well, what can I do about it now? It's done."

"That doesn't mean you should do it again." I couldn't believe Robyn was taking this so lightly. "Does your mom know?"

"No way," she lashed out. "She's so into writing her books that she doesn't know what's going on in my life."

"You sound angry with her."

Robyn's voice softened. "In a way, I guess I am. It seems like her work is more important to her than me and my sister."

"You have a sister?"

"Yeah, she's in the tenth grade."

I realized there was a lot about my new friend that I didn't know. "Robyn," I said, "I don't know what to say. Branson and I have been down this road so many times before."

"If you're convicted about it, then you shouldn't do it. I don't care how excited Jackson is, none of that is going to happen tonight."

"What if Branson ends our relationship because I won't do what he wants me to?"

"It doesn't sound like much of a relationship to me if he doesn't respect your wishes."

I sighed. I knew she was right.

When I saw Jackson heading our way, I hopped out of his car and walked back to Branson's. As Jackson drove off to the other side of the parking lot, I realized how grateful I was to have Robyn in my life. Brittany was a good friend, but she was giving me the wrong information. Though Robyn wasn't a virgin, she was telling me to do what was right for me. She wasn't pushing her lifestyle on me. She was looking out for my best interests, and that was a sign of a good friend.

Branson fumbled around with the radio, trying to find something romantic. He glanced over and gave me a deep, rich look. He looked like a predator that wanted to eat me whole! And I didn't want to be preyed upon. But how was I going to say no? I started fidgeting. Branson reached into the backseat and pulled out a glass bottle.

"What's that?" I asked.

"This is just to relax you a little."

Oh, it'll relax me, I thought. But I didn't want to be relaxed. I wanted to be on guard and not give in to temptation. Sipping anything other than punch was not going to help my cause.

He slid as close to me as he could get around the stick shift. I could smell liquor on his breath. "Just try it," he said, still holding the bottle. "It's not that strong. Trust me."

"Branson, you know I don't drink."

He set the bottle on the floor and stretched his left arm across me. Suddenly, my seat back fell and became as flat as a bed. Branson climbed over the shifting lever, and the next thing I knew, he was on top of me. He quickly unbuttoned his jeans and started to unzip his zipper.

"Branson, no," I cried. "We can't do this."

"Sure we can," he said. "I have protection." He reached into his pocket and pulled out a square of red plastic, showing it off with pride. "See, we're all taken care of. I'll put this baby on and it'll be fine. Don't worry, I'll be gentle. I love you. Did you hear me, Laurel? I . . ." He kissed my left cheek slowly. ". . . love . . ." He kissed my right cheek even more slowly. ". . . you."

He pressed his lips to mine and kissed me hard. His tongue wormed its way into my mouth. Even though his breath tasted disgusting, his passionate energy was irresistible. I didn't want to go that far, but I loved him so much. After all, he was the guy I went to bed thinking about every night and woke up thinking about every morning.

I returned his kiss to let him know how much I cared about him. He started kissing my cheek, then went to my neck, and then worked his way down farther. It felt great, but then he touched me in a place that felt extremely uncomfortable.

"No!" I cried out.

"What do you mean, no? *No* isn't the word I want to hear, Laurel. Tonight is our night."

"No, Branson!" I said as I pushed him back. "I can't do this."

"Yes, you can. Don't make me wait. I've waited long enough." He started kissing me again.

Naturally I kissed him back. Something inside me made me long to keep going. But then something else took over that made me push him away, hard. His back flattened against the dashboard.

"Ow!" he yelled. He glared at me, then yanked open the door. "Get out! Get out!"

"What?" I asked, tears stinging my eyes. "What's wrong?"

"You can't keep playing these games, Laurel," he said, angrily zipping up his jeans. "You turn me on, then turn me off again. I'm not a hot-and-cold water faucet, Laurel. I'm your boyfriend." He buttoned his fly. "So if you can't give me what I want, then get out of my car!"

I sat there, staring at him. He crawled out of the car and then grabbed my arm and yanked me out too.

"Branson, calm down. You don't have to be like this."

This was a side of him I had never seen. We'd broken up

76

before, but never had he been so angry that he pulled me out of his car. We were in an abandoned parking lot, for goodness' sake.

"What do you want me to do, walk home?" I asked, my voice trembling.

"I don't really care how you get home. I can't deal with you anymore. We're through." He stomped around to his side of the car, but I jumped back in on my side before he got in. The tension was terrible, but I felt reasonably sure he wouldn't hit me. Then again, he was acting so crazy, how could I know what he was going to do? I started to cry.

Branson sat in the driver's seat, his back rigid, staring out the windshield. "I don't want to hear any more of your bawling. Just get out of my car!"

"Why are you being like this?" I whimpered. "I love you, but I'm just not ready for—"

"You've never been ready," he seethed, his face turning red. "And I've been playing along. But I need more, and if you can't give it to me—"

"Don't talk like that," I begged him.

Branson leered at me. "Are you willing to give it to me now? Are you gonna make it all right?"

I took a deep breath and prayed for the right words. "If that's what it takes to make things right between us, then . . . I just can't do that."

Branson stared at me for a long moment. His face started to look a little less red. "Look, I'm not cool to be around right now," he said, obviously trying hard to keep his voice steady. "I'm asking you one more time to get out of the car. I'll drive over to Jackson and see if he can give you a ride home."

Reluctantly, I opened the door and slowly stepped onto the dusty concrete. I was all alone. As Branson drove away, the reality of being abandoned set in. He didn't even go to Jackson's car; he just sped out of the parking lot.

I collapsed to the ground in sobs. The ground was dirty,

but I didn't care about my clothes. All I cared about was my boyfriend, who apparently cared more about my body than about me.

Through my tears, I saw the headlights of his car. He was making a U-turn back toward me. Was he coming to apologize? I stood up with what little strength of hope I had. But he zoomed right past me and squealed to a stop next to Jackson's car.

Branson got out and tapped on the window. Things must have been hot and heavy with Robyn and Jackson because he had to tap several times. Finally, the window came down and Branson talked to Jackson, waving his hands and pointing in my direction. Then he stormed back into his car, slammed the door, and drove away again. A few minutes later, Jackson started his engine and swirled around to pick me up.

"Hey, get in so I can take you home," he said.

Without a word, I crawled into the backseat, tears streaming down my face.

"Tell me where to go," Jackson said, pulling out of the parking lot.

I heard him, but I was in so much despair I couldn't respond.

"Robyn, you've got to talk to your girl," Jackson said. "It's 11:30, and I know you've got to be home by twelve."

Eleven-thirty? I was supposed to be home at eleven. I was going to be in deep trouble with my parents.

Lord, I prayed silently, *I don't have the strength to deal with this. I said no for You, and now I've lost Branson. My heart is shattered. You've got to help me here, Lord. Help me keep it together.*

"Laurel," Jackson said, his voice strained, "you'd better speak up. I don't know where you live."

"I'm sorry," I said, coming out of my daze. I gave him the directions to my house, and he finally got me home around ten minutes before midnight. Several lights were on in the house.

Robyn got out of the car and walked up the sidewalk with me. Halfway to my door, she stopped me with a hand on my arm. "Laurel," she whispered, "obviously, something really horrible happened tonight."

"I don't feel like—"

"No, no, no," she cut me off. "I'm not trying to pry. You don't have to tell me your business or anything. I just want you to know that if you need to talk, I'm here for you. I'll listen anytime. I know you did the right thing, Laurel."

"It sure doesn't feel like it," I said, barely keeping the tears back enough to talk. "Branson is gone."

"But your virginity isn't," she said.

For some reason, that didn't make me feel a lot better.

We said good-bye, hugged, and I headed into my house.

Dad glared at me from the couch. "Laurel Shadrach, do you know what time it is?"

"Man, my night is just getting better and better," I complained.

Dad stood. "I can't deal with that smart mouth right now. You go to your room immediately. We'll talk about this after church tomorrow."

I trudged up the stairs and flopped onto my bed. He could put me on restriction forever, but it wouldn't make me feel any worse. Even if my parents stripped me of every privilege I had, it wouldn't be near as bad as losing Branson.

My mom knocked on my door, then came in. "We were worried about you, Laurel. Where have you been? If you were going to be late, why didn't you call?"

I looked up at her but found myself speechless again. Though my eyes weren't filled with tears, I'm sure their redness revealed my anguish. Mom sat next to me on the bed and held me. She rocked me back and forth like I was still her little baby.

Had I done the right thing? How would I ever know if I'd made the right decision? My heaven with Branson had turned into hell.

My mother began to pray. "Dear heavenly Father," she said, still holding me tight, "I don't know what's going on with my daughter, but I lift her woes and her worries up to You. Father, hold her precious life in the palm of Your hand. I pray that You will continue to guide her in the right direction and let her know that if she gives all her troubles to You, then You will give her wisdom to handle those problems. Help her to know that I am here too. Amen."

"Thank you, Mom," I whispered. "Thank you for that prayer. I'm OK. Well, maybe I'm not OK, but I will be."

She rubbed my back. "Just remember that after you get through tonight, joy will come in the morning."

I just hoped I'd make it through to the morning. When Mom left my room and I was alone again, I was so depressed that I punched my pillow. It felt like a brick. Things were just that heavy.

I seriously doubted that Branson thought God's rules on sex outweighed his personal desires. But if he didn't come around, how could we work through this? I wanted to explode.

When Foster said "Good morning" to me at church the next day, that's exactly what I did. "What's good about it?" I exploded.

"Sorry I spoke," he said, and he started to leave.

"I'm sorry," I said, grabbing his arm. "I've just got a lot going on right now. I know I shouldn't take it out on you. Please accept my apology."

He looked at me with compassion in his eyes. "I can't say that I understand, because I don't. But I do accept your apology, and I hope things get better for you."

Around the dinner table that evening, my father talked around the issues. "When your mother and I set rules for you kids," he commented, "it's not because we want you to have a tough childhood, but because that's how God told us to parent you. Your mother and I submit to His authority, and it is your responsibility to submit to ours. Contrary to popular beliefs, there is nothing good on the streets after 11:00 anyway."

Though he never said my name, I knew he was talking about me. It upset me that my parents were judging me when they didn't even know what happened. And it really bugged me that my father was calling me a disobedient child who didn't follow authority. That wasn't the reason I was home late at all. My dad was a good father, but he didn't know everything, and he sure wasn't God.

"So what happens when you're out on a date and your boyfriend kicks you out on the street and you have to walk home?" I asked angrily. "If thirty minutes go by, is that such a bad thing?" I pushed back from the table and stormed up to my room. I wanted desperately to lock the door, but that was prohibited at my house.

Pretty soon my brother Liam came in. He'd never been too happy about my relationship with Branson, so I didn't want to hear anything he had to say.

"So, what are you here to tell me?" I lashed out. "'I told you so'? 'I knew Branson was no good'? 'Why didn't you call me when you were in the parking lot crying your eyes out'?"

Don't you just love the challenges?
Don't you just love the trials?
Don't you just love not knowing if you can go the last mile?

Because in those times of doubt and fear,
You get to find you persevere.
You win the fight, you win the battle.
And though it gets rough and tough and hard and stuff,
You do, and thank God you did it.

Why do you keep on pushing?
Why do you never give in?
Why do you keep on fighting to eventually win?
Because when it's dark and you can't see the way,
You do not stop until you spot a brighter day.

And that's when you've won the fight,
When you've won the battle.
And though it gets rough and tough and hard and stuff,
You did. With God's help, you did it.

I had told myself that since I was out of Kleenex, I
would have to be all out of tears. But hearing my brother
sing those precious words to me brought on tears I didn't
know I had. When Liam saw the empty tissue box, he
dabbed my tears away with his shirttail.

"Laurel, that song really helps me in my struggle to stay
pure. I'm a guy, so I know how Branson feels. But those lyrics
help me live by God's will and Word. There's gonna be a better reward in the end. And He will help you wait. I promise."

"Thanks," I said, smiling briefly.

"I love you," he said as he gently closed my door.

———————

I dreaded going to school the next day. I told my mom I
was sick, but I knew the story wouldn't fly. Brittany never
did show up, so my mother drove me to school. When I arrived, she was at my locker.

"Oh, Laurel, I'm so sorry I forgot to pick you up," Brittany said. "I was running late this morning."

"You could have called.".

"When I phoned your house, the answering machine
was on, so I figured your mom was already bringing you."
She put her arm around me and walked me down the hall.
"I hear you and Branson broke up."

"How can you say it so flippantly, like it's no big deal?"

"It's a big deal. But I told you it was going to happen. You wouldn't put out, so he put you out . . . of the car, that is."

"How do you know all that?" I cried, pulling away from her.

"It's going around all over school." She chuckled.

Why in the world did she think this was funny? She was supposed to be my best friend and she was practically laughing in my face. I wanted to slap her.

"Why are you looking at me so mean?" she asked. "Did I jump to the wrong conclusion? Everyone knows you're a goody-goody who can't handle the pressures of being in a real relationship."

Everyone knows?

She wasn't jumping to the wrong conclusion, but she was jumping on my nerves, she was jumping on my emotions, and she was jumping up and down on my already wounded heart. She was jumping into tension.

five

hating
the world

get out of my face!" I never wanted to see that stuck-up
Brittany again for the rest of my life.

"What did you say to me?" she asked, her hand perched
on her slim hip.

I walked away.

Unfortunately, she followed me. "You might not want to
get testy with me, Laurel."

I kept walking. I was getting tired of her high-and-
mighty ways, acting like she had authority over everything,
like if I didn't do things her way I was destined for failure. I
had nothing nice to say to her, so I hoped she would just get
the picture and leave me alone.

She didn't. "I saw Branson this morning."

Stick a knife in my back, why don't you?

"He suggested you share a locker with me now."

I had no intention of sharing a locker with Brittany Cox,
and the one Branson was trying to kick me out of was mine.

I had let him share my locker with me. He'd given his back to the counselor, saying he didn't need it and someone else could have it. It wasn't my problem he didn't have a locker.

Ignoring Brittany's advice, I went to my locker and tried to open it. It wouldn't budge. I kept trying but kept getting the same results.

"I shouldn't tell you this," Brittany said as she leaned against the locker next to mine, "seeing as how you're ignoring me and all. But since you're starting to look incredibly stupid, I'll tell you. Branson changed the lock this morning."

"He changed the lock!" I blurted out.

"So, are you sure you don't want to share with me?" she asked, barely able to get the words out because she was trying so hard not to laugh. "It's right down the hall."

"Britt, I'm thinking a lot of things right now, but this being a funny situation is definitely not one of them. Do you know what he did with my stuff?"

"It's in my locker," she said, handing me the textbook for my first class. "Branson and I carried the rest of your stuff over there this morning."

Even in my furious state of mind, I could tell something was fishy. "Britt, you told me you got here late; that's why you couldn't pick me up."

She shrugged. "OK, maybe I fibbed a little. Branson told me to meet him here early so I could put your stuff in my locker."

"He called you? He doesn't even have your number."

"Yes, he does."

"No, he doesn't," I argued.

She rolled her eyes. "Why wouldn't he have my number? Do you think I'm making this up? Do you think yours is the only number Branson Price has? You are so full of yourself, Laurel. No car, no money, no job. All you have is a cute body and you think the world is supposed to fall at your feet. Well, like I told you before, Branson and I are friends and we have been for years. Why do you think I was trying to give you advice? I got it straight from the horse's mouth that he needed more from you. I tried to warn you, but you had to learn the hard way. Well, your way didn't work. If you don't want to share a locker with me, I'll just put your stuff on the floor."

As hateful thoughts raged through my mind, I prayed. *God, I don't believe this is happening to me. I am so mad, I feel like a tea kettle full of boiling water. And as for Brittany—*

Suddenly, Meagan jumped between us. "Hey, you guys! I've been looking all over for you and here y'all are!"

Brittany stormed away, opened her locker, and dumped all my books on the floor.

I had to get my locker back from Branson. He could break up with me, kick me out of his car, even talk to my best friend when he should have been talking to me. But he could not kick me out of something that was rightfully mine.

I was already going to be late for first period, so I turned to Meagan for a big favor. "Do you think I could keep my things in your locker for a while?"

"Laurel, people have been asking me all morning if you guys broke up, but I told them it's not true. It's not, is it?"

"Meagan, please don't—"

"Look, I'm not trying to pry," she said before I could finish my sentence.

"I just don't feel like talking about it, OK?"

"No problem. And you can keep your stuff in my locker as long as you want." She told me the combination, then said, "I've got to get to class now. Are you going to be OK?"

I said yes, but neither of us believed it.

I spent all day looking for Branson so we could straighten out this locker business, but he was nowhere in sight.

That evening I went to my first gymnastics lesson of the season. I was not looking forward to it. Coach Milligent's rough tactics were effective, but they were too much to take on bad days. I was already stressed out, and having him pick me apart was not going to help matters at all.

"Laurel," he screamed at me, "how do you think you're going to win State if you can't stay up on the beam? Have you been practicing? Do a round-off for me, right now!"

My coach didn't care about my personal problems; he just wanted to see me do what I had to do and do it right. Even if it killed me, he insisted that I rise to his expectations.

After finally performing the task to his high standards, I was exhausted. The love I used to have for this sport was fading quickly.

I don't want to do this anymore, I said to myself. I felt like I was just being used for three hours after school each day and two hours every Saturday. The worst part was, Saturday practice was at the same time as my weekly Bible study, so I couldn't attend the church group during gymnastics season.

But was I a quitter? Was I the kind of person who couldn't finish what she started? I'd wanted a college scholarship ever since I was little, and though I might not be good enough to go to the Olympics, I definitely had potential to get an education, with help from this sport. Some way, somehow, I had to find the motivation to stay on course.

Branson seemed to be going on with his business. So I decided to take the advice my mom had given me and focus on Jesus Christ. As I started to concentrate on Him, even through the grueling practice, I felt a true joy in my soul.

When the lesson finally ended, I walked home. It took forever and gave me a lot of time to think. And get angry again. As soon as I got home, I ran up to my room, closed the door, and started on my homework. Before long, Lance knocked on my door.

"What do you want?" I called out angrily.

"I need to talk to you about something," he said.

"I'm doing my homework. Go away."

"Look, it'll just take a second. I need to talk to you."

I sighed, got up, and opened the door. "OK, what?"

"Remember I told you about the girl I like, Caitlin?"

I leaned on the doorjamb. "The girl who cheers for J.V. What about her?"

"Well, at football practice today, I was gonna say hi to her but I didn't," Lance explained. "I guess I got scared. I just wanted to ask your advice."

I shook my head and trudged to the bed, leaving my door open for him. "I gave you advice three weeks ago. Are you saying you still haven't asked for her number yet?"

Lance lingered in the doorway. "Well, I was going to say something to her, but a guy on the football team walked over to her first."

"It's no big deal," I said, trying to focus on my brother's problems instead of my own. "You can win her over with your boyish charm."

Lance played nervously with the door handle. "I don't think I can compete with this guy," he said.

"Why not?"

"Well, he's a senior, for one thing."

"So what?" I got the impression my brother was trying to tell me something, and I was getting tired of the guessing game.

"He's also . . . the quarterback on the team." Lance raised his eyebrows at me.

My heart dropped. Branson was the quarterback on our team! Apparently he'd been flirting again in a major way . . . and with a sophomore!

"Get out," I screamed, throwing a pillow at him.

He ducked out of my room, and the pillow thumped against the closed door.

I sat on my bed and stared at the pillow. I had to face the fact that Branson was over me, and now he was out to get what he could from whoever would give it to him.

I threw my homework on my antique desk and watched

its legs wobble. I felt exactly like that desk. Tired, worn out, and barely able to stand.

A few days passed, and the distance between Branson and me grew. Though I could see that we had two different agendas, and it would be best if he went his way and I went mine, that knowledge didn't lessen my pain. Everyone at school wanted to console me and comfort me. But I didn't want their pity. I wanted my boyfriend.

Meagan called me after school and asked for the millionth time how I was doing.

"If one more person asks me that, I'm going to scream," I said bitterly.

"How can you talk to me like that?" Meagan whispered, stumbling over the words. "Why are you so mean to me? Do you think I'm not your friend?"

I didn't want to shut her out of my life. Just because I hadn't let her into my every thought, that didn't mean she'd become a lesser friend. "Meagan, you know what I've been going through. Why are you making me feel worse by telling me I'm mean? A friend knows when to drop a bomb on someone, and I think your timing is way off."

"Gee, I never thought about it that way."

"That's my point, Meagan," I said. "You're always thinking about yourself. It's not that I don't care about you, but I can't try to make you feel better right now. I feel like I'm drowning in a pool right now. And if I can't swim myself, I can't jump in and try to save you."

Meagan paused. "Could you just hear me out? Please?"

I sighed. "Sure, go ahead." I braced myself, knowing what she was going to say. Part of me wanted to put down the phone and not listen, but I decided to hear her out.

"I just don't think we're as close as we could be. I always offer to pick you up for school or spend the night with you or ask if you can come with me to the mall, and you always say no. But you hang out with Brittany. Whenever you have trouble in your relationship with Branson, you turn to her. I just want to know if I did something or said something to make you not want to hang out with me."

I had no idea how to answer her. I'd never really thought about our friendship that way. "Meagan, I . . ."

"It's OK. You can answer honestly."

"It's not that I purposely choose Brittany over you. It's just that we like some of the same things, or at least we used to."

"I guess that's my point. It seems to me you guys are always mad at each other. And now she's going around school talking about you, and you can't say you didn't know because yesterday she walked right past you and called you an awful name. Someone like that is not a friend, Laurel. I hang with Britt a lot, too, but we are nothing alike. I'm sorry you and Branson are having trouble, but I always thought you deserved better."

Now I really felt bad. "Thanks, Meagan," I said. "I'm sorry I made you feel like I didn't want to be your friend. I never meant to do that. You're so shy and Brittany is outgoing, so maybe I responded to her personality more. Right now I'm just trying to establish where my relationship is with Christ." My heart suddenly filled with love for this girl who cared so much about me. "Meagan, you really are one of my closest friends."

"You're one of mine too," she said.

"And I have heard Brittany talk about me. I've listened to her and other people tell me I was stupid for not giving Branson what he wanted."

"Oh, I don't think that," Meagan said. "I'm a virgin, too, and that's a special thing."

Meagan and I turned out to have more in common than I thought. "Well, just hang in there with me, OK?" I said, choking a little.

"I will," she promised.

"Look, I've got to get my homework done. I'll call you later. I promise."

In spite of all the flak I'd been receiving in gymnastics, I was determined to turn it around. I was going to put all my energy into this sport, especially now that Branson was no longer around to distract me.

"Laurel, that's excellent," Coach Milligent complimented me. "Way to stick that landing! That's exactly what I'm looking for. This time, I want you to plant your knees in the same position, but give me a little more power in the run so you can flip higher in the air."

"OK," I said.

"I want another landing like that last one, Laurel. Stick it! Stick it!"

I did a double-twist layout vault with a star value of 9.9. Most of my routines had a star value of 9.8, so this vault was exceptional. I approached the bag, fixed my leotard, and took off with all the power in me.

With each step I chanted to myself, *Forget Branson! Forget Brittany! Forget all the people who said I can't! I can! I can! I can! I'm gonna show them all I can!*

When I flipped into the air, it felt magical. I had the height, the form, the grace. Everything was flawless. But on the landing my leg almost came up from under me and I twisted my ankle.

The assistant coach, Miss Weslyn, ran to my side. "Are you OK?"

"It hurts! It hurts!" I screamed. During all my years of gymnastics, I had never had a serious injury. I guessed there was a first time for everything, but why did it have to be now?

As a trainer helped me to the examining room, I cried, *Lord, how could You let this happen to me? It's my senior year and my life is a mess. I did the right thing. I said no to Branson and now You're going to let this happen?*

91

The trainer examined my ankle carefully. Then he crossed the room and spoke to Coach Milligent. I held my head in my hands. The shock had sapped all my strength. Soon the coach came over and helped me up on a bench.

"Laurel," he said softly, "I have good news and bad news. The bad news is, you've got a deep sprain. It's going to take six to eight weeks to heal."

"Are you serious?" I cried. "All my training time—"

"Calm down," he told me. "The good news is that you still have another six to eight weeks to train before January. You can do this. What I saw out there today is something I have never seen from you before. I saw a champion's heart and a person who wants to win. I saw drive and determination. There are exercises you can do to keep your upper body strong so when you come back you won't have to start from scratch. This isn't the end, Laurel."

Though he sounded positive and there was some good news, I knew I would have to work twice as hard as anyone else to achieve my goal. That didn't seem fair. It was one more complaint to add to the list I was keeping for God.

Miss Weslyn drove me home. When I walked in the door, my mom was shocked to see my ankle wrapped in a long, brown Ace bandage. I told her everything the trainer had said to me. I had to soak my ankle in warm water before I went to bed every night. And several times during the day I was supposed to wrap it in a heating pad for five to fifteen minutes, then do a series of exercises with special weights. Then I had to rub my ankle with ice to reduce the swelling. How I was supposed to do all that and still get on with my life, I had no idea!

Mom waited on me like I was a queen and she was my handmaiden. She propped my ankle up with three pillows to try to keep the swelling down. She even fixed my favorite food for dinner. Before I went to bed that night, while my ankle was soaking in a bucket of warm water, she brought in a cup of apple-cinnamon tea and a pink rose she had picked from her garden.

"Mom, you are so sweet," I said, hugging her.

Just as I thought she was about to leave, she sat down beside my bed. "I know this is difficult, honey. I want you to know that I'm praying for you. You know, everything happens for a reason."

Now, why did she have to say that? Yes, God knows, sees, and is in control of everything. But what could possibly be the reason behind this? Why was the Lord punishing me? And if He wasn't, why did it feel like He was? I couldn't take two steps forward without having to take five steps back. I had said no to Branson and it took everything I had to keep my commitment to the Lord. Surely a blessing should come from that. Gymnastics was the only thing that mattered and now that was practically gone too.

Hearing my mother talk about all the good reasons God had for this made me uncomfortable. I had grown up in church, studied God's Word, and tried hard not to sin against Him. And for what? Brittany was against me and Branson had left me. I didn't understand the Lord's actions at all.

I couldn't tell my mom what I was really thinking, so I changed the subject. "Mom, since tomorrow is Friday, can I stay home?"

"Of course, dear," she said with motherly concern. "Here, take your Tylenol." She handed me the pills and a glass of water. After I swallowed, she dried my foot in a big, fluffy towel, then wrapped the covers over me and left with the bucket of water.

Life was so unfair. I wondered what things would be like if I had surrendered to Branson. Maybe I'd made the wrong choice. I had no guy and my best friend was gone. I felt sick to my stomach because of it.

Maybe I should tell Branson that I want to try it his way. Things can't get any worse, that's for sure.

When I awoke the next morning, there were muffins and orange juice on my nightstand with a note that said, "Running errands. Be back in a little while. Mom."

My sprained ankle made it difficult to take a bath or shower, so I just washed up and put on my robe. We only had one television in the house with cable, and that was in the family room, twenty-four steps away.

I hopped down the stairs, clutching the railing. When I made it to the bottom, I smiled with relief. After hurling myself onto the couch, I realized that I needed a blanket and a pillow to prop my foot on. That meant I had to go back upstairs.

I worked my way up to my room and stuffed a pillow under one arm and a blanket under the other. On my way back downstairs, I got tangled in the blanket and did a flip down five steps, screaming all the way. I lay there in pain, unable to move. It hurt so bad I thought I'd probably twisted my ankle again. I wondered if I'd done some damage that couldn't be undone this time.

I didn't lay there long before Mom walked in the door. "Laurel, are you all right?" she asked, nearly dropping the bags in her hand.

"I fell down the stairs," I sobbed.

She set the bags down on the nearest table. "What are you doing out of bed?" she asked as she hurried back to me.

"I wanted to watch TV," I explained. "Mom, it hurts bad!"

She knelt beside me. "Come on, honey, let's get you to the couch." She wrapped her arms around my waist. "Be careful not to put any weight on it."

She struggled to get me to the couch. Then she checked my bandages and set the pillow under my leg.

"Why do these things keep happening to me?" I cried.

Mom wrapped the blanket around me. "Laurel, honey, try to relax. It's not as bad as it seems."

94

"It hurts! Even worse than before."

"I'll go get your heating pad," she said, and off she scurried.

"I'm sure I couldn't feel any worse than if I'd gone ahead and done it with Branson," I grumbled, my ankle throbbing. "But I didn't and I still feel horrible. I don't know why I even bothered."

"What did you say?" Mom said as she came back with the heating pad.

Oh, no. What had I just done? I was venturing into dangerous territory now!

"So that's why Branson broke up with you, huh? He was trying to push you to do something you knew was wrong." She shook her head sadly. "He always seemed like such a nice boy." She plugged in the heating pad and wrapped it around my ankle.

I was already on thin ice, so I decided to go a little further. "Mom, Branson acts all polite at church, but when we're together he is totally different."

"And now you're saying you should have gone all the way with him?" She raised her eyebrows.

I had never directly lied to my mom. I'd skirted around certain issues before, but I had never looked her straight in the eyes and told a lie.

She sat next to me on the couch. "Laurel, I want you to answer me."

The heating pad felt great, and I just wanted to relax in its warmth. But I knew my mother was waiting for my response. "Mom, I'm not as sweet and innocent as you think I am. You're not gonna like hearing this, but I love Branson. I melt whenever he kisses me."

I expected my mom to faint when she heard those words, but she remained calm, cool, and collected. So I jumped in and started describing all my inner thoughts and feelings. I even told her about how much I struggled in the area of sexual purity.

"I didn't know you and Branson were experiencing those things," she said.

"Well, we are," I grumbled.

She reached over and tucked my hair behind my ears. "Laurel, I want you to know that you can talk to me about the hard stuff."

"But, Mom," I argued, "now you'll never let me see Branson again. You'll just condemn him and me and tell me how awful we are."

"No, I won't," she assured me. "But I think I can share some of God's wisdom with you."

"God?" I turned away. "Don't bother."

She touched my arm gently. "Why do you say it like that, with so much frustration and anger?"

I tried not to cry. "Because it's hard, when you're having feelings about sex and stuff, to just turn all that off and think about what God wants."

"I understand, honey, but listen. God sent His only Son, Jesus Christ, to die for you. He loves you and wants what's best for you. He left us His Word so that we can live the best lives possible, free of guilt and sin. You think you're in a bad place now with that broken ankle and no boyfriend. But think of what life would be like if Jesus hadn't died on the cross. Where would you be then?"

Mom paused and waited for me to look at her. I didn't speak. But I was grateful to be having this conversation. I knew God was speaking through her.

"If Christ hadn't died," she went on, "you would have no real power over your sin. But because of your relationship with Jesus, you have the Holy Spirit inside you, giving you the desire to obey. This desire fuels your willpower and gives you the ability to please God and the strength to say no to sin. Our joy and hope comes from pleasing Him. And sweetie, a life without joy and hope is . . . well . . . far worse than a life without gymnastics or a boyfriend."

I couldn't stop from smiling a little. Mom gently kissed

my forehead, then went to the kitchen to fix lunch. My ankle was feeling better, so I turned off the heating pad and rested the remainder of the afternoon, thinking a lot about what she'd said. I was so angry at Branson, I hated him. I knew hate was probably not the right word, but I couldn't shake the deserted feeling I'd had when he left me in the parking lot.

"Laurel, wake up!" My brother Lance stood over me, trying to hand me the cordless phone.

"I'm asleep," I groaned.

"I think you want to take this call."

I gave him a dirty look, then grabbed the phone. "Hello?"

"Laurel," a quiet male voice said.

"Branson?" I said, sitting up. I was suddenly wide awake.

"Laurel, I'm in the hospital."

"What?" I cried. "Are you OK?"

"I broke my arm at the game. They took me to Newton County Hospital. We were playing Eastside tonight."

"You broke your arm?" I asked, too stunned to say anything intelligent.

"Laurel, my chances for a scholarship . . . I probably won't be able to play all season."

I stared at my bandaged ankle. I knew exactly how he felt. But even though I understood the depth of his pain, why should I care? He wasn't mine to worry about any longer. Why in the world was he calling me? If he wanted someone to be by his side and ride the road of depression with him, he should have thought about that before he put me out of his car and out of his life.

"What am I going to do, Laurel?" he whined.

Though I wouldn't have wished it on my worst enemy —and as far as I was concerned, he sure deserved that title —it seemed like sweet justice. The thought of him not measuring up in football during his senior year actually made my ankle feel a lot better.

"Laurel, are you there? What am I supposed to do? I feel like everyone is against me."

God, did you do this? I wondered. *I know the Bible says that loves does not delight in evil. Help me not to delight in Branson's pain.*

As I prayed for Branson, the Lord gave me a new perspective on my own situation. I sensed God's love and peace and finally stopped hating the world.

making
it right

i had dreamed of this moment for days. Branson was on
the phone, and he was extremely emotional because he
missed me. Well, he hadn't said that exactly, but the fact that
he had called me in his darkest hour was inviting. Was I going to answer his call to me? All the voices in my head said,
No! Don't do it! He's still a jerk! You're better off without him! But
those voices were drowned out by the whisper of God in my
heart.

"I'm sorry this is happening to you," I finally said. "But
you're a fighter, Branson. You might fall, but you'll get back
up. This is only temporary."

"It doesn't feel that way," he moaned.

"I understand, more than you know," I said.

"What are you talking about?"

I took a deep breath. "I was at gymnastics practice yesterday and I had a lot on my mind. I did the first couple of vaults
perfectly, but when I tried the last one, I sprained my ankle."

"Are you serious?" he asked.

"Oh yeah."

"Are you OK?" He sounded genuinely concerned.

"Well, it wasn't too bad, but I did something dumb today."

"What?"

"I fell down the stairs at my house."

He laughed a little, and I had to chuckle too.

"So I know how you feel," I said. "There's only a fifty-fifty chance I'll be able to compete this year. I'm devastated."

"I'm sorry you didn't have me to call," he said in the sweetest voice. "I wish I would've been there for you. Maybe this is why this happened to me. You're my girlfriend, but I've been such a jerk to you."

He called me his girlfriend! I cringed on the inside, not sure how that was supposed to make me feel. Even though I couldn't say it to him, I was glad his injury had happened. At least now he realized how much he needed me.

"Can you forgive me?" he asked.

"What for?" I asked. "For leaving me in the middle of the street with no ride home? For putting a new lock on my locker without even asking me? Or for flirting with practically all the underclassmen at our school? Exactly what am I forgiving you for, Branson?"

"Wow," he said. "I didn't realize what a jerk I've been to you. I guess I want forgiveness for all of that. When I was lying out on that field tonight, the only person I thought about was you. I need you. Will you forgive me? Please?"

I wasn't able to say anything at that moment. Too many emotions were swirling around inside.

"Look, I've got to go. The nurse is coming in to put on my cast. I'll call you tomorrow, OK?"

"Call me tomorrow for sure," I said.

"I will. Thanks for listening, Laurel."

"You take care," I told him. When I hung up the phone, I was so excited I could have done twelve flips in a row, even with my sprained ankle.

Lord, I prayed, *I know it's been a while since I came to You. I need Your forgiveness now, just like Branson asked for mine. I blamed You, but my lack of faith was uncalled for.* I went on to tell the Lord how sorry I was for doubting Him and how happy I was at that moment.

Then I started thinking. *Before Branson calls me back, I have some serious decisions to make. Should we get back together? What if he doesn't call? That's crazy. Of course he'll call. And when he does, I will forgive him.*

My dad and my brother Lance came home. Lance was excited because he'd won the game. After Branson got hurt, he went in as the quarterback. Lance described every play. I smiled at his enthusiasm.

When Lance left, my dad came in from the kitchen with two glasses of ice water. "So, how's the patient? You seem happier." He handed me one of the glasses.

"Yeah, I'm feeling better. Thanks."

"Did your brother tell you Branson got hurt at the game?" he asked, sitting beside me.

"I heard about it."

"From who?"

I knew my dad was fishing for information, but I didn't mind divulging. It was no secret. "Branson called me. He was in serious pain."

Dad shook his head.

I sighed. "We've been through a lot and I really care about him. He apologized to me and I do want things to work out for us. But I'm a little worried. If I go down that road again, how do I guard my heart?"

Dad took a sip of his water. "To be honest, Laurel, I would love to tell you to stop seeing him. I wish you'd never grown so attached to that boy in the first place. But I realize that I can't tell you who to give your heart to. I can only pray that you will seek to please God and to hear His voice in the matter. The Lord does want you to forgive Branson, but that doesn't mean you have to continue dating him. And it certainly doesn't mean God intends for Branson to be your husband. Laurel, you have a lot to pray about. No matter how much you love Branson, God is very specific about sex. It's His gift for a couple's wedding night, not a date night."

At that moment I felt really convicted. Not in a million years did I want to have this intimate talk with my dad. But it was easier than I thought it would be. So I opened up some more. "Dad, I kinda blamed God for some of the things that have gone wrong in my life recently. I know it was a mistake, but how can I make it right?"

Dad smiled. "By humbly falling on your knees and asking God for forgiveness. Sweetheart, the key is to trust God regardless of your circumstances, whether they seem good or bad to you. When you trust God in everything, that's when peace comes. The Lord knows we aren't perfect, but He wants us to turn to Him for strength. Stay prayerful, Laurel. And know that your mother and I love you unconditionally."

"I love you, too, Dad."

"Now, you get some rest." He hugged me tight and tucked the blanket around my shoulders. Things were looking up, and that was certainly a blessing.

The cranberry-red, pumpkin-orange, and sunrise-yellow leaves looked breathtaking as I sat on my porch swing early Saturday morning. Fall was here and with it came a crisp breeze. It was as if Jesus was whispering to me and I didn't want to miss whatever it was He had to tell me. I needed direction and I wanted to hear His wishes for my life.

I opened my Bible and read Isaiah 40:31. "They that wait upon the Lord shall renew their strength; they shall mount up with wings as eagles; they shall run, and not be weary; and they shall walk, and not faint."

Maybe I don't have to rush the answers, I thought. *Maybe this is my time to stay still and let God truly reveal Himself. Just as He takes care of the changing seasons, the Lord will take care of me. Lord, take my life and use it for Your glory. I love You with all my heart.*

As I opened my eyes, one of those beautiful leaves hand painted by God found its way into my hands. Though it might not have meant anything, for me it was a sign that if I opened my hands and kept my thoughts lifted to the Lord, He would be with me in the most precious and beautiful way.

I gently sang the song, "God Is So Good."

A tear trickled down my face as I realized how openly I had blamed God. I didn't give the Lord any credit for knowing what He was doing. I had let Him down and I hoped I would never doubt Him again. *When you think you know more than God, you find out just how foolish you really are,* I thought.

Brittany pulled up and got out of her car carrying twelve helium-filled balloons and a pretty wrapped gift box under her arm. "Don't say a word," she said as she scampered up the sidewalk. "I came to apologize. I'm sorry I forgot about my best friend, and I'm sorry about your misfortune. Can you forgive me?"

She sounded so sincere. I appreciated the early-morning gesture, but I understood Brittany. She always knew how to talk a good game, then later do something to totally upset me.

"I don't know if I can trust you, Brittany," I said. "I'm not mad at you, but . . . I just don't know."

Again I felt convicted. Didn't Brittany deserve the same grace God had given to me? Certainly she did, but she had broken my trust. I wasn't going to allow her to get too close until she proved herself trustworthy.

"Here, open the gift," she insisted in her own sweet way. She handed me the box as if she hadn't heard a thing I'd said.

"You didn't have to bring me a gift."

"I know, but I'm sure you'll like it." She sat on the porch swing beside me.

I took the box from her and tore into it like it was Christmas Day. Inside was a peach-colored sweater I'd seen in a store once when Brittany and I went shopping together. I had wanted that sweater so badly, but there was no way I could afford it.

"Wow!" I said.

"I just know it fits," she squealed.

I hugged her tight. I knew I didn't want to lose her as a friend. Not just because she'd bought me a gift. The thoughtfulness behind it meant a whole lot more.

"I'm sorry things didn't work out with you and Branson," she said as she tied the balloons to the back of the porch swing. "It's his loss. You did good to stand your ground." She went on and on about how I would find another guy and how I needed to focus on gymnastics anyway.

I appreciated her trying to cheer me up, but I finally had to stop her. "I got a call late last night from a really special guy. He apologized for calling so late, but—"

"Who apologized?" I suddenly had her full attention. "Who's calling your house late at night? Give me names, girl, first and last."

I grinned. "Branson. Price."

Brittany's mouth hung wide open. She was speechless, which was something Brittany never was.

"He called me from the hospital," I explained.

Her eyes narrowed. "Are you sure it was him?"

"Don't you think I would know his voice?" I laughed. "Things might be working out between us."

I thought she'd be bouncing off the walls with excitement for me. But she just stared. It was almost as if she didn't want me to get back with him.

"You don't have to protect me," I told her.

"He just broke your heart. Do you really know what you're doing?"

I thought about her question for a minute. "Maybe I don't know what I'm doing," I admitted, "but I know what I want to do. Brittany, you broke my heart but look at us. We're talking just like we used to. I love Branson, and even though he didn't say it last night, I know he loves me too."

Brittany dropped the subject and we started chatting about other things. I'd really missed our "girl talk" and we spent all night making up for lost time. I quickly remembered why Brittany and I were friends.

That evening she helped me get ready for gymnastics practice and drove me there. I hated that I still had to go to practice. I had a sprained ankle, for goodness' sake! But Coach Milligent insisted that I come in for workouts.

Once I got there, though, I followed his instructions completely, putting my all into getting better. He was remarkably pleased.

"Laurel, this is the kind of determination I need from you. I promise you will get a college scholarship if you keep giving me this kind of effort. Way to go!"

My smile was wider than the balance beam was long. It felt great being praised by someone who almost never made positive comments about anyone!

Miss Weslyn, the assistant coach, cornered me after practice. "How are you, Laurel? I hear you've been down lately."

I could always confide in her. She was kind of like my spiritual advisor. She knew God, too, and lived her life for Him.

"Things are better," I said.

"Really?" She leaned against the balance beam. "Explain."

"I was really doubting the Lord with a lot of stuff that was happening to me," I said. "But when I got out of the way, God started doing remarkable things. I overcame nearly everything. The Lord has done so much in my life."

She gave me a serious look. "Are you saying that you believe the good things that are happening to you now are in God's design, or do you believe that the bad things were

His doing too?" Miss Weslyn always liked to challenge me with the tough questions.

I thought about my answer for a moment. "I guess I would say God knows my heart and He knows what's best for me. If I trust Him, He'll work everything out."

She smiled. "That's the way you should live your life. Let God do it all. Keep surrendering yourself to the Lord daily, Laurel. Even when you don't see immediate reactions, He's still there and He's still working. He loves you, and He wants you to trust Him even when you can't see the good."

If my ankle didn't get well, if Branson and I never got back together, if Brittany and I didn't stay friends, would I still trust God? That's what she was really asking. "Yes," I told her and myself. "I'm at a place now where I can trust God with all of it."

"Great," she said as she hugged me.

That evening as I got ready to go out with Branson, Mom came into my room.

"Laurel, are you sure you've got this thing under control?" she asked. "What's going on with you and Branson?"

"I don't know," I said. "We aren't jumping back into our relationship yet. We're just friends right now. If we continue to be good friends and build a solid foundation, neither one of us can get our feelings hurt. We enjoy spending time with each other, and that's what we're gonna do tonight."

"OK," Mom said. "Looks like you've got it all planned out."

"Yep." I grinned. "I even know what I'm going to wear, thanks to Brittany." I picked up the peach-colored sweater my friend had given me. "It looks good with the bandage on my ankle, don't you think?"

Mom chuckled. "I saw the two of you all chummy this morning, but I never got the chance to ask you about it."

"I found out this morning that she really is my friend," I

explained, pulling on the sweater. "And since I believe that beyond a shadow of a doubt, I can deal with all of her idio-syncrasies."

"Well, look at my daughter. Not only is she beautiful but intellectual as well. I'm so proud of you."

I rolled my eyes but thanked Mom anyway. She tried to help me down the stairs, but I assured her I could manage it on my own.

As Mom helped me get settled on the couch, she said, "Liam is having some of the guys from the band over to practice."

"Am I going to have to go back upstairs?" I moaned.

"Only if you don't want to hear them," she teased, arranging the pillow under my leg. "They'll be in the garage, so it won't be that bad."

I opened the book I'd been assigned to read in English class, but it was kinda boring, and walking downstairs with my sprained ankle had been pretty exhausting, so I ended up dozing off. Some time later, something woke me up. I opened my eyes and was startled to see someone staring me straight in the face. I reacted so suddenly my leg fell off the footstool.

"I'm sorry," Foster McDowell whispered. "I didn't mean to scare you."

"Oh yeah, just standing over me while I'm asleep wouldn't scare me at all," I said sarcastically, trying to put my leg back up.

"I didn't know you were asleep," he said, acting like he wanted to help me but didn't know how. "Your brother told me about your ankle so I came to tell you I hope it gets better soon. I know how much gymnastics means to you."

"How do you know?" I grumbled. "I never talked to you about gymnastics."

"I just know." He tried to help me with the pillow, but I grabbed it from his hands. "I guess I'll go now. I didn't mean to bother you." He started to walk away.

"Wait," I said. He stopped and turned. "I'm sorry I was rude. I was just asleep. You're not bothering me."

Foster McDowell had an intriguing presence. His dark hair and copper-brown eyes were very different from the blond hair and blue eyes that usually gazed at me. Comparing him to Branson wasn't my objective, but it came naturally. And Foster definitely held his own. I knew I really liked what I saw because my heartbeat started racing.

"I sprained my ankle during baseball season back at my old school," Foster said, sitting down next to me.

"Where are you from?"

"Spokane, Washington."

"Wow! Conyers, Georgia, must be a big change for you."

"Yeah," he admitted. "But being active in the church made the change easy."

"You know, my friend likes you," I teased.

"No, I didn't know that. Which friend?"

"Oh, never mind," I said, trying to jokingly dismiss the issue because I wasn't sure if Meagan still liked him after all.

He looked like he wanted to pursue the subject, but I avoided his gaze by pretending to fluff the pillow.

"So," he asked, "what are you doing to overcome this injury?"

I told him about all the things the doctor and my trainer had advised me to do to regain the strength in my ankle.

"You forgot one thing," he said.

"What?" I thought I'd covered everything.

"The most important thing you can do to make sure you get back on the right track."

"What?" I asked again.

"Pray. Place your ankle into God's hands. He is the ultimate healer." Foster got off the couch, knelt down on the floor, and laid his hands on my ankle. He closed his eyes and prayed a quick prayer, thanking God for my healing. Before I could say or do anything, he said, "Amen," got up, and took off to sing with the band.

I was very impressed with Mr. Foster McDowell.

That night Branson and I went to a scary movie. I hated horror films, but Branson loved them. We got there early so we could get the handicapped seats with the railing in front of them. Branson placed my pillow on the rail so I could prop up my ankle. The seat next to him was empty, so his arm cast wouldn't be in anyone's way.

At one scene in the movie, I jumped and screamed, then cowered in embarrassment at my reaction. Branson put his good arm around me. "I've got you," he whispered in my ear. "It's OK, I'm here."

He stopped watching the movie and looked me in my eyes. "Laurel," he said romantically, "I've been a jerk. How could I have been so cruel to someone I love so deeply? A lot of guys at school envy me. I'm so lucky to have you."

My insides melted as I savored every sweet word he said. "For real?" I asked him. "Do you mean all of this?"

He kissed me softly. Then he said, "What do you think? What did that kiss say?" When I didn't answer right away, he added, "Just in case you still don't get it, I love you."

I fought the urge to kiss him back. There was an issue I needed to settle first. "What about wanting to go further? How do we deal with that? What happens when I say no?"

"It's good to have you back in my life, Laurel. I don't want to risk losing you. I will wait."

"I'm scared," I admitted.

"Don't worry," he said, giving me a kiss on the nose. "We're gonna make this work."

My heart wanted desperately to believe him. "How?" I asked.

"Do you love me?"

"Of course I do. You left me in the parking lot, but as you can see, I'm still with you."

"We're both learning, and we both need each other. Together, we're making it right."

bonding
through doubts

that night, as we snuggled on the couch at my house, I wondered how in the world I would be able to control myself. I had recommitted my focus to the Lord. I'd apologized to God for feeling that He wasn't with me when things didn't go my way. Now things were right. I wanted Branson to keep touching me, to continue stroking my hair. I wanted him to tell me again and again how much he loved me.

But I had to shake those thoughts from my mind. This was going to be a challenge, not just physically but mentally too. Honestly, I was 90 percent sure that I would stay pure. Maybe even 95. But when it came to controlling my thoughts, I figured there was a fifty-fifty chance I'd win that war. Those weren't good enough odds for me. The more I thought about sex, the more I knew I'd be tempted to give in.

Even as Branson stroked my hair, I prayed in my heart, *Lord, somehow, Branson is back in my life. So I come once again needing assistance. Clearly I am too weak to stay strong in this area. Keep my thoughts pure. Show us how to date. Show us how to be close without getting too close.* I felt God's presence as I prayed. I knew He was with us, even right there on that couch. *Thanks again, Lord. I love You. Amen.*

"It's getting kind of late," Branson said softly. "I'd better go."

God must have heard my plea. Normally, I was the one who called it a night and Branson always gave a pretty strong argument to stay. But now, he was saying he needed to go. Was this our first step toward solid ground? Would he be able to keep this type of attitude? I didn't know. Only time would reveal the answers to those questions. But the realization that we were doing better than we ever had was reason for my heart to celebrate.

Branson stood. "See ya later." He slipped his coat on, struggling a bit to fit his cast through the sleeve. "I really had a good time talking to you about my thoughts," he confessed. "You truly are my best friend, Laurel Shadrach. I'm glad I realized how important you are to me."

"You drive home safely," I told him.

"I'll call you when I get in."

"Thanks."

The following Monday, Brittany picked me up for school on time for a change. I had truly missed hanging out with her. Unfortunately, it didn't last long. Even before we got to school, she said some things that really got under my skin.

"You seem too good for Branson," she said as she drove. "I'm tired of you going back and forth with him. You really should get a clue. He's just not the guy for you."

I pretended not to hear her. I knew she cared about me and was looking out for me, and I appreciated that. I didn't condemn her for it. If we were going to be friends, I needed to realize that I didn't have to like what she said, but I had to respect her opinion.

Fortunately, she didn't say anything more about Branson. But she did say something else that made me burn. "Are you going to the concert next week?" she asked. "It probably costs too much, huh?"

The condescending remark irritated me. Why did she assume that I had no money just because I didn't have fifties and hundreds in my wallet like she always did? She had her eyes focused on the road so she couldn't see how angry I was.

How does she know I don't have a bank account somewhere with scads of money accruing interest? I don't, but she doesn't know that.

I didn't want to believe that she was looking down on me because we weren't on the same economic level. But she was making it hard to think differently. Sometimes the things she said were so belittling. They always made me feel small and inadequate. I wasn't sure I could hang out with someone who thought I was a charity case.

Father, please help me find my value in You and not let these kinds of comments anger me.

As soon as we pulled into the parking lot, I let it go. Branson was standing beside his car, his music blasting. A little crowd surrounded him, but as soon as he saw me, he pushed through the group to help me out of Brittany's car. He picked me up with his good arm and swung me around so hard that all my books fell to the ground. It was the best hello I'd ever received.

"Put me down so I can pick up my stuff," I joked.

He obliged and even helped me pick up my books. When I turned around, I happened to look directly at Brittany. She had an unsupportive look on her face, as if she didn't like seeing me happy. What in the world was going on with her?

Branson put his arm around my waist and helped me inside. I wanted to have a heart-to-heart talk with Brittany, but maybe this wasn't the right time. I was so perturbed that if she'd gotten smart with me, like she often did, who knows what I would have said. I calmed down, enjoyed my guy, and decided to deal with her another time.

Branson and I walked to my locker, which he and I were sharing again, then went to our classes. I was finally starting to understand my lessons, which was a good thing because midterms were right around the corner. The apprehension I had felt about my studies at the beginning of the year was slowly fading. I realized that when I applied myself, I really could comprehend everything.

At lunch Branson and I sat beside each other. A lot of people looked at us, whether out of envy or curiosity or just because we both had injuries I wasn't sure. All I knew was that it felt great to be back with my guy!

Just before the last class of the day, I waited for Branson at our locker. Though I had seen him less than an hour before, I wanted to see him again. But the minutes passed and Branson didn't show. I knew the bell would be ringing soon, and it would take longer to get to class with my aching ankle. Just as I decided to give up, I heard laughter down the hall. Hard, loud chuckles. I recognized both of the voices. They were Branson's and Brittany's.

In seconds I became really angry again. Whatever they were kidding around about couldn't possibly be more important than my boyfriend meeting me at our locker. I knew it was wrong to be so mad, but something about the way they were laughing irritated me. I slammed the locker shut and hobbled down the hall, right between the two of them.

"Wait, Laurel! Wait!" Branson called after me.

I stopped and turned around. But he couldn't even keep a straight face because he was still laughing.

"I *have* been waiting for you," I said. "I thought you must have stayed after class to talk to a teacher or something, but no. You were just hanging around with her!"

Brittany got a shocked look on her face. "What's that supposed to mean?"

"I was talking to my boyfriend, Brittany. Please let us work this out."

"Ooh, sorry," she said sarcastically. "Your best friend dare not take any time away from you and your boyfriend."

"We were just talking," Branson defended himself. "Don't come down so hard on her. I'm sorry I was late. We lost track of the time, that's all."

"I'm going to class," I said, limping away.

"I've got practice after school," Branson called after me. "So maybe I'll come over later or I'll call you."

"Whatever," I grumbled, doing my best to get away from the scene before I said any more angry words.

Just as I turned the corner, I bumped into Foster.

"Ouch," I screamed.

"Where are you going so fast?" he asked. "You're gonna sprain your ankle again."

"I was trying to get to class!"

"Do you need any help?" he offered.

His soft voice soothed my wrath, but now my ankle was throbbing. "No, thanks," I said. "I'll be OK." I tried to walk, but the minute I put pressure on my ankle, it responded with intense pain and I collapsed onto the floor. I screamed louder.

Branson came dashing around the corner. "Laurel, are you OK?" He saw Foster standing over me and said, "Get back. I've got her."

"Some help you are, man," Foster snapped at him.

"I'm OK," I said, getting up ungracefully but on my own. "Don't you guys even start with me."

In spite of my protests, Branson helped me up and assisted me to my class. Although he was there for me, I was still upset with him. I could tell by the things he was saying that he didn't know I was still perturbed.

Branson got me settled into my seat, then he talked to my teacher. He told her he wanted to make sure someone would be available to help me out to Brittany's car after school. "I'd do it myself," he said, "but I've got football practice."

I was going to have to learn to let Branson go and trust God with him. I couldn't keep my eye on him twenty-four hours a day. I may have been his girlfriend, but I wasn't his only friend. I was seeing some jealousy in my heart and I knew it was not from the Lord. Keeping this whole thing right with Him was getting harder and harder.

At the next football game, I used my dad's binoculars to watch Branson pace back and forth on the sidelines. His face was in total despair. I knew he wanted to be out there playing so he could lead his team to victory. We were playing Rockdale High, and it was my brother leading the way, not my boyfriend.

Branson had told me he was cool with not playing but he still hoped for a miracle so his arm would get better. He said he was really excited that Lance would get his opportunity to shine on the field. However, my brother told me that during practice Branson was acting totally jealous. I'd accused Lance of making wrong assumptions, but when I saw Branson's face, I knew my brother wasn't making anything up.

As I watched, I saw Branson kick over the Gatorade carton. I knew I had to do something when I saw him after the game. But what in the world would I be able to say to get him out of this mood?

I remembered the time when Coach Milligent allowed someone to have my spot on the gymnastics team. I was really upset about being bumped down and I worked harder than ever to regain my previous position. I knew Branson could rise above this. The question was, how could I let him know that he could?

My brother did an outstanding job, but Salem lost again. When our group met at the Waffle House after the game, I wanted to ask Branson what he thought of Lance's plays, but I didn't want to start any trouble. Lots of folks were talking about what a good ballplayer my brother was. I could tell Branson was letting every comment sink down deep under his skin.

Finally, I got Branson alone at a table. "Look," I said, "I know a lot of people are saying really great things about Lance, but that doesn't negate the kind of player you are."

"You don't understand, Laurel," he seethed. "Don't pacify me."

"Branson Price, I do understand. If you keep filling your head with all the negatives, you won't have room for what you need to do, and that's get well."

He glared at me. "All the scouts were there tonight to see me, and instead they saw your brother. He's got two more years to prove himself in high school football, but I don't have one more season."

"If what you want doesn't happen," I said lightly, "then you just have to walk on."

He stared at me as if he wanted to knock me across the room. "How dare you say that? If you just walk on, you don't get any respect."

I shook my head. "Branson, I watch college football games all the time, and I see guys walk on a lot."

"There are a few success stories," he conceded, "but not many."

"Come on, Branson," I pleaded. "You can still get a football scholarship. But if you don't, it's not the end."

I wrapped my arms around him and kissed him on the cheek. I was trying to lighten the mood and let him know not to take things so seriously. Though I wasn't trying to take his future lightly, I knew he had to change his outlook on it or he was going to be doomed by negative thinking.

"Thanks," he told me.

"You're welcome," I said, glad that my attempts had worked.

"So, how's your ankle?"

"Better. I go in tomorrow to work with Coach Milligent on it."

"That man is rougher than a football coach," Branson said with a chuckle. "From what you've told me about him, I'd say you're his favorite."

"Favorite? I don't even think he likes me."

"He probably likes you as more than just an athlete," he teased.

I smacked him playfully in the head three or four times. "What are you saying?" I asked. "Coach Milligent is married, and he's at least fifteen years older than me."

"So? You act like an older man can't find a younger girl attractive."

"You should see how mean that guy treats me! The only thing he sees in me is a gold medal, and if I can't get one, then he has no use for me."

"Have you been working on your own?" he asked more seriously.

"Yeah, working and praying."

"Praying?" His eyebrows raised. "What's that going to do? Prayer without works is dead, you know."

"Yeah, but works without prayer, faith, and trust in God leaves you dependent on yourself, not the Lord. God is a miracle worker. I hope you've been praying about your situation."

"Well, if it works for you, then maybe I'll pray a little bit more for myself." He tried to sound like he was just kidding around, but the things he was saying sounded a little off. I was thankful that God blesses His children because He wants to, not because we deserve it. Hopefully, Branson would soon be the benefactor of such a gift.

Branson and I snuggled up in the booth. He was drinking coffee and I was sipping on a hot chocolate with lots of whipped cream. When the cheerleaders came in, everyone started hollering.

"Hey, there's Meagan and Brittany," I said. "Let's call them over."

"No," Branson said. "I want to spend time with you tonight. Can't it just be the two of us?"

"What am I supposed to say when they want to sit down with us?"

"I don't think they're gonna bother us."

"Look, here they come."

"It's just Meagan," he said. "Tell her we want to be alone."

"Branson, that's rude. If we wanted to be alone, then we shouldn't have come here."

When Meagan walked over, Branson turned the other way.

"Hey, guys," Meagan said, slipping into the booth opposite us. "Your brother was great, Laurel. Hey, Britt, c'mon, let's sit with Laurel."

"Meagan, we were kind of talking," I said.

"What?" she asked. "You don't want me to sit here?"

Branson wasn't helping me at all, and it was his idea.

"Meagan, I'll call you, OK?"

She stood and glared at me. "Sure, if I'm good enough to make time for." She flipped her hair, turned around abruptly, and sauntered off.

I punched Branson's good arm. "See what you did? Now she's mad at me."

"She's just a big baby," he grumbled.

I got up. "I'll be right back."

"Where are you going?"

"I want to let Meagan know that what I said was nothing personal."

"Laurel, we're talking," he whined.

"Now who's being a big baby?" I said jokingly.

I looked around for Meagan but didn't see her. After checking the ladies' room, I went outside to the parking lot. I still couldn't find Meagan, but I spotted Jackson Reid. He had a girl pinned up against his car, and from the looks of it, they were extremely into each other. I knew it had to be Robyn. She'd been sick all week, but it seemed she was feeling better now!

Unable to resist the temptation, I sidled up to the girl

inside Jackson's embrace. "You're going to get him sick, you know," I teased. "Didn't the doctor tell you not to spread your germs?"

"What?" an unfamiliar African-American girl shouted at me. I had never seen her before, but she was nowhere near as cute as Robyn. The lipstick she wore was tacky, and it was all over Jackson's lips. "How dare you?" she hollered.

Even though I wasn't sure if he and Robyn were an item, I knew they were exploring the possibility.

"Laurel," Jackson said, "can't you give a guy some privacy? Why are you all up in my business?"

"I thought it was Robyn," I said lamely.

"Robyn?" the girl shrieked. "Who she talkin' 'bout?"

Who she talkin' 'bout? I thought to myself. This girl was so unrefined. Robyn used slang, too, but she was much better and had a lot more class than this chick. I couldn't wait to get home and tell Robyn what a jerk Jackson was.

Jackson cooed into the girl's ear. "You don't need to know who she's talkin' about, baby. You just need to concentrate on me. Come on, let's go."

Jackson started to lead the girl away, but before they got too far, she turned back to me. "You go tell yo' li'l white Robyn friend to leave ma man alone. Tell 'er Jackson don't need no milk in his coffee."

She'd assumed that Robyn was white just because I was white. I guess she thought I couldn't have a black friend. I wondered if that was the way most of the world saw it.

When I walked back into the Waffle House, I noticed Brittany and Meagan sitting with Branson. Britt was in my seat. Next to my boyfriend.

"Hey, Britt," I said coolly, "could you sit on the other side?"

She pouted. "First you don't want me to sit with you at all, and now you want me to sit on the other side?"

Branson smiled. "I told them it was OK because there aren't any other seats," he said, just like a real gentleman. He was making me look like the bad guy!

"Branson, can you take me home?" I asked, gritting my teeth.

"My food is coming."

"What's going on?" Brittany asked. "Don't you want to socialize with us?"

I sighed. "You don't understand."

"Obviously not." She turned to Meagan. "Do you see what's happening here? She doesn't want to be around us."

"That's not it, Brittany. Don't put words into my mouth," I said, getting louder.

Brittany moved to the other side and Branson pulled me down beside him. But my relationship with Brittany, and now Meagan, was definitely strained.

I sat there faking it with my friends. They didn't even seem to notice. Branson, of course, was the life of the table, thrilled as always whenever the spotlight was on him. After about an hour, I noticed it was twenty minutes before my curfew. Although my house was only ten minutes away, I wasn't going to blow curfew for anyone or anything. Branson had no more excuses. He'd gotten his food and eaten it.

"It's time to go." I said.

"Yeah, I guess," Branson mumbled. "I don't want the reverend mad at me."

I ignored his comment and headed toward the door. I couldn't even bring myself to say good-bye to my girlfriends. With the way they were treating me, it didn't seem as if we were friends at all.

Branson drove me home in silence. There were a million and one things I wanted to say to him, but since none of them were nice, I decided to keep them all to myself.

When he pulled into my driveway, he finally broke the ice. "I did want to be alone with you tonight, but Britt came over with a long face saying there was no other place to sit, and before I could say anything, they sat down and started talking. I didn't mean to put you in a tough situation. But thanks for not letting them know it was me who didn't want them to sit down."

"I thought you'd tell them yourself, since you couldn't care less about having either of them as your friend. Now you've damaged both of my friendships. Thanks a lot, Branson!" I stepped out of the car and slammed the door.

"Wait!" he yelled, jumping out of the car. Since I was limping, he easily caught up to me before I reached the front porch. "I'm sorry."

"Save it," I said.

"Come on, Laurel. You know it was a horrible night for me. When your friends came over and started lightening up the mood, it let me know that I didn't need to have you all to myself to enjoy the evening."

"All you had to do was tell them you didn't want them to sit there. But no, you couldn't do that."

"All right, I'll tell them."

"No way." He just wasn't getting it. "They'll think I put you up to it. You had your chance to come clean and you didn't."

"Ladybug," he purred, "you know I love you."

"Ladybug?" I said, stunned. "Where did that name come from?"

He fidgeted, obviously caught off guard by my question. "Well, you are definitely a lady. And you crawl under my skin." He wrapped his arms around my waist and pulled me close to him. I hated this part. I was livid with him, but when he held me—even with one arm in a cast—all the anger faded away. Though he wasn't totally off the hook, the kiss he planted on my lips put some points on the scoreboard for his side.

I felt his hands leave my waist, and as they touched my rear, the porch light flipped on and the door flew open.

We were both startled to see my mom standing there with her hands on her hips. "Laurel, you have one minute to make curfew, and having been on restriction, I think you might want to make it this time."

"Hey, Mrs. Shadrach," Branson said, stumbling over his words. "How are you doing this evening?"

"I see your arm is better," she said, her lips tight. "Seems like it can stretch to all kinds of places."

He quickly took his hands off my body. Both of us were red faced, and I was too embarrassed to even say good night. I waved good-bye, shooed him off the porch, and jetted in the house.

"Wait a minute, young lady," my mom said, closing the door. "We need to talk."

"Mom, I feel pretty yucky. It was drizzling at the game earlier. And my ankle is really sore."

"You didn't seem to feel so bad a few seconds ago. I think you can survive a five-minute discussion. In the kitchen, please."

I followed her into the kitchen. What else could I do?

"What's going on, Laurel?" Mom asked sternly, her arms across her chest.

"We were just saying good night," I said, sitting at the table and propping my leg up on the chair next to me.

"You're playing in dangerous territory."

"It was just a kiss."

"You're struggling with his physical needs. You said you had it under control, but what I saw didn't look that way to me."

And who asked you? I thought to myself. *Did I ask you to peep out the window? Who told you to come outside? I still had one minute.* I wished she would just mind her own business and stay out of mine. "Tell you what, Mom. It won't happen again, OK?"

"I have my doubts."

"Are you saying you don't trust me?"

"I don't know, Laurel. Do you trust this guy? Seemed to me like he had you eating out of the palm of his hand."

"We were just kissing," I huffed. "What did you think we were gonna do? Provide entertainment for the whole neighborhood?"

"I don't know where you're getting this attitude from, young lady. If you want to keep seeing that boy, some ground rules will have to be set and followed. Do you understand?"

"Yes, ma'am," I said, trying to hold my tongue. Then I decided to go ahead and tell her what I thought. "Mom, I love Branson. And no matter how hard I try to fight it, those weird feelings just keep coming up. I'm sorry you witnessed what you did, but if you want to be my friend as well as my mom, there are some things you need to know about what's going on between us."

"I got an eyeful of what's going on between you two. What I want to know is what you're going to do about it."

"I've been praying about it, for one," I said in my defense.

She sat next to me at the kitchen table. "That's good for starters."

"And for most of our date we were at the Waffle House."

"Well, it's good that you weren't alone."

"Then, when we got into the car, we didn't do anything until we got home."

Mom took a deep breath and stared at her hands. "Laurel, you can't fix a relationship with physical activity. The bond has got to be Christ. I know Branson is a member of our church, but I don't see him there regularly." She looked at me, and I knew she was telling me these things because she cared about me, not just because she wanted to give me a lecture. "Why don't you invite him to the church youth retreat in the Blue Ridge Mountains? They're having a workshop about this kind of thing. Maybe the two of you can take it together."

"Maybe," I said, although I wasn't sure Branson would be really excited about it.

"Honey, I don't want to tell you that you can't see him anymore, but if dating him continues to put that kind of pressure on you, then I will stop it. If you want to continue seeing him, you need to work on this."

"Yes, ma'am," I said, with a better tone of voice than the last time I'd said those words. I got up and kissed her on the cheek. "Good night, Mom. And thanks."

I went upstairs, read a book while I soaked my ankle in the bucket of warm water, then tried to go to sleep. But I just tossed and turned. Around 11:50 the phone rang. I hoped it wasn't for me. But moments later, my youngest brother, Luke, brought me the phone. I knew I had to make it quick. I didn't want to anger my parents any more than I already had.

"Hello?" I asked quietly after Luke closed the door.

"Hey, I just wanted to let you know I made it home," Branson said.

"You're just now getting home?"

He hesitated. "I stopped back at the Waffle House on my way."

"Why?" He couldn't have still been hungry.

"I just wanted to hang out with some of the guys on the team."

I decided to take what he said at face value. "Branson, are we OK?"

"Why would you ask that? Of course we are. I don't know about your mother, but you and I are fine."

"Good, I'm glad." I knew he thought I was crazy, but I had to know. "And Mom's fine, don't worry about her."

"I'm sorry she caught us," Branson said, "but your lips sure tasted good."

"Please don't say that." Our relationship had been so up and down, it felt like we were on an unending roller coaster.

"Don't say what?" Branson asked. "That I like having my hands all over you?"

"Good thing one of them is in a cast."

"And it wanted to come out of the cast."

I laughed. "You are so bad."

"I'm just being honest."

"Listen, I'd better get off the phone. I've got practice in the morning. What are you doing this weekend?"

"I'm going on a recruiting trip for Georgia."

"Oh yeah, I forgot."

"I hope Coach Eckerd likes me."

"Is he the head coach?"

"Yeah. Some of us recruits are gonna try to talk to him after the game. I hear he's pretty selective about who he speaks to, but I'm hoping I can get some one-on-one time with him."

"I can't wait to hear all about it. I'm sure it'll be great." I decided to try out my mom's idea on him. "Hey, that youth retreat's happening in a few weeks. Mom said she thinks we ought to go to some of the workshops. There's one she says we both need to attend."

"Let me guess. It's all about fornication, right?"

"Something like that. So, what do you think?"

"My mom wants me to go, too, and that is my free weekend. I guess I probably will."

"That's good!"

"Don't get your hopes up, though. If something else comes up, I might not go after all."

I wanted to tell him, *Sometimes you have to make the things of God a priority.* But I knew he didn't want to hear that.

———————————

The following Monday, right after school, I called Coach Milligent and begged him to meet me at the gym an hour before practice started. My ankle still hurt, but I really wanted to see what I could do. It took some convincing, but he finally agreed.

Unfortunately, every time I tried to vault I stopped because I was afraid of reinjuring myself. I could tell Coach was frustrated with me, and I was getting so irritated with myself that I was in tears. He said all his usual mean things to me, but they weren't working, so he tried a new tactic.

He sat me on the mat, then pulled me so close there wasn't room for a hand between us. "Laurel," he said, stroking my hair, "I've always liked you. And now that you're a young lady, you're perfect. You have the best body, the best moves, and the most adorable presence. I need you to give me what I want."

All I could think about was Branson telling me that my coach of three years had the hots for me. Could my boyfriend be right? I remembered having a crush on Coach Milligent in the ninth grade, when I first started taking lessons. Though he was absolutely gorgeous, he was my coach. And he was married.

"I need water," I said as I hopped up. I took my time at the water fountain. I had no idea what was going to happen next or what Coach Milligent was expecting.

"Laurel," he called out, "I know you might not be ready, but now is the time to do this. We need to connect. It's just me and you. I know you're afraid, but it'll be OK."

So Coach was going to demand that I give him what he wanted regardless of how I felt! I was horrified. He wanted us to be bonding through doubts.

eɪɢʜt

witnessing
total betrayal

top right there, Coach," I yelled. "Don't come any closer!"
He stopped in his tracks. "Laurel, what's wrong with
you?"

My whole body shook, but I stood my ground. "I respect you very much. Even when you yell at me, I never say
anything back to you. But this is going to stop. I want to get
a college scholarship and I want to make it to the U.S. gymnastics team, but I'm going to do it the right way. Your wanting to be intimate with me is all wrong."

His eyebrows came together in a frown. "You've got me
confused," he said, backing up. "What are you talking
about, Laurel? Intimacy? Me and you? Where are you getting these crazy accusations?"

So he was going to play dumb. Now that I'd called him
on it, he was acting as if I'd made it all up. Was I here by
myself? Was someone besides him saying those things to
me?

Since he claimed to be confused, I decided to tell him where I was getting these ideas from. "My boyfriend, Branson, told me—"

"Laurel," he said, holding up his hands in defense, "you misunderstood me. I would never betray our trust like that. The bond we have as coach and gymnast is one I believe in wholeheartedly. And in case you don't know it, I love my wife. She gives me everything I need and more. Maybe playing with your hair was too much, but I do that with my niece when she's upset and she says it helps her calm down."

I was starting to feel like a fool.

"I guess I need to be more conscious about my choice of words. When I said I wanted you to give me what I want, I meant performing the vault. You tried and retreated three times in a row. That's just as frustrating for me as it is for you. I have big expectations for your gymnastics career."

Coach Milligent sat in a chair against the wall and stared at his hands. "Do you remember Mandy Drew?"

"Yeah," I said. She'd been on the gymnastics team the year before, but I hadn't seen her around lately.

"She accused me of having inappropriate contact with her. That's why she's no longer on the team. She was making it all up, but her accusation severely damaged my relationship with my wife for several months. I almost lost the love of my life. After that I promised myself I would never be alone with a female gymnast again." He looked up at me. "But you begged me to meet you here early, and I know how badly you want to work your way back after the injury, so I made an exception."

Now I felt really horrible. His only agenda was for me to be the best gymnast I could be, and here I was telling him off.

"Laurel, if I did anything to make you feel that I had ulterior motives, I just want to assure you that nothing like that is on my mind. My interest in you is strictly professional."

"Coach," I said, "I'm really sorry for accusing you like I did. I was wrong. I hope you'll accept my apology."

"Of course." Coach Milligent smiled. "Now, how about trying that vault again?"

"You mean, right now?" I said.

He nodded. "Why not? The rest of the class will be coming in soon."

Believe it or not, after that whole crazy ordeal, and in spite of my ankle throbbing like mad, I did one of the best vaults of my life. It's too bad there weren't any judges around to see it! But, since I was always my toughest critic, at least I proved to myself that I could do it.

The next day, as soon as I saw Robyn in class, I told her all about my run-in with Jackson. Unfortunately, before she had a chance to say anything, the teacher started class. She showed a video, which was really boring.

"Are you sure you saw him kissing someone else?" Robyn whispered to me, her eyes wide.

"It's not like I don't know what Jackson Reid looks like!" I understood that she didn't want to believe it. Even though Branson and I had our problems and he flirted quite a lot, I would have actually had to see it with my own eyes to believe that he was cheating on me, at least on the level that Jackson had. "Are you guys dating seriously?" I whispered back.

"Not really," she admitted, "but things have been pretty hot and heavy."

"Ladies," our teacher called to us. "Pay attention to the video. No talking."

I knew Robyn had the hots for Jackson, but I had no idea how deep her affection was for this guy. I could see in her eyes how hurt she was. Her whole demeanor had changed. She was acting like someone close to her had just passed away.

Finally, Robyn stood and asked the teacher if she could

be excused. After she left the room, I knew there was a lot more to the story than I knew. I raised my hand and asked the teacher if I could go check on Robyn. After receiving permission, I ran to the closest girls' bathroom and was relieved when I recognized her shoes under one of the stall doors. "Hey, Robyn," I said, "it's me."

She didn't answer, but I heard her weeping.

"I know you like Jackson, but this is too much. At least you found out what he was like before it was too—"

The stall door flew open and she finished my statement. "Before it was too late? It's already too late, Laurel!"

"What do you mean? I'm confused. How is it too late?"

Robyn came out of the stall and yanked a paper towel out of the dispenser. "Jackson came over to my house last Friday," she said, blotting her tear-streaked face with the towel.

"Tell me you didn't . . ." I said, fearing her next words.

She turned to me. "Yeah, Laurel, we did. Jackson Reid and I went all the way. He told me it meant a lot to him, and it meant a lot to me too." She leaned against the wet sink. "Now you tell me he was out with someone else. Laurel, I feel like such a prostitute. I was so sure it was right. But I was wrong. I wish I could take last Friday back." Her whole body started shivering.

I gave Robyn a long hug, trying to comfort her. Pretty soon I started quivering too. I wanted to tell her that sex is not a toy or a game. It's not something to be used to reel a guy in or to keep him for that matter. When the relationship doesn't work out, sex is an action that can't be reversed. It's never worth the price. There was a clear reason why God tells us to wait until marriage.

But I knew it wasn't the right time to say those things to Robyn. Not yet. So I just stood there in the girls' bathroom and held her.

Two nights later, as I approached my parents' room to ask them a question, I overheard them talking.

"You're going to have to do something," I heard Mom say to Dad. "If you don't talk to Laurel soon, it's going to be too late. She is seriously contemplating having sex with that boy."

I stopped right there, forgetting all about the question I'd come to ask. I couldn't believe what I was hearing. How could my mom betray my confidence and talk to Dad about my private matters? If she thought I was still having the problem, then all she had to do was talk to me about it. She didn't have to bring it up with my father. I knew that because they were husband and wife they were supposed to share everything, but I didn't appreciate her breaking the trust I had bestowed upon her. My dad didn't talk to me when my period started. He didn't say anything when my body began to develop. Why would I want to discuss sex with him?

"Sweetheart," Dad said to Mom, "are you sure this is going through her mind?"

"I caught them on the porch in a compromising position," Mom said quickly, like a balloon that had just been waiting to bust. "I'm telling you, Dave, you have to do something. I don't want Laurel to make the biggest mistake of her life. You know this is totally wrong. She's been in and out of a relationship with this Branson boy for almost three years. I never know when they're together and when they're not. Maybe we should just stop them from seeing each other altogether."

That sounded pretty harsh. And it didn't seem right. Even if they both agreed to this, there was no way I could go for it. I imagined seeing Branson at school behind my parents' backs. The last thing I wanted to do was be dishonest with them. But how could I handle this if they stepped into my life and gave me such strict boundaries? I held my breath to see what my dad's response would be.

"No, Laura," he said. "I'm not sure if that's the way to go. Maybe I should go talk to her."

Good idea! I thought. I boldly stepped into their room, determined to get this all out in the open. "Talk to me about what, Dad? What do you think you can tell me that I'm not already thinking about? Do you think I don't know that the thoughts I'm having are sinful? Do you think I want to be impure?" I started to cry. "I'm struggling in this area because Branson is more than a friend. I love him, Dad."

"You love him?" he questioned.

"Yes, a lot." My tears threatened to keep me from being able to speak. "I can't even talk to you guys about this. Mom, how could you do this to me?"

"Do what?"

"How could you bring Dad into this? I thought it would just be between you and me!"

"Don't raise your voice at your mother!"

I tried to calm down. "Mom, I just wish you wouldn't treat me like a child, like I have no mind of my own. And don't talk about my life behind my back. How can you not want me to see Branson? Are you crazy?"

Mom glared at me. "Contrary to popular opinion, Laurel, you are not an adult. Nor are you to speak to me in a disrespectful way."

This conversation wasn't doing anything except getting me more and more angry. "So, are you gonna put me in time-out now?" I asked sarcastically.

"Yeah, that sounds good," Mom said. "You go to your room right now!"

I rolled my eyes and tried to stomp off. With my stupid ankle, all I could do was limp. But I made sure my good foot hit the floor hard with every step.

I knew I was acting like a brat and I couldn't figure out why. I just wanted their respect and trust. I knew God wanted me to show honor to my parents, but when they treated me like a child, I responded like one. It led to a no-win situation. My mother and I had had issues before, but now I couldn't even trust her with my secrets!

I needed to talk to someone. I dialed Brittany's number. We hadn't spoken since the misunderstanding at the Waffle House, and I really missed her.

"Hey, Britt," I said when she answered the phone. "It's me, Laurel."

"Laurel who?" she asked coldly.

"Please don't be like that," I begged. "I'm going through some stuff with my parents and I really need to talk to someone."

"Well, that someone is not me," she said bitterly. "I'm not gonna shove off every time you feel like being alone with your boyfriend and then be there for you whenever you feel like having me around. What kind of friend are you?"

"I'm sorry if it seems like I've been ignoring you this week," I tried to explain. "But Branson's the one who didn't want you guys to sit with us on Saturday because he wanted time alone with me. I just went along with him, but then he made it seem as if I didn't want you to sit there."

"Oh, so I have 'stupid' written across my forehead?"

It irritated me that she didn't take my explanation seriously, so I responded with sarcasm. "Well, I don't know, Britt. I can't see your forehead."

She slammed down the phone.

I didn't mind apologizing to her. I didn't even mind telling her I'd made a mistake. I wanted her to know the truth. But her response really made me mad! Some kind of friend she turned out to be, not even being there when I really needed to talk to someone.

Less than five minutes later, my phone rang. I was sure it would be Brittany calling to apologize. So I was surprised when I heard Branson's voice.

"I didn't see you much at school today," he said. "I waited at our locker after every class."

"I was there," I snapped.

"When? A couple seconds before the bell rang? I can't wait for you that long."

"Whatever," I grumbled.

"Laurel, what's wrong with you?"

"I thought you were gonna talk to Brittany and Meagan about last Saturday. This is a really big deal to me, and you haven't taken care of it."

"How do you know?" he asked.

"Brittany just hung up on me."

"Well, I sort of explained it to them. I just told them what they already knew."

"That I didn't want them to sit with me?" I yelled.

"Yeah, but I told them you didn't really mean it."

I was so mad my brain started swimming. "And when did you talk to them about this?"

"In school."

"When? Today is Thursday."

"I told them on Monday."

"Branson!"

"I'm sorry. You're right, I didn't tell them until yesterday. And I didn't really explain the whole truth. But it's water under the bridge now, right? So let's just leave it there, OK?"

I slammed down the phone. Then I quickly dialed Meagan's number. It was busy. I tried again. Same result. I figured she must be on the computer, so I logged on. Meagan's name popped up on my buddy list.

"Meagan, it's me," I typed. "Are you there?"

I waited a few seconds and finally read her reply. "Laurel Shadrach? You never talk to me on-line. What do you want?"

"I need to apologize." My fingers flew across the keyboard. "I'm sorry I didn't call sooner. Branson didn't tell you guys the whole truth about last Saturday. The reason I told you I didn't want you to sit with me was because Branson asked me to tell you that."

I waited forever for her to read my mail and respond. When she did, it was only one word. "What?"

My fingers raced over the keys again. "He said he wanted to spend some time alone with me and to tell you guys not to sit there. Then you got mad and walked away and I went off to look for you, but I couldn't find you. When I got back, Branson made it sound like I didn't want you guys to sit there."

"Well, yesterday," she wrote back, "he told me you didn't want us to sit with you."

"That was so not true!" I punctuated my remark with about thirty exclamation points.

"Your boyfriend lied to you."

I stared at the words and knew they were true. "When you put it that way, it sounds awful," I typed. "Get off the Internet so that I can call you, OK?"

"OK, bye."

"Bye."

Five minutes later we were talking and laughing on the phone. She was so understanding and I appreciated her hearing me out.

"Brittany is so mad at you," Meagan said. "I think she's jealous."

"What are you talking about? Britt is ten times cuter than I am. Why would she be jealous of me?"

"She's not even close to being cuter than you," Meagan said. "And her grades aren't as good as yours either. She's the cheerleading captain but she can't do one flip, and you can do like ten in a row. She has tons of new clothes, but you look cute in your old ones. And you have Branson."

"What about Branson?"

"She wants him," Meagan said plainly.

"No way," I cried. "That's totally wrong."

"Laurel, I see them together all the time. And Brittany isn't the only one flirting when they're together. Branson flirts back."

My ankle was throbbing and my stomach was twisting. "What am I gonna do?"

"I don't know," Meagan said, "but leave me out of it. Things are bad enough between you and Brittany."

"But I can't just ignore this. Brittany's my friend."

"Really?"

I couldn't imagine not being friends with Brittany . . . not for longer than a few days anyway. "We just had some misunderstandings, that's all. We'll work it out."

"You still want to be friends with that girl?" Meagan asked in shock.

"I don't know. Look, I'll call you back later, OK?"

Lord, I prayed as soon as we hung up, *what is going on in my life? Things seem so out of control. It doesn't feel like I have a handle on anything. Help keep me grounded. And keep me focused. Thanks for always listening. Amen.*

———————

Mom dropped me off at school early the next day. I gathered my books and went straight to Brittany's locker. I had thought long and hard about what I wanted to say to her. I knew we needed to talk. I had to ask her about her feelings for Branson, and I wanted an honest answer. He was my boyfriend and I wanted it to stay that way.

"Britt," I said as soon as I saw her.

"Look, I hung up on you for a reason," she scowled at me.

"I know things aren't great between us—"

"And I think it should stay that way," she cut me off. Then she slammed her locker and walked away.

I caught up to her, grateful that my ankle was feeling a little better. "You were the first friend I had when I got here," I said. "We don't have to be best friends, but we don't have to be enemies either."

She didn't slow down or even look at me.

"Is this about me or about Branson?" I asked. "Are you doing this just because you want to go after him?"

"Whatever you say," she mumbled, walking faster.

I wasn't sure what she meant by that, but it sounded like she wanted to prove me wrong. And that scared me.

I shot up a quick prayer. *Lord, where are You? This doesn't sound good. Show me what's going on here.*

Later that day, Meagan came running up to me, almost knocking me over. "Laurel, you're on the homecoming ballot!" she squealed.

"Yeah, I'm one of five names. Don't get too excited. Look who else is running."

"Brittany?" She rolled her eyes. "Oh, please!"

"Why do you say that?"

"The whole school thinks she's a snob."

"Well, someone must like her," I grumbled, "or she wouldn't be on the ballot."

"She probably nominated herself!"

Meagan and I laughed.

"I've got to get to class," she said. "You need any help getting around?"

"No," I said, grateful that she had at least asked. "My ankle's feeling a lot better. As long as I don't twist it again, I think I'll be fine."

Before we could go our separate ways, my youngest brother, Luke, came running up to me.

"What are you doing down here?" I asked him. "Freshman classes are upstairs, you know," I added, pretending to act like a stuck-up senior.

Meagan chuckled.

"I ran into Brittany," he reported. "She told me to tell you that she wants to apologize. She needs to explain some stuff and wants to show you something." Luke started off down the hall. "Meet her under the stairs," he called over his shoulder.

I couldn't believe this. Was God answering my prayers already?

"Are you going?" Meagan asked me.

I shrugged. "Why not?"

"You'll be late for class."

"This might be worth it! I'll make it quick."

Meagan smiled. I was glad she understood. She wished me luck, and I headed for the stairs to meet Brittany

I felt really nervous, although I wasn't sure why. I decided not to do any talking. I'd just let Brittany say her piece, then take it from there.

When I rounded the corner, I stopped dead in my tracks. Brittany was pinned up against the wall, being kissed heavily by a guy. And the guy was someone I knew all too well. It was my guy, Branson Price! Except he apparently belonged to Brittany Cox now.

I wanted to go break them up, but my legs wouldn't move. My heart felt like it had stopped beating. As I stood there, watching them kissing, the chemistry between them seemed to intensify. She kissed his ear, stroked his hair, rubbed his neck. I heard him tell her how much he enjoyed being with her, how beautiful she was, how much he wanted her. As I watched, numb with shock, I noticed the top buttons of Brittany's blouse were unbuttoned.

Lord, I prayed with what little strength I had left, *this hurts. It hurts worse than anything I could ever imagine. I asked You to work this out. Now You're showing me the truth. You're showing me two people that I love but that I need to let go. But how can I let go when I can't even walk away?*

Brittany had always told me that Branson needed more than I was willing to offer, and if I didn't give it to him, someone else would. I just didn't know that someone would be her.

When I finally got up the courage to turn away, Brittany saw me. She smiled at me with a look that was cunning and almost wicked. She was enjoying this! I was witnessing total betrayal.

wishing
to reverse

i can't believe this!" I cried as I watched my boyfriend and my best friend embrace in uncontrollable passion.

I hadn't meant to say anything out loud. But the look Brittany gave me just made me scream.

Branson heard me and quickly pulled away from Brittany. He turned and looked at me with a face full of pure guilt.

But there was nothing he could say to me now. Could he tell me I was just making up everything I had just seen? Could he say that this was a mistake? Or would he tell me the truth, that he was happily kissing Brittany Cox and wanted to take it a lot further?

I ran off as quickly as I could, not even caring whether I twisted my ankle again or not. The halls were empty because everyone was in their last-period class. Branson took full advantage of that and started yelling down the hall.

"Laurel!" he called.

His plea didn't phase me at all.

"I'm sorry you saw that. It wasn't what it seemed."

That last statement made me stop and turn around. *"It wasn't what it seemed?"* What was that supposed to mean? Had he lost his mind, or did he think I had lost mine?

As I looked at his pitiful face, I suddenly knew that the guy coming toward me was not a good match for me. We were going in two different directions. Why should I waste any more time hearing anything coming from his lips? We were no longer on the same page, no longer thinking the same thoughts, no longer a couple.

Brittany came flying around the corner, pathetically fixing her clothes. She caught up to Branson, wrapped her arms around his neck, and tried to whisper something in his ear. He shoved her back and took three more steps toward me. Brittany had to feel foolish. She was practically giving it up in school, then when she tried to show him off, he pushed her away.

Brittany's true colors had finally shown through. She had used my brother to show me that she and my boyfriend were making out. Well, they could have each other!

I turned around again and kept walking. I was devastated but I refused to cry. I hurried to the bathroom to collect myself.

The minute I turned on the faucet, I heard someone burst through the door. I didn't even have to look up. I knew it was Branson. He had some nerve, coming into the girls' bathroom!

"Laurel, just hear me out."

I shut off the water and looked him straight in the eye. "What do you think you can possibly say to me? I don't want to hear anything that comes from your mouth, Branson Price. You are so full of lies. I have no more respect for you."

"Don't say that," he pleaded. "I know you're torn up about what you saw, but I can explain. I need you to let me explain."

"Like I really care about what you need!" I yanked a paper towel out of the dispenser. "You lost all of those rights and privileges when I saw you kissing my best friend a few minutes ago." I yanked out another towel. "I am through being there for you." One more for good measure. "I wish I could erase the day I met you!"

"Don't say that, Laurel. We've had so much joy, so many good times. We've gotten through so much; I know we can get through this."

I wadded up the paper towels in my hand and stared at him, tapping my foot on the tile floor. He wanted to explain, fine, let him explain. It wouldn't make any difference to me.

"Brittany just said some things that sounded good to me. I was weak."

That was it? That's the best he could come up with? I couldn't believe this guy. "Look," I said, trying to keep my voice from echoing off the walls, "even if what you're saying is the truth—and I doubt it—if you really cared for me, you wouldn't have done what I just saw."

Suddenly a stall door opened. I had no earthly idea anyone else was in the bathroom. It didn't even cross my mind to check under the doors. But I never would have thought Branson would burst into the girls' bathroom either.

I was somewhat relieved to see that it was Robyn. Then again, I was kind of embarrassed to discover that it was someone I knew.

She strutted right up to Branson, her hands on her hips. "I think you need to leave," she said boldly.

"Yeah, OK," he mumbled, backing down in front of my righteous girlfriend. "But please, Robyn, talk to her."

"What-ever," she sneered at him. "Now get out!" She pushed his chest until he backed out the door. Then she brushed her hands together like she'd just taken out the garbage.

"Are you OK?" she asked, coming back to me. "What he did was horrible."

"I need to wash my face," I said lamely, as if splashing water on it would make all the shame disappear. I tossed the crumpled ball of paper towels into the trash, then walked over to the sink and turned on the tap.

"Did you really see Branson kissing Brittany?" Robyn asked, looking at my reflection in the mirror.

"Oh yeah," I admitted, then soaked my face with the cold water. "You thought hearing about Jackson was bad. My walking up on Branson and catching them in the act was a whole lot worse." I pulled out two more paper towels and dried my face. "Hey, what are you doing in here anyway? Aren't you supposed to be in class?"

"I didn't feel good," she said as she washed her hands. "Hey, at least Branson felt sorry about what he did. It is definitely clear that he wants you more than he wants your friend."

"Don't call her that," I grumbled. "The last thing I want to call Brittany Cox is *friend*." I tossed the used towels into the trash. "You know, she set this up."

"What?"

"Yeah. She told my brother she wanted to meet me under the stairs to apologize, but what she really wanted was for me to catch them together. When she saw me, she gave me this evil look. It was scary. She was clearly sending me a message that she had him. It was horrible."

"Well," Robyn said, drying her hands, "at least the only thing he walked away with is your heart. That's something I can't say. Jackson took a lot more than my pride. But you know, he didn't even take that. I gave it to him, and he just ran away with it."

"I'm sorry," I said, feeling bad for someone other than myself for the first time in a long while. "Are you OK? Have you talked to him?"

"Yeah," she said, digging through her purse. "At first he tried to deny it. Then he realized that he didn't have to come at me with lame excuses. He told me a lot more than I wanted to hear." She pulled a tube of lipstick out of her purse and yanked off the top.

"What did he say?"

"He didn't even try to get back with me like Branson did with you. He was just plain coldhearted." She stared into the mirror. "I wish I could take back last Friday."

"I told Branson that I regretted the day I met him. I loved him. But Branson and Brittany stomped on my heart and now I hate them both. I know hating is a sin but I do." I watched Robyn smear lipstick on her full lips. "I need counsel, Robyn, but I don't know who I can go to."

"What about your folks?" she asked, pressing her shiny lips together.

"No way," I said. "I can't talk to my parents right now, especially not my mother."

"I'm sorry," she said, not even asking for details. I was grateful that she was respecting my privacy. "Are you ready to go back to class?" she asked, dropping her lipstick back into her purse.

"No," I said. "I wish I could stay right here forever and never have to go on with the rest of my life."

"Girl, don't say that," Robyn said. "He's not worth all of that."

"That's easy for you to say."

"No, it's not. I've been there and I'm still there. We both need to go on with our lives. Branson was no good for you. At least you're still pure."

We hugged each another. Robyn understood. God knew I would need her. He sent her to me in my time of despair. He sent her as a glimmer of hope.

I wanted to lock myself in my room and cry my eyes out when I got home that sad Thursday afternoon, but homework wouldn't allow me to do that and neither would my brothers. I was downstairs using my family's computer when the Three Musketeers, as I sometimes call them, busted into the room.

"So, our big sister has been nominated for homecoming queen, huh?" Lance teased me.

"Everyone in the ninth grade thinks I'm cool," Luke added, "because my sister's on the ballot."

I shrugged my shoulders and tried to ignore them, but it was hard to concentrate with the three of them hovering over me.

"You've gotta admit, this is a pretty big deal," Liam said to me.

"No, it's not," I said. "I can't win. Whichever one of you nominated me wasted your time."

I looked up from my work. They all stared at me with innocent faces. That got me thinking. Who in the world *did* nominate me for homecoming queen? "I wish my name wasn't even on the ballot," I admitted, slumping in the chair. "Did you see my competition? It would be a miracle if I won."

"You've got one advantage the other girls don't," Liam responded with confidence.

"And what would that be?"

He grinned at me. "None of the other candidates have brothers in the ninth, tenth, and eleventh grades who will be campaigning for them. The underclassmen vote decides the winner, you know."

"Now that Liam is the new starting quarterback," Lance bragged, "you're in for sure."

"I suppose the *old* QB might be able to get you a few votes too," Luke added.

My brothers started laughing. Though they didn't know it, they had hit a sore spot. I appreciated everything they were willing to do for me but winning the crown meant nothing. I had already lost the one thing that meant the world to me.

"What's wrong?" Lance joked. "Did you and Branson break up again?"

I turned my attention back to the computer.

"Give us a break," Liam said. "We never know when you guys are together or apart."

"Well, we aren't together, so don't bring up his name anymore!" I stood and stormed outside, where I plopped down in the tree hammock. The air was crispy cold, which was exactly how I felt. I had been dealt a bad blow, and I was determined to take it like a punching bag. I wanted to toughen up and get over Branson.

"Lord, how am I supposed to do this?" I uttered to the sky above. "How am I supposed to not let this affect me? Today was the worst day of my life. I know You're up there, and I know Your Holy Spirit lives inside me. But, Lord, I feel so defeated. Father, this is a heavy load to carry. Help me to trust You and focus on Your truth and not my circumstances."

I closed my eyes and tried not to think about my problems. In my mind, I started singing my favorite praise songs. Whenever thoughts of Branson started creeping in, I started a new tune. Soon, one song was running into the next and I started really focusing on the Lord and His goodness. Just when I thought I had finally accomplished my goal—no more horrible thoughts about Branson—I thought I heard his annoying voice. "Laurel! Laurel," the voice in my head said. "Wake up!"

When I opened my eyes, I saw Branson standing in front of me holding a dozen peach-colored roses. I loved peach roses and he knew it. My attempt to get out of the hammock was ungraceful. It flipped over and I fell to the ground with a thump. Branson transferred the roses to his left hand, the one that wasn't attached to a broken arm, then extended his right hand to assist me.

"I would rather be helped up by a rattlesnake," I said, pulling myself to my feet.

"I deserved that," he said humbly. "Laurel, you wouldn't talk to me during school so I didn't get a chance to explain what happened."

"I heard your lame excuses already," I said, dusting off my jeans.

He stood there, holding the bouquet of roses. "Laurel, please don't be like that. You know I love you. You're my one and—"

"Don't give me that," I cut him off. "I should have seen through you a long time ago."

"What do you want me to say? Tell me what I can do to make you forgive me."

"Why are you looking for my forgiveness? You did what you wanted to do. You showed me who you wanted to be with. You might as well give those flowers to Brittany. Or have you already given her some?"

"Laurel, don't be so mad." He extended the flowers toward me. "Please take these. I bought them for you."

I grabbed the flowers from his hand and threw them at his feet. The stems flew apart, and several petals came loose and fluttered across the ground in the breeze. "Oh, look, the bouquet is shattered. Just like our relationship!"

"So it's like that, is it? You won't even give me another chance? You're not going to forgive me?"

"Branson, unlike your mother, I cannot live with infidelity." I knew I'd struck a low blow, but I really didn't care.

"Why are you bringing my mother into this?"

"Just because your parents accept this kind of lifestyle, that doesn't mean I have to put up with it. That's not the way we're going to be. But just because I don't want to go further, that doesn't mean you shouldn't try with someone else. If you're looking for somebody who doesn't care about unfaithfulness, of all people, Brittany's a perfect choice."

"But she came on to me," he wailed. "She wanted me."

"We're finished, Branson Price." I left him standing alone in the cold and stomped into the house, glad that my ankle was healed enough for me to stomp again. I slammed the door behind me.

Even though I'd talked like I didn't care, I was still hurting inside. I knew, however, that God was with me. Could I survive without Branson? With God I could.

I returned to my homework on the computer.

Later that evening, my mom came in with the cordless phone. "It's for you," she said, handing it to me.

I hoped it wasn't Branson. I hadn't found the right words to tell my parents that he and I were no longer together. If it was him, I decided, I was going to tell him not to call anymore.

"Hello?" I said nicely.

I was so expecting it to be Branson, I was surprised when I didn't hear his voice. But it was just as bad—it was Brittany.

"I just wanted to tell you I'm really sorry things had to end up this way," she said. "I shouldn't have hurt you like that, but I felt pushed to the limit. Branson has been coming on to me for weeks, so I finally decided to let him have a taste of what he's been wanting."

"Why are you calling me?" I yelled. "Do you think I want to hear this?"

"You can't have him," she said, getting defensive. "He just left my house."

She was probably telling the truth, but I didn't care. "If you're calling to challenge me, there's no contest. You can have Branson."

"Oh, I know. Branson is going to be my one and only," she said, rubbing it in my face. "As soon as we're intimate, I'll be sure to tell you all about it."

I screamed into the phone. "How could I have ever been friends with you? I am so ticked at you for betraying our friendship!"

"You're just mad because you lost your guy and I got him," she bragged.

I couldn't believe this girl was saying such hateful things to me. I asked God to help me know what to say back. Before I really thought about it, words started tumbling out of my mouth. "Look, Brittany, regardless of how I feel about you at this moment, I have to tell you the truth. You are destroying your life. You probably couldn't count the number of guys you've been with if you used all the fingers on both hands and some of your toes too. And that's sad! Branson might want to get with you now, but I promise, if he does, it will be a mistake for both of you."

"You're wrong, Laurel," she said. "You don't know what you're talking about."

Obviously, she wasn't going to listen to a word I had to say. "Look, Brittany, from now on, let's just say our friendship is over. We don't need to hang out with each other anymore."

"Fine," she said, her voice as cold as ice.

"Fine," I said lightly.

We hung up. I didn't like ending a friendship this way, but I didn't do it; she did. She had maliciously tried to destroy my life. Though it hurt to let her go, I knew I was much better off without Brittany Cox.

That Saturday morning, I took a walk to try to clear my mind. My ankle hardly hurt at all anymore, except when I neglected to keep up with my heat-exercise-ice routine. Unfortunately, I hadn't done that for a few days, so I figured I could use the exercise.

I ended up near the church, so I decided to wander into the sanctuary for a little alone time with God. I'd only been sitting there for a few minutes when I heard someone come in.

"Laurel," Mrs. Meaks, my youth director, said in her tiny voice. "What are you doing here all by yourself?"

I looked up. "I just needed to come and pray for a while."

"Mind if I sit with you?"

"Sure." I shrugged. "I'm not very good company, though."

She sat in the row in front of me and turned around, resting her chin on the back of the pew. "What's up with you these days, Laurel? We haven't had much chance to talk lately."

"I know," I said. "I miss that." When I was younger I used to spend the night at Mrs. Meaks's house whenever her husband, who was a professional baseball player, was at an away game. We talked about everything. I wanted to be just like her. She used to give me advice whenever I had a problem, but after I got older, my problems got bigger and I hadn't shared them with anyone.

"Is something bothering you?" she asked.

"There's just a whole lot of stuff going on in my life right now," I said honestly. "I've been praying, but I'm still kind of weighed down by it."

"Is it Branson?" she asked gently.

"Yeah. We aren't gonna be together anymore. I couldn't give him what he wanted so he found someone else."

"Laurel," she said. Then she got up and slipped into my pew, where she wrapped her arms around me and hugged me tight.

Her unexpected gesture got my tear ducts going again. "What am I supposed to do, Mrs. Meaks?" I sobbed. "How am I supposed to move on?"

"Well," she whispered, "you've come to the right place to look for the answers."

"I need help," I cried out.

She pulled back and smiled at me. "You may be better off than you think." She patted my knee. "Maybe I can disciple you one-on-one. I could teach you how to walk closer to God and be a soldier for Him."

I didn't know what to say. I'd never thought about doing such a thing with anyone.

"Why don't you pray about it and we can talk about it tomorrow, all right?"

"OK."

She smiled at me, her whole face lighting up.

"Look, I've got to get to gymnastics practice. But I'm really glad I came here today."

"So am I," she said.

I walked back home at a much brisker pace than before. Not only was my spirit lighter, but I needed to find Liam so he could take me to the gym for practice. I desperately needed a car!

When I got home, I heard beautiful piano music coming from the back room. When I got to the doorway, I saw Liam at the keyboard and Foster standing nearby with his eyes closed, lifting his hands toward heaven.

"You can come in and join us," one of the band members said when he saw me.

I was really tempted to take him up on his offer. I'd always been a little jealous of Liam's band. I loved to sing, but I'd never had a chance to perform other than when I was in children's choir. Still, I didn't want to impose. "I'm sorry. I didn't mean to interrupt. You guys go ahead. I'll just wait out here for Liam."

As I pulled back into the hallway, I heard Foster say, "Hold on, fellas. I'll be right back." He stepped into the hall. His dark eyes were shining like stars in the night. "How are you?" he asked with concern.

I hesitated. "Why do you ask?"

"I saw you in school yesterday. You seemed . . . different."

"I was just tired." It was true. Branson really made me tired!

"I don't think that was it," Foster said. "I also noticed that you and Branson were ignoring each other. Are you guys broken up again?"

"Forgive me if I don't want to talk about this. It's kind of personal."

"Your brother said you have a beautiful voice," Foster said, graciously letting the subject drop. "Why don't you join us?"

"No, thanks. I'm really not in the mood. I've got a lot to deal with right now."

"I'm not trying to push you into doing something you don't want to do," he said carefully, "but when I'm down and out, I sing praises to God. And a lot of the stuff I'm feeling on the inside disappears."

I stared at him, unable to figure this guy out.

"Think about it," he said, then he went inside to tell Liam I was waiting for a ride.

When I got home from gymnastics practice, my mother called me into the kitchen and asked me to sit down at the table with her.

"Mom, I really don't want to talk right now," I said.

"I know you're angry that I told your father something you said to me in confidence, but I need to explain."

"What is there to explain?" I said, still standing. "You betrayed my trust."

"Your dad and I do not have secrets."

"You should have told me that before I spilled my guts to you."

"Your father is the head of our household and God speaks to this family through his leadership. Besides that, he is also your pastor."

I pulled out a chair and sat down. This was going to take a while.

"Honey, you didn't even hear the whole conversation. Your dad came to me because he already knew you were struggling in that area. He asked me if I knew anything about it. Your virginity is a precious thing, Laurel, and once it's gone, it is gone forever. We want you to give it to your husband, not lose it to some high school boyfriend."

I didn't want to be there hearing all this, but I knew every word she said was true. Seeing Robyn's situation put my mom's words in a whole new light.

I finally told her that Branson and I had broken up. Though I wanted to tell her the whole reason why, I couldn't. It was too unbelievable to repeat. I was just glad it was over between us. He was such a jerk.

Mom prayed for me and we hugged. Though I was still angry about her telling Dad, I understood. I needed their prayers and guidance.

At church the next day, when the choir sang "That Name Jesus," every note touched my soul. Jesus' name was so precious to me at that moment. When I concentrated on Him, my burdens didn't seem so heavy. I thought about how much I loved God because He saved me from losing my virginity to Branson. I asked to see the truth, and even though it hurt, it set me free. Jesus calmed me. I knew God and loved God, so I didn't have to be alone.

I wished I hadn't told Foster I didn't want to sing because I really did want to sing for the Lord. God was too good for me to not want to praise Him. That was what I really wished for, more than anything. Just to praise my Lord! I found myself wishing to reverse.

sobbing
for days

f or the next several days, I was tough—strong to the core. Then Thursday came, exactly one week since I had caught Branson in the arms of my "friend" Brittany. That night I couldn't sleep. My stomach was twisting into knots and my heart felt shattered. I started wailing. Branson was gone! He wasn't dead or anything, but he might as well have been. We weren't speaking and he hadn't called or anything. I had turned him away, but now I wished he would come back. Maybe this time I would be more receptive. I dismissed that thought as quickly as it came because I knew I couldn't let him into my life again.

My heart ached. Everything was so unfair. Life wasn't supposed to be like this!

I turned on the radio next to my bed and tuned it to the hip-hop station. They were playing slow, sad songs that made me weep even more.

"I loved you, Branson," I sobbed as I pulled out last

year's prom picture from the dresser drawer where I'd thrown it last week. "I loved you so much. Why did you have to do this to me? Why did you have to break my heart this way? And why did you have to do it with Brittany?"

I didn't realize how loudly I was moaning until my door opened and my father walked in. I quickly wiped my tears. But when he held out his arms to me, my weeping started all over again.

"Oh, Daddy!" I said, rushing into his embrace.

"It's OK, sweetheart," he whispered into my hair.

He could have said, *"You don't need that no-good boy who is only after one thing."* Or, *"I can't believe you're still thinking about that jerk. Get over him already."* He could've said a lot of things but he didn't. He simply said, "It'll be OK," as he stroked my hair. Then he said, "Believe it or not, I know how you feel."

"What?" I said as I wiped more tears.

Dad smiled at me. "I had a girlfriend in high school before I met your mom. Her name was Sally Jane."

I raised an eyebrow. "Sally Jane?"

"Yeah. She was so beautiful! Every guy liked her but she liked me."

"Really?"

"Yep. And I felt honored. I was flattered when she approached me. I really cared for Sally Jane. She had a reputation, however. A reputation with the boys. I thought it was all a bunch of rumors, but I found out they were true. She wanted me to be on her list of conquests. When I refused because I knew it was right to stay pure for God, she dismissed me quicker than a second thought."

"You're kidding." I'd never heard my dad talk like this before.

"Naturally I was devastated. However, a bigger and better blessing was around the corner when I met your mom in college." He sighed. "I know you're hurting right now and life seems unfair, but joy will come in the morning. I'm not

155

going to let you drag this thing on forever, but if you need a shoulder to cry on, you can always use mine."

"I love you, Daddy." I gave him another hug. "And I'm sorry about not wanting Mom to tell you about my problems."

"Yeah, what was that all about? Do you think your dad is an old fuddy-duddy? I may not be as hip as you but I'm cool."

I laughed. "Yeah, you are. Thanks, Dad."

The next week the push was on for choosing a homecoming king and queen. My heart was definitely not in it, and I didn't do any campaigning for myself. But my brothers sure did. And thanks to their efforts, I actually won!

That Friday afternoon in assembly, when my name was called, I sat there in shock. I couldn't believe it. Then Brittany stormed out of the room, and the look on her face told me she was not a bit happy with the outcome. That's when I knew I'd heard right and I really was the homecoming queen!

I didn't want her to be hurt, but it did seem to even up the scoreboard a bit.

It felt great walking up to the podium with everybody cheering for me. And the homecoming king turned out to be a really cute guy. Of course, he already had a girlfriend. I didn't even have a date for the homecoming dance. Fortunately, my brother offered to take me.

My mother took me shopping that night and she bought me the most beautiful dress in the world. It was a sparkling navy blue that glistened in the moonlight. It made me feel like a real queen.

The next night, as Liam escorted me through the gymnasium doors, some people snickered because I was with my brother. I tried to act like I didn't care. But then I saw Brittany stroll in on Branson's arm. The girl who lost had a better prize than I did! I didn't shed a single tear, but inside my heart was drowning.

The principal walked up to the mike. "It is now my pleasure to announce the homecoming court," she said, her voice echoing through the room. Everybody gathered around the platform. I knew what would happen after the announcements were made. School tradition was that the homecoming king and queen danced the first song with their respective escorts.

I jetted out the double doors, raced down the hall, and ran outside. I couldn't take this. There was no way I could go out on that dance floor with my brother! That would be way too humiliating.

I plopped down on the concrete steps outside the building. They were cold and I started to shiver. The tears on my cheeks chilled my whole face.

"Here," a sweet, husky voice said. "Take my jacket."

I looked up into the very handsome face of Foster McDowell, there once again to lift me up. He took off his jacket and wrapped it around my shoulders. "They're waiting for you to start the first dance."

I huddled into the warmth of his jacket. "I can't go out there and dance with my brother."

"Who said you had to dance with him? I'd be honored if you would dance with me."

My heart skipped a beat. My lips wanted to say yes before my brain could think about it. A few more tears fell, but they were tears of joy. He didn't have to be so kind. He didn't have to make this all better for me.

Before I could answer him, my brother called out from the doorway, "Laurel, c'mon!"

Foster took both of my hands in his and pulled me up off the cold concrete step. "I saw Branson in there with Brittany. I know how hard this is for you. Give me a chance to make tonight what it should be for you, a night full of good memories. It'll be OK," he whispered. "Trust me."

Moments later all eyes were on us. Foster was twirling me around and I felt like Cinderella. All the negative feelings I'd had before floated away. Foster was just the medicine I needed. I was finally enjoying being the homecoming queen.

After the first dance, everyone else joined us on the floor. To my surprise, Foster didn't flee the minute the music ended. As a matter of fact, when the next song began, he started dancing with me again! But Branson and Brittany ruined my moment when I saw him rubbing his hands up and down her back. Those arms used to be around me.

"Ignore them," Foster said, noticing my look in their direction.

"How can I?" I whined. "They're everywhere."

"They aren't inside you. Christ is. Branson is the stupid one. Laurel, you are gorgeous. If he let you go to be with her, then he's the loser. Don't sweat it."

"Thanks," I said. When the song ended, I exited the dance floor. Foster followed me to a table and sat down with me.

As people came over and started congratulating me, Foster offered to bring me a glass of punch. Just as he left to get it, Branson and Brittany made their way over to me. With all the congratulations surrounding me, I'd almost forgotten about them.

"Look, honey," Branson said to Brittany, his voice dripping with sweetness, "there's the homecoming queen."

Honey? A week ago he said it was a mistake and he didn't want to have anything to do with her, and now he was calling her honey?

"What do you two want?" I asked, knowing they had only come over to try to upset me.

"I just wanted to introduce my current girlfriend to my former girlfriend," Branson said as he kissed her on the cheek right in front of me.

Foster was right. Branson was such a loser.

"Yeah, I may not be queen, but I sure got a king." Brittany looked at me and then wiped lipstick from Branson's mouth.

"Don't you mean jester?" I said, standing. "He looks like a joke to me. Actually, both of you do. You two belong together."

I burst between the two of them and walked away. I hated saying such mean things, but the only way I could keep from shedding tears was to get angry. Who would have thought that Brittany and Branson would be a couple? But that was the way it was and I was going to have to accept it.

Foster found me in the back of the room. He was carrying two cups of punch and handed me one. "Something happened when I was gone, didn't it? Are you OK?"

"Not really," I said with a small smile, trying to hold it together.

"But you're going to be OK, right?"

"Right." This time my smile was more sincere.

Two weeks later, Robyn invited me to spend the night at her house on Halloween. It was the first time I'd spent the night with an African-American and I wondered if it would be any different. Her house was more lavish than mine. But other than that, being there was a lot like being at home.

Robyn's dad was gone for the night, which I found out was pretty normal since he was an airline pilot. But Robyn's mother was really nice and her little sister, Bunni, was in awe of me. It was great having a girl going into tenth grade admire me, especially since I lived with three brothers who mostly just teased me. Robyn told me Bunni was named for a nonfiction author, P. Bunny Wilson, who was a good friend of their mom. I thought it was great that Robyn and Bunni were both named after writers.

"I changed the y in Bunny to an i," Mrs. Williams explained, "just like I changed the i in Robin to a y."

If Robyn's mom put as much creative detail into her books as she did into naming her children, I knew I was going to love reading them.

During dinner Mrs. Williams asked if I had time to take a look at the manuscript she was working on. I jumped at the chance! I was really excited about reading a book before it got printed and even having the opportunity to give the author my input.

After a great meal, Robyn and I went into her room. She closed the door and pulled the twin-size trundle bed out from under her own bed. But as she finished, I noticed she was sobbing.

"Robyn, what's wrong?" I asked, joining her on the bed. "Why are you crying? It's Jackson, isn't it? You still like him, don't you?"

"You don't understand, Laurel," she said.

"Why would you think that? My boyfriend betrayed me, too, you know. The only difference is he betrayed me with my best friend. I know how you're feeling, Robyn. But we don't have to be gloomy about it. We both have bright futures ahead of us and our dreams can come true in the end."

"Believe me, you don't understand," she said more firmly.

"Then talk to me. Help me understand what's going on with you."

Robyn's tears flowed down her face. "Laurel, I'm . . . I'm pregnant."

Pregnant? I couldn't believe what I was hearing. She told me she'd been intimate with Jackson, but I never gave a thought to the consequences. It was bad enough that he'd been with another girl, but the fact that he'd done it while she was carrying his child was unthinkable.

"Are you sure?" I asked.

"I'm two weeks late," she groaned. Robyn explained that they had used protection. But I knew the only 100 percent sure method of being safe from diseases or conception was to stay pure.

"Laurel, what I am gonna do? By graduation I'll be eight months pregnant. My body is already changing and I can't keep any food down. This is horrible. It wasn't supposed to be this way. I really liked Jackson. I just wanted him to like me."

"I know," I said, trying to comfort her.

"I can't believe I made such a huge mistake. What am I supposed to do now?"

I had no idea what to say. I couldn't think of anything that would make this load lighter for her, so I just hugged her and joined in her crying. Somehow that made me feel better. I hoped it made Robyn feel a little better too.

I thought about how easy it was to only think about the pleasure of the moment when we're with a person we like. Then later we have to suffer the consequences. I realized how close I'd come to acting on those desires myself. It had taken everything I had to stay pure in the heat of the moment. But for the grace of God, Robyn's situation could have been mine.

As I hugged her I prayed. *Thank You, Lord, for sparing me. Please help my friend Robyn.*

We discussed her dilemma all night. We brought in a new day with our conversation. Unfortunately, we didn't come up with any solutions that she was comfortable with. As a matter of fact, she was more confused after our hours of talking than she was when we started.

I was glad I didn't have gymnastics practice that day, because Robyn and I slept from six until noon. As soon as I got up, I thanked Robyn's mom for not waking me. If I was at home, my mom would have found some chores for me to do. Mrs. Williams handed me a box with her manuscript in it and thanked me for offering to look it over for her. I thanked her back.

Just before I left, Robyn hugged me and made me promise to keep her secret. I promised, then told her I would be lifting her up in prayer.

When I arrived home, the chores I hadn't done were

waiting for me. After two hours of housework, my brother brought me the phone. I didn't care who it was, I was just glad to get a break. "Thanks, Luke," I said. After he left the room, I said, "Hello?"

"Laurel, where have you been? I called you all day yesterday," Meagan said.

"I spent the night at Robyn's. Why? What's wrong?"

"I think you know. As a matter of fact, I think you've been holding out on me. You never told me about the homecoming dance."

"What's to tell? It was just a dance."

"That's not what I'm talking about," she said slyly.

"Oh, you mean about Brittany and Branson?" It suddenly occurred to me that she probably didn't even know they were dating. "I really don't want to relive that."

"I understand. I mean, you and Brittany have been best friends for ages and she really stabbed you in the back."

"Exactly," I said, wishing she would change the subject.

"So, I guess now you know how I feel," Meagan said.

"What?" I asked, totally confused.

"You're doing the same thing to me," she said quietly.

"I have no clue what you're talking about."

"Look, Laurel, I heard all about it."

"About what?" I said, trying not to get impatient with her.

"You were dancing with the guy I have wanted all semester. I've been trying to get Foster McDowell to notice me, but Brittany says he has the hots for you now."

"That's crazy! Don't listen to anything that traitor says. She's just trying to start trouble between us."

"Are you telling me you weren't in his arms the night of the homecoming dance?"

"Sure, I danced with him," I admitted, "but only because I didn't want to dance with my brother."

"Knowing how I felt about Foster, you should have danced with your brother."

"What are you saying, Meagan? Are you trying to compare this situation to my problems with Branson and Brittany? Because that makes no sense to me. I know you like Foster, but Branson was my boyfriend. You and Foster haven't made any commitment to each other. He was just being a gentleman by helping me out that night. If you would have gotten the story from me instead of trouble-making Brittany, we could have straightened all this out."

Meagan started yelling and crying, and I couldn't understand a thing she was saying. I told her to calm down but she didn't. She was totally over the edge.

"Meagan," I said, "stop screaming and listen to me."

"What?"

"Foster doesn't even like me."

After a pause, she said, "Well, he doesn't like me either."

"How do you know? You're always at least ten feet away from him. He's not psychic, you know. He can't read your mind. You need to talk to him, try to find out how he feels."

"I did," Meagan said sadly. "I talked to him yesterday."

"Well, what did he say?"

"He told me he has his eye on someone else."

No way! "Did he say it was me?"

"He didn't have to. I know it's you. Laurel, my heart is broken. The same thing Brittany did to you, you did to me. How could you do that? All you care about is yourself." Before I could say anything, she slammed the phone in my ear.

I had to talk to Foster and straighten this all out. Then I could ask him to call Meagan and talk to her. She always did need a little help when it came to boys.

Ever since Branson and I split, he had stopped coming to church. But just when I'd let my guard down, he walked into Sunday school, all cocky and confident with a smug look on his face. I desperately wanted to slap it off.

The lesson that morning was on loving your neighbor.

"Does anyone want to share how you love your neighbor?" Mrs. Meaks asked the class.

Branson raised his hand. When she called on him, he went on and on about how he had this new girlfriend and how he wanted to be a sensitive, understanding guy around her. I could have barfed.

"I never dreamed I could feel this way about someone," he bragged. I knew he was just rubbing it in and probably didn't mean a word of it. I tried not to let it get to me, but he was really making me sick, so I got up from my seat and headed for the door.

Mrs. Meaks must have thought the same thing I was thinking. As I left the room, I heard her say, "Branson, I think that's enough."

I didn't wait to see if he took her suggestion. I walked out to the grassy area behind the Sunday school classrooms. "Lord," I said out loud, "this is so unfair!"

"Yeah, it is unfair," I heard a familiar male voice say. "But you're gonna get through it."

I turned around to see Foster with his arms out, ready to embrace the pain as if it was his own. I really wanted to enjoy his friendly hug, but after the way Meagan had scolded me, I kept my distance.

"My girlfriend Meagan has a crush on you," I blurted out.

"Yeah, I know," he said. "I told her I was interested in someone else."

"That's what she said." I couldn't help but wonder who his *someone else* might be. "I think you should know that no one can compare to Meagan. She's the greatest."

"That's not true," he said softly. "You're way sharper than any other girl at our school."

"Me?" I blinked.

"Yeah. Look, I know you're just coming out of a relationship, so I don't want to push myself on you. But I do want to be a good friend to you."

Friend. That was what I wanted to hear. "You are my good friend," I assured him.

"Well, then, maybe I want to be a little bit more."

Uh-oh.

"I'm not really attracted to very many girls," he confessed. "Most of them seem too into worldly things. But God has put you into my heart, Laurel. I want to encourage you and be there for you. I want to wipe your tears away and bring you joy." He moved a step closer. "Will you let me do that?"

I was stunned. I couldn't believe it. Meagan was right. How could I have been so blind? I had no idea how to answer his question, so I didn't. I turned away like a coward and headed for the sanctuary.

All during the church service, I thought about Foster's question. How could I not have noticed? Now that I thought about it, he'd given more than enough hints. I was just so fixed on Branson I hadn't been thinking straight.

Could I like him? No, Meagan liked him. But he didn't like her. He was so cute! But I still loved Branson. How could I give my heart to someone if someone else still owned part of it? This was crazy. I needed to pay attention to the service. *Talk to me, Dad,* I thought as he approached the podium.

Dad spoke on a subject related to autumn. His sermon title was "The Harvest Is Plentiful, but the Laborers Are Few."

"All this month," my dad preached, "I am going to focus on 'Whatever you say or do, you reap.' God has called all of us Christians to lives of giving. The concerns of others should be more important than our own. When was the last time you bore someone else's burden? When you care for someone other than yourself, you reap a good harvest. When you concentrate on someone else's interests instead of your own, your life won't seem that bad."

My dad was talking to my spirit. I'd been focused on my

165

own problems way too much. Though my life seemed horrible, I knew many other people had a lot worse problems than mine.

I immediately thought of Robyn and decided that as soon as church was over I was going to call her. I knew it couldn't be easy handling what she was going through. I wondered if she'd told her mom yet. How was she feeling? What would Jackson's response be?

I also knew I needed to call Meagan. But what would I say? I didn't want to depress her any more, but the information I had just learned from Foster wasn't what she wanted to hear.

When the service ended and I started exiting the church, I saw Liam and Foster walking toward me. They were engaged in what sounded like a friendly argument.

"I don't know why you're asking her," I heard Liam say to Foster. "You know she's gonna say no."

"I don't know that. I just want to ask her. Who knows? Maybe she'll say yes."

"Ask me what?" I asked when they got close.

"Our band is performing at church next week," Foster said. "I found this perfect song by Celine Dion and R. Kelly, but it's a duet. It's called 'I'll Be Your Angel.' Have you heard it?"

"Yeah!" I loved that song.

"Would you be willing to sing it with me?"

"Sure," I said, excited about getting the chance to sing with the band.

"When can you make it to practice?" Liam asked.

"Whatever time you want."

"We usually get together on Saturday afternoons," Foster said hesitantly.

"I'll be there," I promised.

"What about gymnastics?" Liam asked.

"Don't worry," I said. "I'll work around your schedule."

"No way," Foster said. "You tell us when you've got gymnastics practice and we'll find a time that's good for you."

I smiled. "Thanks."

Foster handed me a copy of the sheet music and a tape recording of the song.

"It shouldn't be hard to learn," I said, looking over the music. "I know the song pretty well."

"Great," Liam said. "That means we won't have to practice too much."

"Cool," I said, really excited about this great opportunity.

First thing Monday morning, Brittany came running up to me, all smiles and giggles. "Look what Branson bought me," she squealed, showing off a gorgeous silver chain hanging around her neck. Her low-cut V-necked top set it off beautifully.

"I have to get to class," I said. "Please move out of my way."

"Not so fast," she said. "Don't you want to know what I did to deserve such a beautiful present?"

"Why should I care?"

"Well, you know how cheap Branson is. At least, that's what you always told me."

I shook my head. "Whatever you do is your business. I really don't need to know." I tried to move around her.

"Wait!" She grabbed my arm, nearly making me drop my books.

"Let go!" I yelled.

Instead of letting go, she pulled me up closer to her and whispered in my ear, "I gave him what you wouldn't. And he was the best I've ever had!"

I stared at her in disbelief. If this was the choice she and Branson had made, why did she have to torture me with it? The contempt that filled my soul for both her and Branson was so deep it frightened me.

I shoved her aside and ran to class. I was so upset I wasn't really watching where I was going, and as I burst into the classroom, I bumped right into Foster.

He grasped my shoulders to keep me from plummeting nose-first to the floor. When he saw my tear-streaked face, he whispered, "Trust God with it."

I sighed. "What's that supposed to mean?"

"Simple. Whatever is bothering you, trust God with it."

"You don't even know what's wrong," I grumbled, trudging to my desk.

He followed right behind me. "It doesn't matter. If you give it to God, you won't have to worry about it. Besides, you're too cute to frown. Your beautiful brown eyes are too heavenly to let them get so red." He made me laugh in spite of my depression.

"You're silly," I said. "As a matter of fact, you sound just like a poet."

"Do I?" He looked genuinely pleased. "Hey, that reminds me. Did you have a chance to work on that song for Sunday?"

"Yeah." I'd looked over the sheet music while listening to the tape for at least an hour before falling asleep the night before.

"Well, think about the words," Foster said with a grin.

"I'll be your angel?" I questioned.

"That's what I want to be to you," Foster whispered, then he walked to his seat two rows over.

"So," Meagan said from her seat behind me, "I was just making it up, was I? I thought you said he didn't like you. Well, excuse me!"

I'm in deep trouble now!

"Let me talk to her," Foster said, coming back over when he heard Meagan's comments. He walked past my desk and knelt beside hers. He spoke so softly I couldn't catch a word he said, but I knew he was trying to take care of things, just like he'd been handling everything else that was going wrong in my life.

Whatever Foster said to Meagan worked. By the time class started, she was smiling at me. While the teacher was lecturing, Meagan passed me a note. "You've been through a lot with Branson," it said. "Foster is a gem. He really likes you. You should go for it with him. I won't be mad."

"Why the change?" I wrote below her message and handed the paper back to her.

"Foster's going to hook me up with his cousin," she wrote, and she drew a big smiley face beside the words.

It was all I could do not to laugh right there in the class!

Robyn didn't show up for school at all that week. On Friday I picked up her assignments from her teachers and took them to her house. I also brought along Mrs. Williams's manuscript, which I had found time to read through. I'd written a few comments in the margins about ways I thought she could make her characters do and say things that sounded more like modern teenagers.

"Is Robyn OK?" I asked Mrs. Williams when she answered the door.

"She'll be all right," Robyn's mom said as she let me in. "I thought she'd be over the flu by now, but she's really been sick with it. If she doesn't get better soon, I'm going to take her to the doctor."

I gave Mrs. Williams the box with her marked manuscript in it and thanked her again for the privilege of reading it and offering my opinions. She told me how grateful she was for my input. Then she pointed up the stairs. "Go ahead on up to Robyn's room. She'll be real glad to see you. I think there's something bothering her besides that flu bug, and I'm sure she'd like to talk to you about it."

I hauled Robyn's books up to her room. She looked terrible, like she was in a daze or something. She didn't even look up when I walked in.

"Robyn?"

She didn't say anything, but a tear slid down her cheek.

"Robyn, what's wrong?" I said, tossing her books on the desk and rushing to the chair beside her bed. "Is this about the baby?" I asked gently.

She groaned. "What baby?"

"Your baby. Jackson's baby."

"There is no baby."

"You mean, you're not pregnant after all? That's great. Isn't it?"

"Laurel, I had an abortion two days ago."

I didn't have a clue how to respond to that. I sat there in total shock.

"I feel so empty," she said. "I have committed the worst sin in the world. I killed my baby." She twisted a corner of her pillowcase tightly in her fist. "Laurel, what have I done? What am I going to do?" She collapsed in tears on her bed, her face buried in the pillow with the twisted corner.

I couldn't think of a thing to say, so I just slid onto the bed beside her and laid my head next to hers. "I'm so sorry I wasn't there for you, Robyn."

"It's not your fault," she mumbled into the pillow.

"Does your mother know? Does Jackson know?"

"No. My aunt took me to the clinic."

"Do you want to pray with me?" I offered.

"I just want to be alone," she said, not even looking up.

"You don't have to be alone."

"Please, just go." She turned her head away from me.

I suddenly felt afraid of what might happen to Robyn if she was left by herself in this depressed state. "I really would like to stay."

"I'm not in the mood for company."

"Robyn, it's going to be OK."

She bolted to a sitting position and glared at me. "How can you say that? Nothing will ever be OK for me again. How can I live with what I've done?"

I reached up to dry her tears, but she grabbed my wrist.

"No need to do that. I've been sobbing for days and I'm sure there'll be plenty more tears where those came from."

I stared at her blankly. What could I do? She seemed to really want to be left alone. I stood, half expecting her to apologize and ask me to stay. But she didn't.

"Don't tell anyone about this."

"I won't."

I left her house, knowing she would be sobbing for days.

eLeveN

dating
God's way

i went back to Robyn's house first thing the next morning, before gymnastics practice. This time she was ready to talk.

"I'll never forget that room, Laurel. It was so cold. The moment I put on the robe I knew I was doing the wrong thing, but I couldn't stop the process. I didn't want to stop it. When I put my feet in those stirrups and they ripped out my baby, I felt as if a part of me was gone forever." Robyn started crying again. "I don't know how I'm gonna get past that."

"You've got to focus on things above," I uttered without even thinking. It was as if God had told me what to say to her. My eyes were watery and my heart was heavy. This was truly a tragedy and definitely not the way God wanted it to be. Nonetheless, this was Robyn's reality, and even when a Christian falls so far from the Lord, His grace is sufficient.

"You've got to stay in love with the Lord," I told her.

"And just how am I supposed to do that?" she asked.

"You've got to date Him."

"Date Him? God doesn't want me."

"That's not true, Robyn," I assured her. "I came real close to going all the way with Branson. I didn't think God would ever forgive me. I'm still asking the Lord to change me in that area. I want so much to honor Him in my relationships with guys!" I took her hand in both of mine. "Look, Robyn, you made a mistake. You sinned. But that's why Jesus came to this earth. He died to pay the penalty for your sin so you could be forgiven and so you could be changed from the inside out. God changes your heart and gives you strength not to make the same mistake again."

"Laurel, I deliberately killed a baby. Why should God forgive me for that? I should be sentenced to death myself."

"You need to stop beating yourself up over this. When is enough going to be enough? Robyn, the beating has already happened, and the death sentence has already been paid. Jesus paid it for you. You've got to move past this."

"How?"

"The best thing you can do is spend time with the Lord."

"And what good will that do?"

"If you're living close to God, then next time your choices won't be the wrong ones."

She thought about that for a while. "Do you really believe that's true?"

I smiled. "Absolutely."

"Thanks for being there for me," Robyn said.

"Just do me one favor," I asked.

"What?"

"Think about what I've said, OK?"

She almost smiled. "OK," she promised.

I was glad I'd spent this time with her. It was nice to be close to Robyn during this difficult time in her life. I knew her pain wouldn't go away instantly, but I also knew God would help her get through it.

I worked extra hard at gymnastics practice that afternoon and did my best to follow the coach's direction. But it seemed no matter what I did, I couldn't land anything right. Finally, I just gave up and went home early, thoroughly frustrated.

Shortly after I got back from the gym, I had my first real practice for the song I was going to perform the next day in church. Liam couldn't make it, but Foster played the melody for me on the piano in our back room.

I sang the first line, which was about no mountain being too high to climb as long as you have "climbing faith." I stopped him there, like I'd done probably a hundred times in the past forty minutes. I'd been practicing all week, but that evening, for some reason, I just couldn't get past the first line.

"Laurel, what's the matter?" Foster asked as he got up from the piano bench and came over to me.

"These words are so deep," I said in awe. "And they really relate to my life. It's as if the mountains are my problems in gymnastics and wanting to get to the U.S. gymnastics team. But when I sing those words, I feel as if I can do anything as long as I have climbing faith."

"If your faith is in Christ," Foster expounded, "then you can do anything. Anything He wants you to do, that is."

I sat in the chair next to the piano. "What does God mean to you?" I asked.

Foster perched on the piano bench. "Christ means everything to me. He knows all about me and He gives me everything I need. God is all-powerful. The depths of His riches and wisdom amaze me so that I long to study Him more and more."

"You know a lot of Scriptures, don't you?"

"Not enough. I wish I could quote the whole Bible from beginning to end."

I laughed. "Are you serious?"

He nodded.

It was wonderful that Foster had that desire, but it made me sad to realize that I hadn't even been thinking along those lines. My dad was a minister and I could barely recite twenty Bible verses.

"Reciting Scripture is important to me," Foster went on, "because when I go through struggles I can fight Satan with God's Word. If I didn't know what God's Word says, I'd have nothing to keep me on the straight and narrow."

"That makes sense," I said.

"What do you think of God?" Foster asked. "What does He mean to you?"

"He used to be my parents' God," I replied. "I only went to church because they made me go. Now that I have my own struggles, I know God is the only healer. Things only get really bad for me when I take my focus off of Him. I'm learning to let Him be the Lord of my life. I'm getting to know Him for myself."

Foster nodded, encouraging me to continue.

"It hurt when Branson dumped me for Brittany. But then God allowed me to see that he wasn't right for me. The Holy Spirit allowed me to realize that Branson was not seeking God and he was not what I needed."

"So how are things for you now?" he asked.

"Much better!" I smiled. "Let's sing that song." I hoped, now that I'd talked through my feelings, I could get past the first line!

Foster started playing the first stanza. That guy could play the baby grand the way it was designed to be played. Every note sounded perfect. It made me want to sing just as perfectly. I wanted to be an angel in people's lives.

Singing with Foster was more wonderful than I could ever have dreamed. We were like a match made in heaven. His tenor voice and my soprano blended perfectly.

Something about Foster McDowell intrigued me to no

end. As we sang together, I realized what it was about him that most appealed to me. It was his giving heart. I smiled so much when we practiced the duet I had trouble enunciating the words.

When we finished practicing, Foster asked, "What are you doing tonight? Do you want to go see a movie and get a bite to eat?"

"Sure," I replied eagerly. "My dad's in his office; I'll go ask him."

"No, I'm not," Dad said. I turned around and saw him standing in the doorway. "I heard you two singing and you sounded fabulous. You guys were so moving; I'm sure the congregation will be blessed through that song."

I beamed. It felt good to know my dad was proud of me.

"So, you want to take my daughter out, huh?" He smiled at Foster.

"Yes sir," Foster said, quickly standing. "Is that OK? I mean . . . sir . . . do I have your permission?"

My dad reached out his hand to shake Foster's. "Yes, that will be fine."

"Thank you, sir. I promise I'll have her home at a reasonable hour."

"No, you'll have her in by eleven." Dad grinned.

"Yes sir," Foster answered seriously.

"You kids have fun," he said over his shoulder as he left the room chuckling.

"Wait right here," I said to Foster. "I need to go change."

"You look great to me," he said. "You're always beautiful."

I blushed. Then I went and changed anyway.

Foster and I had a great time at the Mexican restaurant across town. When the food arrived, he and I prayed together for the meal. In all the times Branson had taken me out, we never prayed before we ate.

Before, during, and after the meal, Foster and I talked about God. He told me that his favorite Bible story was the one about how God got Shadrach, Meshach, and Abednego out of the fire.

"I love the part where they say, 'God can deliver me from the fires if He wants to, but if He doesn't, He is still God.' It's incredible. That's the kind of faith I want to have."

"Isn't that already the kind of faith you have?"

"No," he said honestly. "It's a daily surrender." He smiled. "But enough about me. Tell me what you're looking for in a guy."

"Foster!" I cried. "I just got out of a relationship."

"So, does that mean you'll never have another one? What if the right guy came along? How would he know if he was the right guy?"

"If he was the right guy," I said with a smile, "he'd know it."

"Really?" He leaned closer. "Then I'm applying for the job. How am I doing so far?" Foster was applying pressure, but it didn't feel heavy. I was totally cool with it. I actually liked his pursuit of me.

"So far," I admitted, "you're doing pretty good."

After dinner Foster asked what movie I wanted to go to. But during the meal, my throat had started to feel kind of scratchy. I told him I wasn't feeling well and thought I should just go home.

He was really sweet and understanding. He took me home immediately, without a word of argument. It was so refreshing after Branson's pushiness!

I sucked on a throat lozenge while I did my homework. I prayed while I did the heat-exercise-ice procedure my trainer still wanted me to do. My ankle didn't hurt much anymore, but he and I both wanted it to heal as quickly as possible so I could get back to doing my gymnastics routines properly. Just as I was putting my foot in the bucket of warm water, I got a call from Meagan. Though I'd seen her at school all week, our relationship had become somewhat strained. She said she was cool with Foster and me, but I wondered how she really felt.

"I'm so bored," she moaned. "It's Saturday night and I have nothing to do."

"You can come over if you want."

"Oh, Laurel, that'd be great. I'll be right there."

Meagan showed up with an overnight bag, misinterpreting my invitation as an offer to spend the night. I didn't mind, but I hadn't asked my mother for permission. I talked to Mom about it privately so I wouldn't hurt Meagan's feelings. Fortunately, she said yes.

When it was time to go to sleep, I knelt beside my queen-size antique bed to pray. I silently thanked God for everything He had done for me, especially for the wonderful date with Foster. I asked Him to help my scratchy throat to heal so I could sing well in church the next morning—not so everyone would think I was a great singer or anything, but because I wanted the congregation to be blessed by my song the way I'd been blessed as I rehearsed it. And I thanked Him for taking care of Robyn. After our talk that morning, I knew she was going to be all right.

When I got up off my knees, Meagan was staring at me.

"What?" I asked as I crawled into bed.

"Do you do that every night?" she asked.

"Yeah, and every morning before school. I pray all the time."

Meagan got into bed next to me. "I didn't know you prayed every day. Do you really think God hears you?"

"Without a doubt."

"What if your prayers go unanswered?"

"No prayer is truly unanswered," I explained. "See, God hears the prayers of all His children. Sometimes His answer is 'yes,' other times it's 'no,' and a lot of times it's just 'wait.' When His answer is 'no,' sometimes it seems like an unanswered prayer, but even 'no' is an answer."

"If God really loves you, why would He say no to something you really wanted?"

"He knows what's best for each of us," I said. "I might ask for something that would end up hurting me, and 'no' is the best answer He could give." It felt great to be talking about spiritual things with my friend. I hoped what I was saying made sense to her.

"Laurel, financially, I have everything. But there have been lots of things I've asked for that I haven't gotten."

"Like what?"

"I'm a senior in high school and I've never had a boyfriend," she said. "I'm lonely."

"You need to concentrate on God," I advised her, "not guys. Trust the Lord to give you what you really need."

"I don't know if God is enough to fill me."

Suddenly, a brilliant idea hit me. "Why don't you come to church with me tomorrow? I don't believe you can truly know God if you don't worship Him regularly. You have to put forth an effort to love God."

"That makes sense," she said.

"Ever since Branson and I broke up, I have been so happy!"

"Yeah, right," she said. "That's because you got Foster right away."

"No," I said honestly. "It's because I put my focus back on God."

We talked all night about lots of things. I even asked Meagan to forgive me for putting Brittany before her, and she said I was forgiven. We were building a true friendship. I thanked God for that. We were finally moving past all the obstacles so we could really enjoy each other's company.

Just as I was about to fall asleep, she asked me about my relationship with Foster. I hesitated, wondering how she really felt about him.

"You can tell me," she said, trying to pull the details out of me. "Foster is a great guy and you deserve a great guy."

"We're singing a duet together in church tomorrow."

179

"Really? Oh, then I definitely want to go to your service!"

"Meagan," I said, "there's something wrong with my throat. I'm not sure what my voice will sound like tomorrow."

She laughed. "You'll be fine. Where's that great faith you were talking about?"

I laughed too. "That's a good one."

"So?"

"What?"

She sighed. "Tell me about your relationship with Foster already!"

She seemed sincerely interested, so I took a chance at honesty. "I really like him," I said, "and he's shaping up to be a pretty good friend."

"Friend?" she questioned.

"Yeah. He took me out to dinner this evening." I thought back to the great time I'd had with him at the restaurant. "I'm telling you, Meagan, he is so much better than Branson!"

Lance suddenly burst into my room. He'd been at a youth meeting at the church all evening, so he didn't realize I had company.

Meagan threw the covers over her head, not wanting my brother to see her in her hair curlers.

"Oh, I'm sorry," Lance said, turning away so she wouldn't be embarrassed. Then he peeked back at Meagan in an adoring way. He liked her! I'd never thought of it before, but the idea of the two of them as a couple was cool!

I acted like I hadn't noticed the way they acted toward each other. But inside I was smiling.

When I woke up the next morning, my throat felt great, not a bit scratchy. I thanked the Lord for answering that prayer with a yes!

Foster and I had sounded great when we'd practiced the song at home, but when we performed on stage our voices sounded like heaven on earth. There was something special there between Foster and me, and it wasn't just the music. I felt as if he really wanted to be my angel. As we sang the last words together, he put his hand in mine. It seemed completely natural, and I felt totally secure.

We received a standing ovation. As I stood there holding Foster's hand, the Lord's presence was so real to me, I felt I could reach out and touch Him. I knew I wasn't alone. There were angels everywhere.

After the service, the church had a fellowship dinner in the basement. The room could comfortably seat seven hundred people, but there were a little under a thousand there that night! By some miracle, it all worked out.

Foster caught up with me after I filled my plate at the buffet line. "Where are you sitting?" he asked.

"I don't know," I said, looking around the crowded room. "Meagan is here somewhere, and I was going to sit with her, but I'm not sure I'll be able to find her."

"I'm sitting with my parents," he said, pointing to a nearby table. "Maybe you can come over and meet them."

"I'd like that."

After my father blessed the meal, I found a table with two available chairs. I put my plate down in front of one of the seats and my sweater on the back of the other, then went searching for Meagan.

When I bumped into Lance, I asked if he'd seen her. Before he could answer, Meagan stepped from behind him with a tray in her hand. Obviously, they were together.

"Meagan," I said, "I saved a seat for you next to me." I glanced at my brother. "But there's only one."

Meagan looked up at Lance. He whispered something to her and then took off, and Meagan followed me to the table. We ate quietly for a few minutes, then I asked the burning question. "So, what were you doing with my brother?"

She swallowed her bite of barbecued chicken. "I was lost with all these people, and then I found him. He was really sweet."

"Sweet?" I asked, wondering exactly what that meant.

"Yeah. And cute too." She smiled. "Is he dating anyone?"

I frowned at her. "I don't know. What did he say to you?"

She giggled. "He told me I looked nice."

She placed her hand on my shoulder and said, "I've never been excited about a guy who seemed excited about me. I really like Lance, but I don't want to get my hopes up."

I grinned. "Yesterday, when my brother came into the room and saw you, I noticed he looked at you in a strange way."

Her face fell. "Strange how?"

I laughed. "Strange good." She relaxed. "I don't know what's there, but it's definitely something."

She bounced in her chair. "Are you serious?"

"Very serious."

Meagan went back to eating, but I could tell her mind was not on the food. When we'd finished our meal and tossed our throwaway dinnerware in a big plastic trash can, we headed for the door.

"Hey, there's Foster," Meagan said.

I looked in the direction she was indicating. "He's with his parents."

"Have you met them?"

"No," I admitted. "But he told me he wanted me to."

"Well, go on, then."

I hesitated but not for long. "I'll be back."

Foster saw me as I approached his table and he stood to greet me. "Mom, Dad, this is Laurel. Laurel, these are my parents, and this is my little sister, Faigyn. She's in the ninth grade."

"Hi, Laurel," Faigyn said. "It's really nice to meet you. My brother talks about you all the time."

I could tell I was starting to blush. "Do you know my brother Luke?" I asked, since he was in the same grade.

"Yeah," she said, "I've met him a couple of times."

"The two of you sounded really good in church today," Foster's mother said. "I'm really proud of both of you."

"Thank you," I said. Now I was really blushing.

"Your voice is lovely," Mr. McDowell said. "You actually made my son sound good!" We all had a hearty laugh and I started to really feel comfortable around these people.

I told Foster and his family that I had to get back to my friend Meagan. Foster followed me as I walked toward her and asked, "Do you think this Friday night we could do the movie we were unable to go to last night?"

Without hesitation I said, "That would be great."

"OK," he said with a smile. "I'll pick you up around seven."

That Friday when Foster pulled into the theater parking lot, he handed me a gold-foil-wrapped box. When I opened the package, I saw a Bible study guide.

"I thought we could go through it together," he said.

I was so blown away by the idea I didn't know what to say.

"I believe the best way for you to get to know me is through Christ. We need to build our relationship God's way so we both remain pleasing in His sight. This is the only way I can do that."

Did he think I needed convincing? "I would love to go through the study guide with you," I exclaimed.

My mom always taught me that a wife was supposed to submit to her husband and follow his leadership. But I figured a woman couldn't expect a man to lead after marriage unless he'd had some practice during the dating relationship. Foster sure seemed like the kind of guy I could follow.

At the end of the night, as he walked me to my door, I told him I'd really enjoyed our wonderful evening, and I thanked him for the book.

"No problem," he said. "Hopefully we can get together soon and do a chapter."

"I'd like that."

We stood there for a moment. Surprisingly, it didn't feel awkward.

"Before I leave," he said, "do you mind if we pray?"

"Sure," I said. I was thrilled that this was what he wanted to do with me at the end of our date!

Foster grasped my hands and we bowed in prayer, right there on the porch. "Heavenly Father," he began, "I thank You for sending Your Son to die for our sins. Thank You for putting Laurel and me on this earth at the same time so we could be in each other's lives to encourage each other to live our lives for You. May we continue to know that You hold tomorrow, and may our only concern be that we please You and allow Your will to be done. Thank You. May Laurel's dreams be sweet. Amen."

"Amen," I whispered.

"Good night," Foster said as he started to leave.

"Wait," I said. He turned. "I just want to say that I have never known dating could feel so spiritually right. Thank you for showing me the proper way to do this. I can see now why God sent you my way."

He smiled that gorgeous smile of his.

When I walked into the house, I saw that my father was working on his next sermon. As I passed his study, he asked me to come in.

"How was your date with Foster?" he asked.

I explained the things we had done on our date. Needless to say, my father was pleased.

"A date with Foster is like . . . Vacation Bible School," I said.

My dad laughed. "When you keep God as your sole focus, He can bless every part of your life. Now that you know the difference, I hope you'll start dating God's way."

twelve

giving much thanks

although I was really enjoying my gymnastics lessons with Coach Milligent, I was ecstatic when my P.E. teacher announced that the principal had hired a gymnastics coach who was going to formulate a school team that year. When I heard the news, I let out a cheer that could be heard all the way in the parking lot!

After the announcement, the P.E. teacher excused me from class so I could meet the new gymnastics coach, Mrs. Turner, one-on-one. What she told me completely blew me away.

"You want me to be the captain of the team?" I shrieked. "You're kidding!"

"Well," she said, "twenty-six girls have signed up for the team, but you have the most experience by far. I've studied your records from Rockdale Gym, and Coach Milligent tells me no one can hold a candle to you. If we're going to have any chance at winning the meets this year, we need you."

Suddenly, my heart sank. "You know, I don't know if I can handle a school team in addition to Coach Milligent's team. And I can't quit on him. He's really been working hard with me."

Mrs. Turner smiled. "Your coach and I already talked about that. He told me he'd be thrilled to let you do this."

"He did?" I was floored.

"He thinks it'll help you get that scholarship you want."

This was like a dream come true. "You have no idea what a blessing this is," I said. "Thank you so much."

"If you need some time to think about this, I understand. There are a lot of things going on during senior year. Are you sure you want to be tied down with this? It means practicing every day after school, not just three evenings a week. And the Saturday practices will be longer too."

I didn't need to think about it for a second. "Mrs. Turner, I can't begin to tell you how much I've wanted a gymnastics team at school. Being captain would be an honor."

"Laurel, it's not just a title. There's a lot of responsibility involved."

"You can count on me."

She smiled. "All right, then." She shook my hand. "Welcome to the team, Captain."

I strolled back to P.E. class in a daze. All I could think about was what the leotards would look like! *Thank You, Lord,* I prayed over and over and over. *I can't believe how You've blessed me!*

When I saw Foster outside the lunchroom, I ran up to him and practically leaped into his arms.

"What?" he asked, chuckling. "What's going on?"

"We're getting a gymnastics team!" I screamed. "And I'm gonna be the captain!"

Foster hugged me tight. "That's fantastic! Whenever I'm not playing in my baseball games, I can come and see you at your meets."

"You'd come to my meets?" I asked. Branson had never wanted to do that.

"Of course," Foster said. "I wouldn't miss it."

"Thank you," I said, hugging him even tighter.

Suddenly, I heard an irritating voice say, "Don't you know how to hold a woman, man?" I didn't even have to look up to know it was Branson. "You look so dorky with your arms around her back like that. Are you trying to perform the Heimlich maneuver or something?"

I turned around and saw that Branson wasn't alone.

"This is how you're supposed to hug someone." Branson grabbed Brittany and put his hands around her hips. "Must I show you everything, Foster? Perhaps you should come to The Branson Price School of Dating."

I felt terrible for Foster, and I wished Branson would shut up. But he didn't.

"Oh, I forgot," he continued. "You're with Laurel. You guys are probably just friends, not seriously dating. After all, I'm sure you don't want to upset God." His sarcasm about the Lord made me want to belt him.

"We don't have to listen to him," I said to Foster. But he didn't seem to hear me. He just stared at Branson. I could tell he was trying hard to hold back his anger.

"You know I'm telling the truth," Branson sneered. "If you keep holding hands with her, sooner or later she'll want me back."

Foster started to lose it. "Why would she want something used when she could have something new?" he seethed.

"Is that supposed to be funny? Brittany, why don't you tell Laurel what she missed out on. In detail!"

Brittany broke into an evil laugh.

"I don't need to hear anything Brittany has to say," I said, walking away. Foster grabbed my hand and walked into the lunchroom with me.

"You sure sounded calm back there," Foster said. "Didn't those things they said bother you?"

"Those two used to make me absolutely miserable," I admitted, "but I'm getting over it. If they were really so happy, they wouldn't have to brag about it."

"I guess you've got a point."

"Hey," I said, "is it OK if I have lunch with my friends today? I can't wait to tell them my news!"

"Of course," Foster said with a smile. "I'll go eat with my guys."

"Great," I said. It felt so nice having a guy who understood my need for girlfriends and didn't get all jealous!

While I stood in the cafeteria line, I looked everywhere for Meagan but couldn't find her. I did spot Robyn, though, and she and I hadn't talked for a while, so I wandered over to her, my tray in hand.

"Is this seat taken?" I asked.

"No," she grumbled, "but why would you want to sit here?" She looked around and made a point of showing me all the blacks at her table.

I'd never sat on this side of the cafeteria, and I hadn't really noticed the segregation. Obviously it bothered Robyn a lot.

"Look," I said, "I really want to talk to you." I put my tray on the table and slid into the bench beside her. Though I didn't feel uncomfortable being on that side, it was a little weird being a minority. "How have you been?" I asked, opening my carton of milk.

"Is that what this is about?" Robyn said defensively. "You want to baby-sit me now? I'm over it, Laurel. You don't have to worry about me like I'm a charity case or something."

"That's not what I was trying to do."

"It seems that way to me. This may come as a shock to you, but you can't fix everything."

"I'm not trying to fix anything," I said, starting to get angry. "I just wanted to make sure you were OK." I softened my voice. "I've missed you."

"I know," she said, changing her tough stance. "I've missed you too," she admitted.

I leaned closer to her. "Have you told anyone yet?" I whispered.

"No," she said. "And I don't want to. I'm trying to get over it, but with you bringing it up, it's not easy."

"I'm sorry. I'm just concerned."

"Laurel, I'm not doing great, but it's not all grim. God is good even when I'm really bad, and I'm making it one day at a time. I'm learning to depend on Him, and I'm asking Him to show me what He wants me to do."

"Wow! Sounds like you're doing great."

"Not that great," Robyn admitted. "I had a dream that my baby came back to haunt me."

"Oh, Robyn," I said with compassion, not knowing what else to say. "I've been praying for you. And I won't stop."

"Thanks," she said. "I know your prayers are helping. I'm really thankful that God sent me a friend like you to help me cope with all this." She smiled. It was the first smile I'd seen on her face in a long time, and it was really refreshing. "Imagine, a white girl who isn't afraid to step out of her comfort zone and eat on the other side of the cafeteria just to make my day. You're cool, Laurel Shadrach."

"Thanks."

As I walked into the Rockdale Gym on Thanksgiving morning I realized what a huge part of my life gymnastics was. None of the other students was coming in on the holiday. I was grateful that Coach Milligent agreed to meet me for an extra practice. He said it would pay off for both of us next year. I was also glad that Miss Weslyn, the assistant coach, agreed to come in. I didn't want Mr. Milligent to break his rule again about not working alone with female students.

So, while Coach worked with me one-on-one, Miss Weslyn sat in a small room off the gymnasium doing paperwork with the door open.

"That's it, Laurel!" Coach said. "Perfect landing!"

I never had to guess whether Coach Milligent liked or disliked something I did because he always told me what he was thinking. Now I needed to do the same with him. "Coach, can I talk to you for a second?" I asked.

"If you want to get home and eat some turkey this afternoon, we need to finish practicing."

"This will only take a second."

Coach looked at me, obviously trying to guess what was on my mind. "Sure, Laurel," he said, taking a seat. "Go ahead."

I took the chair next to him. "I really appreciate you talking to Mrs. Turner about letting me be on the gymnastics team at school. But I'm still surprised that you let me do it."

"You've been a real blessing to us here at Rockdale, Laurel. I know you want to get a scholarship, and this school team is just what you need to do that." He grinned. "And who knows? Maybe you'll learn something there that will help me be a better coach!"

I laughed.

Coach Milligent's tone grew more serious. "I told Mrs. Turner that if I saw you slipping I would ask you to drop one of the responsibilities, either Rockdale or the school team. But I really hope you don't have to make that choice."

I threw my arms around his neck. "Thanks, Coach. I won't let you down."

"Enough of that, now," he said, his voice gruff again but with tenderness behind it. "Get back out there and let me see that floor routine again."

When we finished practice, Miss Weslyn took me home. My family was at the Thanksgiving service at church. Even my grandparents, who were in town from Arkansas for the holiday, were there, so I had the house to myself.

My ankle was a little sore from all the extra work, so I sat down on the couch with a Robin Jones Gunn novel and propped my foot up on pillows. Five minutes after I got settled, the door opened. Luke came in with both of my grandmothers.

"Laurel, honey!" my mother's mom called out. She hurried over to the couch and hovered over me, asking how my ankle was feeling and how I was doing in school and if there was anything she could do to make me more comfortable.

"No thanks, Grandma Ma," I said with a smile. "I'm fine."

"Let me get you a cup of tea," she offered, then scurried off to the kitchen.

"Hello, my dear," Dad's mother said as she sat next to me. Her sharp navy-blue suit dress was quite a contrast to Grandma Ma's bright, flowery outfit. I loved both of my grandmothers, even though they were total opposites.

"You look beautiful, Grandmother," I said. "How was the service?"

"Oh, it was lovely," she said. "I wish we could have stayed longer and chatted with the folks in your congregation, but your Grandma Ma and I wanted to get over here right away to get the meal started."

"Oh, I can help," I offered, getting up.

"Are you sure your ankle is up to it?"

I smiled. "I feel fine, Grandmother." I followed her into the kitchen, where Grandma Ma was already busy pulling things out of the refrigerator. When I started to set out the good china, I noticed Luke setting up the extra table. "What are you doing?" I asked him.

"We've got four more people coming," he said.

Grandma Ma explained. "We met this nice young man and his family at church this morning."

"They're new in the area," Grandmother said, tying an apron around her dress. "So your father invited them to join us for dinner."

"His name is Foster McDowell," Grandma Ma said.

I almost dropped the stack of dishes I was holding. "Foster is coming over here?" I shrieked. "Now?"

191

"Laurel," Grandmother asked, "do you know this young man?"

Grandma Ma stopped what she was doing and looked at me with a twinkle in her eye. "Looks like something might be going on here," she said.

Fortunately, Luke thought of something he had to do in another part of the house just then, so I went ahead and told my grandmothers about my relationship with Foster McDowell.

As they prepared the turkey and stuffing, they went back and forth explaining to me their different takes on dating. I had never seen this side of them, and I had to admit it was rather fun. Though we were two generations apart, we were talking like girlfriends.

"Don't like him more than he likes you," Grandma Ma said, rubbing salt on the turkey.

"Never let a date cause you to miss curfew," Grandmother suggested as she measured seasonings into the stuffing.

"Don't spend your time with only him," Grandma Ma said, "or he'll think he's the center of your world."

None of these things were biblical, I thought, but they were probably good advice anyway. When my grandmothers got past the "don'ts" and got on to the "dos," they did have some spiritual advice for me.

"Make sure you get with someone who believes the same things you do," Grandmother offered.

"And always pray on a date," Grandma Ma added.

Grandmother stirred the stuffing vigorously. "Remember to honor God in your relationship."

"No matter what," Grandma Ma said, opening the turkey so Grandmother could stuff the dressing into it, "stay pure."

"No matter how attractive the young man is," Grandmother said, "nothing is worth throwing away your purity."

I smiled as I set the silverware and glasses on the table. I'd already come up with these wise guidelines myself, but it was amusing to hear them coming from my sweet grandmothers.

"It was easier to stay pure back in our day," Grandmother said. "Now it seems as if it is expected for a young couple to have premarital relations. But on your wedding night, you want to give your husband a prize—one that no one else can have. So you must hold onto it."

My grandmothers were just getting the bird into the oven and starting on the side dishes when the rest of my family arrived home. As soon as they walked in I grabbed my father's arm. "Can I talk to you for a second?" Without waiting for an answer, I pulled him aside. When Mom and my brothers and grandfathers were out of earshot, I whispered, "You didn't have to invite Foster over here. We aren't boyfriend or girlfriend or anything."

"What are you talking about?" Dad said innocently. "I didn't invite the McDowells over here for you. Liam wanted them to come."

I rolled my eyes. "I need to go get dressed."

As I flew up the stairs, I heard Dad mumble, "Yeah, and you say there's nothing between you two."

I really liked Foster as a friend. And although he certainly made me feel good, it was still too early to be jumping into anything.

After I changed clothes and ran a brush through my hair, I ran to the bathroom to touch up my lipstick in the better lighting.

"You look mighty cute, Sis," Luke said as he leaned against the wall outside the bathroom. "So I heard the McDowells are coming over."

The doorbell rang and I almost smeared my lipstick.

"You sure are going all out for a friend," Luke said with a chuckle.

I threw a towel at him.

I sat between my parents at the dinner table and across from Foster, who sat between his mom and dad. His sister, Faigyn, sat next to their mother. It seemed strange to have them over for Thanksgiving, but it felt good.

My dad's father said grace. He wasn't a minister, but he was a very religious man and he said a beautiful prayer. Dinner was delicious, as always, and the conversation during the meal focused mostly on how good everything tasted.

When the pumpkin pie was served, my mom's father decided we should go around the table and each say what we were thankful for.

My brother Liam started. He talked about being thankful for God giving him the gift of music and song. Lance followed, humbly thanking God for his gift in athletics. Luke, my youngest brother, articulated the gospel in a way I had never heard him do before. My mom, dad, and grandparents all spoke about how thankful they were for family. The McDowells talked about how grateful they were to God for allowing them to live in Conyers. Faigyn thanked God that she had finally stopped crying about having to move. That gave us all a good laugh.

When it was Foster's turn, he looked directly in my eyes and said, "I don't know what's going to happen with baseball next season, so I don't want to thank God in advance for anything in that area. But I am grateful to God for one of His greatest gifts on earth, the soft and gentle-hearted creatures called women."

My face grew hot, and I knew my cheeks were totally red. If Branson had said something like that, it would have come across as a crude joke and would have made the moment awkward and uncomfortable. But the way Foster said it just made me feel special.

It was my turn to speak, so I cleared my throat. "I am thankful because, through all of my trials and tribulations, God has never left me. He allowed people and circumstances to change my heart so I could become a little bit more like

His Son, Jesus Christ. I don't know what tomorrow holds, but I know whatever comes I will be OK as long as I am living my life for the Lord. For that I am truly thankful."

We were having such a beautiful time of praise I didn't want it to ever end. It was the best Thanksgiving I had ever had because that year, I was truly thankful.

Meagan sat beside me on the bus in the church parking lot. We were about to leave for a three-day retreat in the Blue Ridge Mountains, which would take up what was left of our Thanksgiving weekend. She was jabbering away, something about not believing I had talked her into coming. I didn't hear much of what she said because I was searching for Foster. We hadn't had a chance to talk after the dinner, since we were surrounded by so many family members. But that hadn't bothered me too much because he'd said he was coming on this retreat. Now it was almost time to take off and he hadn't shown up.

When Meagan stopped talking for a minute, I tore my gaze away from the bus window and looked at her. The expression on her face told me she'd asked a question I was supposed to have heard. "I'm sorry, Meagan. What did you say?"

"I knew you weren't listening," she complained. "I asked, is this retreat going to be any good?"

"It should be," I said. *I wouldn't be going if it wasn't*, I thought. "People are coming from five different states."

"So there are going to be a lot of other kids there, huh?"

"Uh, yeah!" I said in an irritated tone.

"What's wrong with you?" Meagan asked. "Why are you so touchy?"

"Look, if you're having second thoughts, maybe you shouldn't go after all."

"I never said I was changing my mind," she said. "Something's going on with you. What is it?"

"Nothing," I mumbled.

"Foster isn't here and it's bugging you. That's it, isn't it?"

"That is so not true," I argued. But as the bus pulled out of the parking lot, I felt completely dejected. "I'm sorry, Meagan," I told her. "You're right, I was looking for Foster."

"I know," she replied softly. "I understand."

I leaned back in my seat and tried to relax. The more I thought about it, the more I realized that maybe it was better that Foster wasn't there. This way I would be more likely to spend the weekend focusing on God, which was the purpose of the retreat in the first place.

After everyone got settled into their cabins, we gathered in the main hall for the first group meeting. The subject was "Accepting the Call."

The speaker was a dynamic, good-looking man who strode across the stage while he talked. "Some people say that teenagers don't have to know anything about Christ," he said, his miked voice booming throughout the large room. "I'm here to tell you, that is hogwash!"

The place exploded with cheers.

"Can you accept the call to abandon worldly pleasures for heavenly gain?"

Suddenly I knew why I was there. God wanted to make me aware of my purpose in life. He wanted to make me a stronger Christian. I listened to the rest of the talk with every ounce of my attention. By the time it was over, I had nothing on my mind or my heart but following the call of God on my life.

When the meeting ended, Meagan and I joined the crowd of people leaving the main hall. During the talk, the sun had set and I was a bit surprised to notice that it was already getting dark outside.

Just as we got through the big double doors, I bumped into Foster. "You made it!" I said.

He smiled at me. "I rode up with Marcus."

"Who?"

"One of the youth directors. He was as late for the bus as I was."

I turned around to talk to Meagan, but she had already taken off and was hanging around with a group of other kids. She saw me looking for her and gave me a wink that said she was happy I'd found my guy.

I gently grabbed Foster's hand and pulled him away from the crowd. "I missed you," I whispered. "The whole drive up here, I was looking for you."

He gave me a sweet, simple hug. Then we took a walk through the trees, still holding hands. In the fall night air, his grip was cozy and warm.

"Did you get a lot out of the lesson?" he asked.

"Yeah, it was really convicting."

"I'm sorry I missed it," he said.

"Me too."

"I'm really glad your brother invited me to have Thanksgiving dinner with you," he said.

I smiled.

"I just wish my family hadn't chimed in and said they'd love to go too!"

"Well," I said, "I suppose you really should spend Thanksgiving with your family."

We stopped walking and looked at each other. I was digging him and I could tell the feeling was mutual.

Foster definitely had a place in my heart. Despite all the hurt I had felt in the past, I was thrilled to discover that I was still able to care for someone. In my heart, I was giving much thanks.

trying
to return

foster and I finally decided to head over to the mixer. This retreat always had a mixer the first night so everyone could catch up with people they'd met in earlier years and meet some of the new ones. We walked slowly toward the building, listening to the sounds of music, laughter, and conversation filter through the night air.

"Laurel," Foster asked, "would you like to sing with me for the Christmas concert this year? Everyone's been asking me when I'm going to do another duet with you."

"I hadn't thought about it," I admitted. "I'd really like to, but I have so much practice with gymnastics, I don't know if I'll have the time."

"We'd only need to practice a few times before the concert."

"Really?" I said.

"Yeah. I've been practicing with your brother's band for a while now, but if you're interested I could bring you up to speed. You pick things up quickly. Besides, your voice is always beautiful."

"Stop flattering me," I said, though I didn't really want him to stop.

We paused just outside the mixer building. "I really like singing with you," Foster said.

I sighed. "What did I do to deserve such a sweet guy?"

He gazed at me with a look that made me lose my breath. "No," he said with sincerity and charm, "I'm the one who's blessed. You're a very special woman, Laurel Shadrach." He opened his arms and I immediately walked into them. He held me tenderly. I didn't want him to ever let me go.

"We'd probably better get inside," I said. It took all my inner strength to pull out of his arms. Holding hands, we walked into the building. It was crowded with people dancing, laughing, and having a good time. As we wound our way through the people, we tried to stay close together but it was impossible to continue holding hands.

"How many times have you been to this retreat?" he asked me over the noise.

"This is my fourth time," I answered back.

"So you must know a lot of people, huh?"

"Some," I said. "But there are a lot of new ones here too." I realized the truth of my words when I didn't recognize a single person around me.

Just then a girl I'd met a couple of years before came up and grabbed my arm. "Laurel Shadrach! It's so good to see you! Remember me? Rachel Humphrey! I feel so bad that we haven't been writing or calling. How have you been doing?"

"Good."

She wrapped her arm around my shoulders and pulled me away. I was sure she hadn't even noticed I was talking to Foster. "Laurel, I have to tell you about this guy I met here last year. Turned out he was from my hometown. And guess what? He's my boyfriend now!"

"Are you serious?" I said, glad to see my friend so happy.

"Yes," she said. "And he's here with me this year. Right over there." She pointed across the room to a guy with slicked-back hair, a tight black tank top, and a bandana around his neck.

"I'm really excited for you, Rachel," I said.

"Thanks. Do you want to meet him?"

"Sure," I said.

"Great! I'll go get him."

"OK."

She left before I had a chance to catch her up on all of my recent drama. I turned around to look for Foster, but I couldn't see him anywhere.

As I slowly made my way through the crowd, I heard some guy behind me say, "Hello, beautiful!" The voice was unfamiliar but sounded as creepy as a loan shark's.

I had zero desire to talk to such a sleazy-sounding guy. I didn't even want to acknowledge that type of come-on. So I kept looking for Foster without even glancing back.

"Hey, why are you ignoring me, beautiful?" the voice behind me asked. Apparently it didn't occur to this jerk that I didn't want to talk to him.

When I turned around to explain, my mouth dropped open. The guy behind me, leering at me with hungry eyes, had slicked-back hair, a tight black tank top, and a bandana around his neck. Rachel's boyfriend! What a creep.

I thought about giving him a piece of my mind right there. But then I decided to act polite and get out of there as fast as I could. "Hi," I said as nicely as possible. "What's your name?"

He acted crushed. "Oh, c'mon. You remember me, don't you? I tried to talk to you last year but you wouldn't give me the time of day. You said you already had a boyfriend."

Now that he mentioned it, I did remember him. Last year he'd been a sweet, preppy boy, and I felt bad for brushing him off. But I was dating Branson at the time and didn't have any interest in anyone else. This guy had changed dramatically in one year.

His leer returned. "So, is that boyfriend of yours still around?"

"I'm sorry," I said, avoiding the question, "but I don't remember your name."

"It's Kline," he said with a cocky jerk of his head. "So, do you want to blow this joint and go talk somewhere quiet?"

Before I could say, "No thanks," he put his hand around my waist. I was so shocked I couldn't even think of how to tell him what I thought of his rudeness.

Like a knight in shining armor, Foster came up at that moment. "She has a new boyfriend now," he said, smoothly removing the guy's hand from my waist. Foster gave me a look that told me I should play along. I was ever so happy to do so.

"Kline," I said sweetly, "I'd like you to meet Foster McDowell. Foster, this is Kline, a friend I met here last year."

Just then I spotted Rachel walking toward us. "There you are," she said as she walked up to Kline. "I've been looking all over for you. Laurel, this is my boyfriend," she said, placing her hand in his.

"Oh, this is your guy?" I said, trying to play it off. "I didn't realize you were talking about Kline. Are you sure he's your boyfriend?" I asked, trying to bring a little conviction to that boy's heart.

"Why wouldn't I be sure?" she asked, totally oblivious to what had just gone on.

I didn't answer her. Instead I looked at Kline and said, "Are you sure you're her boyfriend? You don't seem like the kind of guy who likes being tied down to one girl."

His cheeks got bright red. Now, he was the one who was speechless.

Rachel answered for him. "Oh, he loves being tied down to just me. Things have been great for us. We have hardly had any problems."

"Really?" I said.

"Look, not to tell all of our business, but our relationship has been getting kind of heated." She said it almost like a brag. "I'm really excited about the seminar tomorrow on dating God's way. It's so hard to resist temptation sometimes." She giggled. "But maybe you don't know what I'm talking about." She gave me a look of pity.

"Oh, I think she might," Kline said, finally getting enough guts to speak. "That's her boyfriend right there."

"Oh, really?" Rachel exclaimed. "My goodness!"

Foster and I had played along with Kline. But Rachel was my friend, and I didn't want to deceive her. How was I supposed to get myself out of this one?

"You have to tell me all about it!" Rachel said excitedly.

"Maybe later," Foster said, rescuing me again. "I want to talk to Laurel right now." He escorted me to a chair in the corner, where we busted up laughing.

"So," I finally asked, "what made you say you were my boyfriend?"

He shrugged. "It just seemed natural."

I wasn't sure what he meant by that. Did he want to take our relationship to the next level? Surely he knew I was not entirely over Branson. I was in no position to be anyone's girlfriend. But I knew, if I was ready, I would want to be Foster's.

For a few minutes we sat in silence. Part of me wanted very much to be his girlfriend, and I think he knew that.

Foster walked me to my cabin. When we got to the door, he gave me a warm, sweet embrace. I suddenly wanted to do much more than hug him! I realized that the comment Rachel had made really did apply to me. The feelings I used to fight so hard against with Branson were resurfacing. I was experiencing desires that were definitely against what God wanted for me.

But then I thought about how nice it would be to do this all the time. To hold hands and hug and talk and not worry about anything else.

We said good night, and I floated into the cabin like I was walking on air. When I got inside, I saw Meagan relaxing on the bottom bunk.

"I didn't feel good so I came to lie down," she explained. "How was your night? Did you have fun with Foster?"

I didn't feel comfortable talking to her about Foster. After all, she liked him first. I said, "Fine," then tried to change the subject. "So, what's going on with you and my brother?"

Meagan blushed. "He's really nice." She giggled. "He kissed me tonight."

"He kissed you?" I exclaimed.

"We're going to that seminar on dating tomorrow."

"I'm going to that one too."

"Laurel, I know you really like Foster. And I can tell he really likes you."

I didn't know what to say, so I just opened my suitcase and started unpacking my pajamas and toothbrush.

But Meagan wouldn't leave it alone. "There's nothing wrong with that, you know. Foster's not a bit like Branson."

"I know," I said.

"Laurel, why won't you talk to me?"

I looked at Meagan, wondering if I should tell her what my hesitation was all about.

Fortunately, she understood. "It's OK to talk with me about Foster. You deserve someone great. Sure, I wanted him when I first met him. But you two are terrific together, and I'm really happy for you."

I knew she was telling the truth. "I do have feelings for him," I admitted, "but I'm not sure what they're all about." Now that she'd given me the OK to talk, it felt great sharing my worries with my girlfriend.

"I know you'll do the right thing," Meagan assured me.

I sure hoped she was right.

I was excited to see that the person teaching the seminar on dating was the same one who'd given the opening night's speech. Meagan and I arrived in the room after most people were already seated. When we saw that Lance and Foster had saved seats for us, we looked at each other and grinned.

The speaker made some great points, things I knew I'd remember for a long time after the retreat. "You don't want to strain your dating relationship," he said. "Being alone with your partner for too long is one way to place unnecessary strain on your partner. There is no reason for you to sit at home alone in the dark with the person you're dating. Nine times out of ten, something negative is going to come from that situation."

I glanced at Foster, glad to see that he was as focused on the seminar as I was.

"Keep physical touching to a minimum," the speaker continued. "You should always be more concerned about your partner as a brother or sister in Christ than as your girlfriend or boyfriend. Don't let the devil kill your focus. Don't let him steal your intimacy with God by convincing you it's OK to be intimate with the person you're dating."

When the talk concluded, the speaker asked if there were any questions.

Kline's hand immediately shot up. "I've been dating Rachel here for a while now," he said. She smiled up at him. "I don't go to the same school she does, so we don't see each other every day. When I do see her, I want to touch her to let her know how much I've missed her. Why can't I do that?"

"What is your purpose for touching Rachel?" the speaker asked, not the least put off by the question. "Isn't it enough just to tell her you missed her?"

"I'm not really a talking kind of person," Kline responded. "I'm more the touching type."

A few people in the audience giggled. It bothered me that Rachel was dating someone who seemed so much like Branson. I wondered if he really cared about her as a person.

"There are several ways to express love," the speaker explained. "Touch is certainly one of those ways. It's exciting when someone we love holds our hand, hugs us, or kisses us . . . even when that someone is our mom or dad."

More chuckles.

"We also like to hear words of affirmation from people we care about. 'I love you' sounds great, but so does 'I appreciate you' and 'I respect you' and 'I understand you.' You can show Rachel you love her by giving her thoughtful gifts, even when it's not Christmas or her birthday. And doing little things to help her is a great way to show how much you care about her. If you're not sure what to do, just ask her. I'm sure she'll come up with some ideas."

This guy was good. He had some great points, and he was expressing them in a way that kept everyone's attention. Several people in the group were taking notes.

"Spending time together whenever you have the opportunity is wonderful, as long as you plan activities for that time so you don't end up just sitting around with nothing to do but get physical. That's when touching becomes the most obvious way to show your love for each other. Unfortunately, once you get started, it's not easy to stop."

"That's sure the case with us," Rachel said. "When Kline hugs me and stuff, I just want him to keep touching me more."

"That's playing with fire," the speaker said, "because it can go too far before either of you realizes it."

This was really hitting close to home. Even though Foster was sitting right next to me, I kept thinking of Branson and how hard it had been to stop touching once things got going. I started feeling down on myself, but the speaker didn't leave us there.

"None of us is perfect," he said, "but we need to keep trying to be. Kline, if you really love the Lord, then you need to ask Him to help you find other ways to show Rachel that you love her."

Kline shrugged, not looking convinced.

"Sometimes, the best way we can let our partners know

how much we love them is to do everything we can to *re-frain* from touching."

That sure made sense to me! I hoped it did to Rachel too.

Rachel raised her hand. When the speaker called on her, she asked, "But what are you supposed to do when you really want the person you love to touch you? When it's all you can do to keep your hands off the guy, especially when you don't really want him to keep his hands off you?"

Some of the people in the room started whispering about Kline and Rachel like they were terrible sinners to be talking the way they were. But I knew they were just trying to be honest. And if the rest of the people in that room were truthful, they'd probably have to admit they had the same temptations themselves. I recognized that I was having some of the same feelings for Foster that Kline and Rachel were struggling with.

The speaker interrupted my thoughts. "I hear a lot of mumbling going on. Are Kline and Rachel the only ones in this room who have felt like this?"

The mumbling ceased immediately.

To my surprise, Foster spoke up. "I've never felt the kind of temptation you've been talking about until recently," he said. "My focus has always been on the Lord and baseball. Then one day, as I was going into church to praise the Lord, I saw the prettiest sight I'd ever seen. And I started wondering if I was good enough for the pastor's daughter."

"Aw," Rachel sighed, "that's so sweet."

Was this out of the movie-of-the-week or what? I had to be dreaming. I squeezed his hand. But he wasn't done.

"Then the girl I thought I could never get ended up with a broken heart from a guy who didn't appreciate her. And the next thing I knew, there she was in my arms. It was the greatest thing I've ever felt."

Meagan gave me a big smile. I felt like the luckiest girl in the world.

"Then last night," Foster continued, "when she was in my arms again, I had to ask the Lord to give me the strength to fight those feelings."

"The best way to resist temptation," the speaker said, "is to keep yourself out of tempting situations. But if you find yourself there, you've got a very powerful weapon to use against it. It's called prayer. If you sincerely ask God to deliver you from temptation, He will."

"Does that really work?" Rachel questioned.

"It sure does!" I blurted out.

Foster smiled at me and squeezed my hand. "When you love the Lord more than you could ever love anyone else, your love for Christ keeps things pure."

"Wow," the speaker said. "Thanks for sharing with us, you two."

It felt great to think that our honesty and insight might have been able to bless some of the people in that room.

"Let's all stand in a circle and pray," the speaker suggested. "I'd like each of you to mention one thing that you want God to give you."

Foster started. "Lord, give us strength to battle unwanted thoughts."

I added, "God, give us love for You that is greater than our love for any person on earth."

Lance said, "Father, give us wisdom to know what pleases You in our dating relationships."

After it went around the circle, the leader closed by saying, "Heavenly Father, we know You have heard all of our prayers. Please bless these young people as they struggle in the area of dating. Equip their minds and hearts with things above. Don't let them be weighed down with things of the world. May they find partners who are gifts from You. Lord, I thank You in advance for allowing them to stay pure for You. I pray against sexual desires and temptations and against wrong partners who harm their walk with You. In Jesus' precious and holy name we pray. Amen."

A unanimous "Amen" filled the room.

————————————

As soon as I saw Meagan at school on Monday morning, she asked, "Hey, remember Justin Townsend?"

Everybody knew Justin Townsend. He'd graduated from our school last year. He was more popular then than Branson was this year. He lettered in every sport and caught the eye of every girl—even mine, and I had a boyfriend. Justin and Brittany were quite an item for a while, and he was the first guy she had ever been intimate with.

"He has AIDS," Meagan whispered.

I was shocked. "AIDS? Are you sure?"

"Yeah," Meagan said. "He called Brittany and told her she needs to get tested."

This was unbelievable. Could Brittany lose her life because she slept with the wrong guy? "Where is she?" I asked, forgetting our past differences. "I need to talk to her."

"She didn't come to school today."

"Then how do you know about this? It's not just a rumor, is it?" I hoped that's all it was.

"I got it firsthand, Laurel. When I came home from the retreat yesterday, she was at my house crying. My mom said she'd been there for about an hour."

"She must be devastated," I said.

"That's an understatement."

"Has she told Branson yet?" If she did have AIDS, he could have it too.

"I don't think so," Meagan said.

"We'll have to pray for both of them."

"I always wondered why God says to wait," Meagan said. "Now I know."

The bell rang and we had to go our separate ways. As I walked to class I thought about Robyn. She had gone against what God said and paid dearly for it. She created a life and then took it away. That is something she would have to carry with her until she died. Now Brittany might lose her life for the same reason.

Lord, I prayed as I walked, *I sure hope Brittany and Branson don't have AIDS. And I thank You for not allowing it to happen to me. Help me walk closer to You every day so I won't fall.*

Robyn was waiting for me when I walked into the classroom. She had a huge smile spread across her face.

"What's going on with you?" I asked. "Why are you so happy?"

"Jackson called me last weekend. He asked me why I hadn't been talking to him lately, so I let him have it. I told him everything. I thought he'd get angry but he didn't. Instead, he apologized for everything and we both got emotional. So I went out with him."

"Is he your boyfriend now?"

"Not a chance, girl," Robyn said with a smile. "We're taking it real slow. I told him not to have any expectations in a relationship with me because I'm not down for sex anymore. He said he understood."

"I'm glad you put your foot down. Saying no in a relationship isn't easy."

"Remembering the day I got an abortion will make me say no until I get married."

We hugged.

"What are you doing after school?" she asked me.

"I have my first day of gymnastics practice for the school team," I said excitedly.

"You've got to let me know when the meets start so I can come and support my girl."

"Great. I'll need all the yelling and screaming I can get."

I was on my way to practice when I heard a familiar voice. "Laurel, wait. Can I talk to you?"

What in the world did Branson want? I turned around slowly.

"Did you hear about Justin?" he asked me.

"Yeah."

"Laurel," he said nervously, "I might have AIDS. I have to get a test. I never meant for this to happen. Brittany and I were only together a couple of times. Do you think I might have it?"

"Branson, I'm not a doctor. I wish I could tell you it will be OK, but I can't."

"Thanks a lot," he complained.

I didn't have any patience for him. "What are you getting mad at me for? I didn't make you sleep with Brittany. You made your choice."

He stared at me with large eyes. "So you're glad this is happening to me?"

"Branson, you know me better than that." I softened my voice a little. "I've already prayed for you guys."

"Great," he said sarcastically. "Your prayers are probably what did this. You must have told God to punish me."

"I can't believe you'd say that!" I spun around and stomped away, trying not to lose my cool. I had a practice to get to and I didn't have time to argue with him.

"Laurel, I'm sorry," he said as he ran to catch up with me. "I can't even look Brittany in the face. She's scared to death and so am I. I made the worst mistake of my life when I left you."

I stopped and glared at him. "You're only saying that because of what's going on."

"No, Laurel. Even when I was with Brittany, I kept comparing her to you."

"Yeah, right," I said, tapping the toe of my tennis shoe. "If that's true, then why didn't you come back to me when you had the chance?"

"Pride got in the way," he said without hesitation. "But pride's not important anymore. Laurel, I'm begging you. I can't go through this alone. I need someone who really cares about me. I need you. Do you think you can find a way to forgive me, take me back, and let me be your boyfriend again?"

His words were sincere. I had dreamed of this moment so many times before. And he was right, I still cared for him deeply. But I was shocked that he was trying to return.

laughing
and loving

aughter slipped out of my mouth as I stood before Branson. I couldn't believe he had asked me to be his girlfriend again. I knew his situation was serious, but for some reason I found it hilarious that he would have the nerve to try to get back with me after everything that had happened.

Branson didn't think it was funny at all. "What are you doing, Laurel? I'm being honest here. Don't laugh at me."

I managed to stop giggling, but I couldn't force the smile off my face. His sincere words couldn't change what I was feeling inside.

"I love you, Laurel. I have never stopped loving you. Give me one more chance. I could die from this. And if I do, I want you by my side."

Now he was laying a guilt trip on me. Did he think I couldn't figure out what he was doing? I didn't have time for this. I had to get to practice and he had already made me late. "Branson, I have to go."

"Will you at least think about it?"

"Think about what? Branson, I am not going to get back together with you. There's no way. And that's final!"

I started to leave, but he stopped me with a soft request. "Would you be willing to go to the doctor with me?" he whispered. "For the test?"

The tears in his eyes broke my heart. "Do you really think me being there with you will help?" I asked.

"I honestly don't know if I can do it without you." His voice broke. I'd never seen him so frightened.

Perhaps God was going to reach Branson through this. Maybe He could use me to show him the Lord's love. I knew there was no hope of a relationship between us, and I had to make that clear to him. But did that mean I couldn't be his friend in this time of need?

"All right," I said. "I'll go with you. But—"

"Great," he said before I could finish what I was saying. He grabbed me and squeezed me so tight I felt like a tube of toothpaste with just a tiny bit left inside. "I'll meet you right after your gymnastics practice."

"You're going today?" I asked.

"Yeah. It takes two weeks to get the results and I can't wait any longer."

"All right," I said slowly. "But I'll have to call my mom and make sure it's OK first."

His eyes teared up again. "I knew you'd be there for me, Laurel. I just knew it. Thanks." He placed his lips on my cheek to show his appreciation and then darted away.

How am I supposed to explain this to my mom? I wondered.

───────────────

That afternoon I went to the clinic with Branson for his testing. I'd tried asking permission from my mom without giving her all the details, but she drilled me until I let it all out. I was afraid she'd be really upset and maybe even tell me I couldn't go with Branson. But she said it was fine with her. I was really appreciative of the fact that she understood. This was something I just had to do.

The clinic's waiting room was cold. Branson was shivering, but it wasn't just because of the air temperature. I knew he was scared.

While we waited, I talked to him, hoping to calm him down. I asked him some tough questions, like whether or not he'd used a condom.

He assured me he had. "And it was only a couple of times," he said.

I knew it only took one time. But I didn't think that's what Branson needed to hear right then.

Eventually I ran out of words to say, so I just started praying in my mind. *Father, help me give my friend what he needs right now. Lord, You know I'm still angry with him, but there is a possibility that AIDS is infecting his body at this very moment. Help him get through this. Please spare his life."*

As I prayed, an overwhelming sense of peace came over me. It was so strong it felt like a revelation.

Branson put his hands over his face and started sobbing like a baby.

"It's gonna be OK," I told him calmly and sincerely. "You're going to be fine."

He looked up at me and sniffled. "How do you know that?"

"You've got to trust God with your life."

Branson looked astonished that I would say that. "Do you think God is proud of me? Do you think He's happy that I dogged out one of His own to be with some chick who doesn't even believe in Him? God probably figures this is what I deserve."

"The Lord isn't like that," I explained. "He loves you, not because of anything you've done, good or bad, but because of who He is and who you are in Him. You are a child of the King, Branson. Don't ever lose your faith in Him."

"But if God loves me so much, why would He let this happen to me?"

In an instant, the Holy Spirit gave me an answer to Branson's tough question. "Maybe this is a wake-up call for you to get it together. You need to stop playing with life and take it seriously."

"You're right, Laurel," he said, staring at the floor.

"Look," I said, taking his hand, "I really do believe that it's going to be OK. You can't give up hope."

"Branson Price," a lady in a white uniform called out.

Branson looked up. "Yeah, that's me."

"You can come on in, sir."

As he followed the nurse through the door, he looked back at me with sad eyes.

"You'll be OK," I whispered. Though I didn't have any evidence to prove that fact, I trusted God to take care of him. In my heart I hoped the Lord would not allow Branson to have AIDS. But I knew that, if he did, God could give Branson the grace to handle it.

Moments later the nurse returned. "Miss," she said, "would you mind coming with me? I need to talk to you for a moment."

"Sure," I said, grabbing my things. As I followed her down the hall, I wondered what she wanted to tell me.

She took me back to a conference room and shut the door behind us. "I'm Barbara Jenkins," she said. "Mr. Price asked for an AIDS test because he has just learned that his girlfriend's ex-boyfriend has been diagnosed with the disease. He also said that his girlfriend was timid about being tested herself."

"Yes?" I said, waiting for her to continue.

"Well, I just want to encourage you to go ahead and take the test. I know it's frightening, but it will be much more soothing to your soul if you clear your mind of any uncertainties."

I started to laugh. "Oh, no, no, no," I said. "He wasn't

talking about me. I'm his old girlfriend. I'm just here for moral support, as a friend."

She looked at me as if she didn't believe me. "Mr. Price said you are his girlfriend."

I took a deep breath. "He must be assuming that we're back together because I'm here supporting him on this. But as soon as we leave here, I'm going to let him know that he made the wrong assumption. Even if he doesn't have AIDS, I don't see a future for us. The girl he left me for was my best friend."

"My, my," the nurse said, shaking her head. "You teenagers sure have a lot going on these days."

"Yeah, tell me about it!"

"Well, I guess what I was saying wasn't for you after all. But if you talk to this girl, please encourage her to take the test. And all of the people she has been intimate with should be tested too. If there are any more," she added, prompting me for information.

"Oh, there are more," I said, half laughing and half wanting to cry for my friend.

"There's nothing funny about this," the nurse said seriously. "Having multiple partners is very unsafe. This isn't a fictional story where we can rewrite a happy ending. Whatever the test results say is what it is going to be."

"I know," I said, getting serious too. "I'm practicing abstinence myself."

She gave me a small smile. "That's a very smart move. I wish more teenagers would adopt that practice."

"Well, I plan to stay pure until I'm married. I believe God will honor that."

Her smile grew. "I like you, young lady. Make sure you continue to stay on your knees and pray. It's tough, but since you've been successful so far, the Lord can give you the strength to continue. You're a good friend to come here with your ex. I pray this works out for him."

"Yeah, me too."

After the test, Branson and I went to Burger King for dinner. Neither of us were sparking conversation. Suddenly I felt his warm hand touch my fingertips. He was trying to slide his hand into mine. I knew he needed comfort, but I could not let him think that we were more than friends. He needed me to lean on, but that was the only reason I was there.

"Branson—"

He cut me off. "Laurel, I want to thank you again for being here with me. I care about you so much. I don't know how I could ever have been so stupid. I'm glad you can put that behind you, forgive me, and let us pick up where we left off."

I leaned back in the seat and put my hands in my lap so he couldn't reach them. "The nurse told me you said I was your girlfriend. How could you think that? You hurt me in ways I could never get over. I only came with you today because I didn't want you to have to go alone."

"I'm going to win you back, Laurel. I love you."

"Branson, look," I said. "I don't want you to suffer. I don't want you to be sick. But a romantic relationship with you is nowhere in my mind."

"Just think about it," he pleaded.

The fact that he could even suggest us getting back together showed his lack of respect for me. He had cheated on me with my best friend, and that fact alone was enough to make me never trust him again. I grabbed my coat and headed for the door.

He was really flipping out. Us, a couple again? No way! It was all I could do to keep from laughing in his face.

As I drove home, my anger at Branson turned to sadness and pity. I still didn't want to have anything to do with him as a boyfriend, but the Lord helped me understand his desire to win me back after everything that had happened between him and Brittany. I'd been there for him when he needed me. Where was she? *I can't imagine how lonely he must feel right now. Father, help Branson to know how much You love him.*

When I walked in the door at home, I found my parents in the den having coffee. Mom held her arms out to me and I fell into them. So much was going on at that moment. I needed their love. I needed them to tell me that everything was going to be OK.

"Mom, this is awful."

"Yes, it is," she said, rubbing my back. "But I'm sure you have prayed for Branson, and that's all you can do. You can't carry this for him."

"I know."

"Sex is nothing to play around with, Laurel," my dad interjected. "This is one of the things I have warned you and your brothers about. Sex may be exciting, but there are some moments in life that you can't take back. Those moments cause emotional scars that you can never heal from. God doesn't want that for any of His children."

I'd heard all this before. But for some reason, I didn't mind hearing it again.

"Laurel, I'm sorry that you're in a situation like this. But I hope you will learn from it, and by God's grace you'll never go through this kind of suffering yourself."

"Oh, don't worry, Dad," I assured him, "I won't! You can count on that."

He smiled at me. "You're a very mature young woman," he said, "and I'm proud of you."

"Thanks, Daddy," I said as I hugged him. "See? I really was listening all those times when you and Mom were talking to me about sex."

He laughed. "Well, keep those ears open because we're not finished talking about this."

"Sweetie," my mom said as she stroked my hair, "we know being a teenager isn't easy. But we're here for you. We want you to be able to talk to us. We may not be cool like your high school friends—"

"Speak for yourself, dear," Dad joked. "I'm pretty hip."

Mom rolled her eyes lovingly at my father, then turned back to me. "The point is that we love you," she said. "And you can come to us for any advice you need."

"I realize that now more than ever," I told them. "I know you guys really do have my best interests at heart. I realize I give you a hard time once in a while, but it's great to know that you both love me and that you know what's best for me. I'm so thankful that I have you two." I kissed them both on the cheeks, messed up my dad's hair, laughed, and headed to bed.

I went out of my way to be nice to Branson over the next few days. It wasn't easy to be his friend when he kept trying to take it further. Several times I was tempted to just give up on him. But I knew he needed a friend, and I was determined to help him get through this.

As I stood in front of my locker that Thursday morning between classes, Branson snuck up behind me and tossed a book onto the shelf.

I pulled the book out and handed it back to him. "No, Branson, we are not sharing a locker. Don't you dare put your books in here."

"Oh, c'mon," he begged. "My class is right around the corner from here. This'll be so much easier."

"No," I insisted. "We've done this before, remember? It didn't work out."

"Please, Laurel," he begged with big puppy-dog eyes. "Just this one book."

I shook my head. It didn't sound as if he was going to give up, and the bell was about to ring. So when he tossed his book back into my locker, I just shut the door and left it in there.

"Thanks," he said with a grin.

"Just one book," I insisted.

Before he took off for class, he planted a quick kiss on my cheek. I was furious! Several people in the hall saw his advance. I knew rumors would start to fly before I even made it to my next class.

Over the next couple of days, I tried to distance myself from Branson, but everywhere I turned, he was there. I didn't want to totally abandon him, but he was taking this too far and getting on my nerves.

At lunch on Friday, I saw Foster sitting alone at a table, so I took my tray over there and sat down. I hadn't realized it till then, but I'd been spending so much time with Branson, I hadn't seen much of Foster that week.

"Hi," I said as I sat in the seat next to him.

Foster took a long drink of his milk without even acknowledging my presence.

"Foster? Are you ignoring me?"

He turned toward me as if he'd just that moment realized I was there. "Oh," he said sarcastically, "so you've decided to speak to me today?"

"What are you talking about?" I asked.

His tone turned from sarcastic to livid. "I've tried to get together with you all week, but you've been too wrapped up in your *boyfriend* to give me the time of day."

I knew he was talking about Branson, but I had no idea why he would think that jerk was my boyfriend. "Foster, I—"

"Don't try to deny it. Your brother told me you and Branson were dating again. And I've seen you guys together all week in school."

"Just because you've seen us together, doesn't mean we're a couple." I was starting to get angry right back at him. "I thought we were friends. Why are you taking this so personally?"

"You're right, it's none of my business." He got up, even though he'd barely touched his lunch. "I wouldn't want you to think I cared or anything." With that he walked off, leaving me alone at the table.

At first it didn't really bother me that Foster had misread things between Branson and me. But the more I thought about it, the more I realized that I was really disappointed that he was angry with me. I had to find out what my brother had said to make Foster so upset.

"Hey, Liam," I said after dinner that evening, "wanna play a board game with me?"

He agreed, so we got the box out of the cupboard and started setting up the pieces. As we played, I couldn't keep my mind on the game, so he was winning by a landslide.

"Liam," I said during one of his turns, "why did you tell Foster that Branson and I are dating?"

Liam casually rolled the dice. "I just told him that you guys went out a couple of times." He moved his game piece. "You owe me $500."

"That is nowhere near the truth," I said.

"That's what it says on the board," he said, pointing to the square his piece had landed on.

"I meant about Branson," I said, paying him the game money.

"I know." He handed me the dice. "Don't get upset."

"How can you tell me not to get upset?" I nearly screamed, squeezing the dice in my hand.

My brother gave me a serious look. "Hey, Foster's a cool guy and I don't want him to get hurt by you. He deserves to know that you're still hung up on that Branson guy!"

I tossed the dice onto the table. "Why does everyone assume that Branson's my boyfriend just because I hang out with him?" I moved my game piece around the board, slamming it onto each square.

"You guys have broken up and gotten back together a million times. No one knows when it's truly over with you two. Even if he does have AIDS, you're probably going to stick with him."

221

"That's messed up, Liam!" I yelled, picking up the dice and throwing them at him.

Liam retrieved the dice from the floor and placed them on the table. "OK, maybe I didn't have to say that. But the creep leaves you for your best friend, and then he gets AIDS—"

"The results haven't come back yet."

"Why do you keep defending him, Laurel? Make up your mind. Which guy do you like?"

"Branson and I are just friends," I argued. "And I would appreciate it if you wouldn't tell people anything other than that." I reached for the dice, but Liam grabbed my hand and looked me in the eye.

"Why are you getting so upset? You really like Foster, don't you? I mean, as more than just a friend."

"Yeah, Liam," I whispered, nearly in tears. "I do."

Liam looked at me, his anger finally cooling. "I'm sorry, Laurel. Really. Hey, maybe I can fix this."

"No, thanks," I said, "you've done enough damage already."

"Look, if you like him so much, you've got to let him know. Laurel, that boy's heart is broken."

"Really?" I asked, concerned.

"Really," he assured me. "Now, can we please finish this game?" He chuckled. "Or are you willing to concede defeat?"

As I went to bed that night, I had a big smile on my face. Foster was all broken up because he thought I was with someone else. That told me he really cared about me. A lot. Now the question was, what was I going to do about it?

Mom walked into my room before I woke up the next morning. "Laurel," she said, "you have company downstairs."

"Company?" I looked at my bedside clock. "It's seven o'clock in the morning." Who in their right mind would come to see me at seven o'clock on a Saturday?

"It's Brittany," Mom announced.

My heart almost stopped. "Brittany?" I questioned.

"She said she needs to talk to you desperately," Mom explained. "She told me she would drive you to gymnastics practice."

"Tell her I'll be down in a minute." As I got dressed, I decided to protect my emotions. I knew Brittany could switch personalities quickly.

I walked down the stairs and saw her sitting on the couch with a worried look on her face. When she noticed me, she stood, clutching a tissue in her fist. "I know you're surprised to see me here," she said.

"Yeah, I am," I said coolly. "What's going on?"

"I'm sure you've heard what's been going on with Justin."
I nodded.

"I'm really scared, Laurel. What if I have it too? And what if I gave it to Branson? You probably think this is what we deserve. If he had stayed with you, he wouldn't be facing all this." She collapsed back onto the couch and started crying.

The bitterness I'd felt toward her dissolved. I sat beside her and put my arm around her trembling shoulders. Brittany wasn't the greatest friend, but this whole situation was frightening.

"Branson broke up with me," she told me. "He said he never stopped loving you, but I know the real reason. Why would he want to be with someone as dirty as me?" Brittany started bawling again. "Can you ever forgive me, Laurel? I really want us to be friends again."

Lord, I prayed, *I've missed Brittany a lot. And now she's asking for my friendship again. Do You want me to give it to her? I know You want me to forgive her. Give me the strength to love my friend again.*

"Laurel," Brittany whispered, "I know I'm going to die. Please talk to God and tell Him I'm sorry."

I knew Brittany had to tell God herself that she was sorry for what she'd done. But I could tell she wasn't ready to do that yet. "Brittany," I said, "God allowed this to happen to show you that He is in control. He loves you very much. The Lord wants you to please Him more than anyone on earth. Your sin has separated you from Him. But because He loves you so much, He sent His Son to pay the penalty for your sin so you could have a right relationship with Him. If you feel the weight of your sin and see how it controls you, yet you want to live for God, then you need to cry out to Him to save you. Let Him heal your heart, Brittany. He's the only one you need!"

Brittany stared at me for a moment. Then she got down on her knees right there beside the couch. I joined her and listened as she cried before God. I could tell she was broken because of all that she had done wrong. She asked the Holy Spirit to come into her heart and make her new. By the time she said amen, we both had tears all over our faces.

We got up and hugged each other tightly.

"Can I ask you one more favor?" Brittany asked.

"Sure," I said, although I had no idea what she was going to ask me.

"Would you let me use some of your makeup before we leave? I just know mine's a mess!"

We laughed and ran upstairs, where Brittany freshened up and I got dressed and ready for gymnastics practice.

In the car on the way to Rockdale Gym, Brittany and I rode in silence for a while. Then I broke the ice. "I need to talk to you about something, Britt."

"What is it?" she asked.

I could tell I'd broken into her thoughts, so I waited till I had her full attention before I continued. "Branson told me you haven't taken the test yet. I really think you should."

"I suppose," she said, obviously not convinced.

"Did you use protection with Justin?" I asked.

Brittany was quiet for a long time, then she finally spoke. "We were together several times," she admitted. "But I think he used something most of the time."

"You *think*?" I asked, trying not to sound as upset as I felt.

She pulled into the parking lot of the gym. "Now that I think about it, I guess there were times when he didn't."

"Brittany, you've got to take that test," I urged.

As she parked, she looked at me, her eyes wide. "But what if it comes back positive?"

"Then you'll take the first steps to educate yourself."

Her hands slipped off the steering wheel and fell into her lap. "I'm going to die," she whispered.

"We're all going to die someday, Brittany," I said. I could tell that didn't help. "Look, you could be worried about all this for nothing. The test could come back negative. I bet you're fine. In fact, I'll make you a wager. If you are fine, you owe me . . ." My voice trailed off as I tried to think of an appropriate finish.

"My cream-colored sweater?" she suggested.

I grinned. "Yeah! The cream sweater."

We laughed.

"You know, I always thought that sweater looked better on you than it did on me. That's why I never wanted you to borrow it." She looked embarrassed for a minute, then she smiled up at me. "But I'd be happy to let you have it now!"

That Monday I sat with Meagan and Brittany at lunch. "So, how did you guys do on your first final?" I asked as I ate my sandwich.

"I think I did OK," Meagan said.

"It's hard for me to concentrate on anything." Brittany had gone in to take her AIDS test while I was at gymnastics practice, and she hadn't been able to think of anything else since.

"Don't focus on that, Brittany," Meagan advised her.

"Yeah, think positive," I said. "That cream sweater is all mine!"

Robyn and Jackson walked by, entwined in each other's arms.

"Robyn," I called out.

"Hi, guys," she said, coming up to our table. "How have y'all been?"

"Good," I answered. "What about you? Looks to me like things are going pretty well for you."

She grinned up at Jackson. "I can't complain." Then she asked if she could talk to me for a second. Jackson gave her a kiss on the forehead and I excused myself to my girls. Then Robyn and I went over to a table to talk alone.

"My heart still hurts real bad about what I did," Robyn admitted. "But all in all, I'm doing great. I'm sorry I haven't called you. I never had the chance to thank you, but your friendship meant the world to me. You were there for me when no one else could be. Thank you. You were my angel."

We hugged. "I'm just glad God was able to use me," I whispered. And I was. I had really grown since my first semester of high school.

As I walked across the lunchroom to rejoin my other friends, Branson caught me. He spun me around and said with a smile, "I got my test results. They were negative!"

"Branson, that's great," I shouted, then gave him a quick, friendly hug. To my relief, he didn't try to make it last longer.

"I have to be retested in six months," he said. "But I'm taking it one test at a time."

I told him how happy I was. Then I looked over at Brittany. She was watching us, and I knew she had figured out what our excitement was all about. Her face looked dejected. I knew she was happy for him, but she was more concerned about her own results.

"You should talk to Brittany," I told him.

"I guess you're right," he admitted reluctantly. "But it's her—"

"Don't even say that," I interrupted him. "You can't

blame her for this. You did it too. You need to encourage her. It's the right thing to do."

"I know," he said. "But first I want to talk about us."

"Us?" I asked. "What about us?"

He took my hand. "We can move on now. Now that we know it's safe."

I pulled my hand out of his grasp. "That is not why we haven't moved on."

"Laurel," he said, grinning, "don't tease me. You don't have to pretend anymore."

I looked at him like he'd just escaped from the nuthouse. "What are you talking about, boy?"

"Liam told me you're crazy about some guy," he said. "Who else could it be but me?"

"Hopefully, it's me," said a sweet voice behind me. I turned around quickly and saw Foster. "I've been trying to find the nerve to tell you how I've felt for weeks now," he said. "I'm tired of wondering." He took my hand gently in his. "Laurel Shadrach, will you be my girlfriend?"

"I'd love to," I answered quickly.

Meagan let out a happy shout. Branson stood back with his arms folded across his chest and a glare in his eyes. Brittany stared at us, completely shocked.

I threw my arms around Foster's neck and gave him a big hug. After Branson I thought I would never have another boyfriend. But being Foster's girl was an idea I loved. With him I knew there would be a whole lot of laughing and loving.

fifteen

celebrating
his birthday

the smile on my face would not disappear. Foster was looking at me with fascination and pride, and the warmth in my heart told me that we had finally gotten it together.

Though the cafeteria was packed, it felt like we were the only two people there. I was enchanted by his presence. I knew the guy standing before me cared deeply for me. The road we were about to embark upon as boyfriend and girlfriend was sure to be a sweet ride.

My wonderful thoughts were interrupted when Branson tugged on my arm and pulled me away from Foster. "You can't go with this guy, Laurel. I want us to get back together. You know how much I care about you. Don't do me wrong the way I did you. It's insulting, agreeing to go out with this guy right in my face."

I vividly remembered watching Branson with Brittany pinned up against the wall under the stairs. But I didn't say anything about that. They had apologized, and even though I hadn't forgotten, I had forgiven them. Branson and I had tried to get it right, but we never did. Now I couldn't imagine myself with him ever again.

"Branson," I said tenderly, "we broke up because you wanted to do your own thing, and because you thought you needed more from me. That hurt but I had to respect your wishes. This is my moment now. Please don't spoil it."

He gave me a look that was anything but joyful.

"Look, if you want to pout, go ahead. But I'm not gonna let you ruin this for me. I'm really happy that your first test came back negative, but it's not my job to hold your hand for your whole life."

"Fine," he said coldly. "Go make a mistake with your life. See if I care."

"So you're going to be a jerk about this, huh? After I forgave you, you're gonna act like this?"

"Laurel," Foster said.

"You'd better go," Branson said sarcastically. "Your boyfriend is calling."

I looked at Branson sadly. "I really hate that it has to be this way. I would have liked for us to be friends. I hope you'll come around someday." I picked up my books, told my girlfriends I'd see them later, and walked arm in arm with Foster out of the cafeteria.

"Are you OK?" he asked when we got to the hallway.

"Yeah," I assured him. "Branson is such a big baby. I just hate that I didn't see it sooner. I went through so much drama with him, and now I realize that I didn't have to."

Foster led me to a bench and we sat down. "I'd like to pray," he said. "Is that OK?"

I smiled. Of course it was OK!

He held my hand. "Heavenly Father, I come to You lifting up this relationship between Laurel and me. Thank You for giving me the courage to ask her to spend time with me. She is so beautiful, and I know we will face temptations. I pray that You will continue to help us see that our relationship is a gift from You, and because it's so special, we won't misuse it, mistreat it, or abuse it. May our relationship glorify Your holy name. Amen."

I thought my heart was full when Foster asked me to be his girlfriend, but at that moment I realized it had only been half full. When he finished talking to the Lord on our behalf, I knew my heart was truly full.

"You know, my birthday's coming up," he said.

"I think my brother mentioned that. When is it?"

"The twenty-third."

"Wow! Two days before Christmas. Are you having a big party?"

"No. My mother got tickets to something. She's a big fan of the theater."

"I am too," I said. "Do you know what play it is?"

His forehead crinkled. "I don't remember the name, but it's something about a toy that turns into—"

"The Nutcracker!" I exclaimed.

"Yeah, that's it. We're going to dinner beforehand at some semiformal restaurant."

It sounded like a perfect night. I would have loved to go, but I didn't want to impose on his night with his mom.

"I'd love it if you could come with us," he said.

"Are you sure it's all right with your mom?" I asked. "Is there an extra ticket? I don't want to take anyone's place."

Foster placed a finger on my lips. "It would make my birthday the best one yet."

I melted. "You know all the right things to say, don't you, Foster?"

"You mean, that was the right thing?" he joked.

I playfully punched his chest. "You're so silly. You told me once that you never had a girlfriend before, but I don't believe it. You're too smooth not to have had some practice."

"Not true," he said, giving me a serious look. "You're my first. And you're all I need and want."

I decided I was going to have to get used to smiling a lot with this guy. I was elated, inside and out.

That December 23 was like a fairy tale. My mother bought me a beautiful pale-blue dress that was as pretty as Cinderella's ball gown. Meagan came over to help me get ready, and she waited on me like I was a princess. Even Brittany put aside her personal problems to do my makeup and twist my hair into a fancy French braid. When my friends finished with me, I checked out my reflection.

"Mirror, mirror, on the wall," I said in astonishment, "who's the fairest one of all?"

My girlfriends cracked up. But I really did feel like Snow White waiting for her handsome prince.

Foster showed up with a dozen red roses for me. A stretch limo was waiting in the driveway. His parents followed in their car, to give us privacy. After I waved to my friends and family, I climbed into the limo, and we toasted with sparkling apple cider.

"I have never seen you look more beautiful," Foster said.

"Thank you," I responded, blushing. "I had a lot of help."

"Well, be sure to thank whoever helped you look like this for me," he said, laughing.

I gave Foster a cross necklace for his birthday. "How do you like it?" I asked, even though I could tell he was thrilled.

"You're the best present I could ever receive," he whispered.

We ate dinner at a high-rise in downtown Atlanta. The top floor was a restaurant that revolved very slowly. The view was breathtaking, and the six-course meal made the night even more memorable. Our conversation was fun and friendly. Foster's parents were extremely nice to me.

The ballet was so moving that I sometimes felt like I was in that make-believe world. Near the end, when the lead character was dancing with her prince, Foster took my hand and I closed my eyes, imagining us dancing in each other's arms. It wasn't until the audience erupted in applause that I came back to reality.

As we walked through the lobby, Foster held my hand. "Did you like it?" he asked, rubbing his fingers across my knuckles.

"Oh yes," I exclaimed. "But I feel bad."

He looked perplexed. "Why?"

"Because it's your birthday, and I feel like I'm the one who got the big present."

He laughed.

"This night was perfectly wonderful," I said. "Thank you so much for inviting me to come with you."

Back in the limo, Foster pressed a button on the CD player and Celine Dion started singing our song, "I'm Your Angel." He took me in his arms and whispered the lyrics in my ear.

I kissed his forehead. Then I decided he deserved a special birthday kiss on the lips, one that only a girlfriend could give.

Our mouths connected. Our heads started moving slowly from side to side. As the passion heated up, thoughts of the flesh started seeping into my mind. I helped him out of his jacket. As his hands caressed my body, I kissed him more. "This feels so good," I whispered in his ear.

Suddenly he pulled back. "I can't believe we're doing this. This is so wrong."

We withdrew to opposite sides of the bench seat. I could see he was shaking. What had I done? Had I destroyed everything with one stupid moment of passion? Would Foster and I ever recover from this?

When the limo pulled up in front of my house, Foster walked me to the door, but he kept a distance between us.

"Can we talk about this tomorrow?" I asked when we reached the porch.

"I don't know," he said softly. "I have to think. I'll call you." He walked slowly back to the limo.

A tear trickled down my face. How could I have ruined such a perfect evening?

Bright and early the next morning, my family piled into our van and headed for Arkansas, like we did every year. Christmas Eve was my dad's birthday and he always wanted to go home for the holiday, even though it was a long ride. I enjoyed spending Christmas vacation with my grandparents. This year, however, I finally had a life that I didn't want to leave.

"Laurel, you haven't said a word the whole trip," my mom said to me about two hours down the road.

I hadn't slept a minute the night before. How could I have ruined my perfect relationship with Foster? I couldn't believe I'd let lust creep through the back door of my mind! In that one moment of weakness, I had let my guard down. I'd forgotten that Foster was a present from the Lord. I had totally abused his trust.

A tear slipped down my cheek when I realized I had become the kind of person I hated. Though we didn't commit the full sin, what we did was impure. There are always consequences to sin. Foster was probably reevaluating our whole relationship.

"Laurel?" Mom asked again.

"I'm OK," I assured her. "I'm just relaxing." Trying to cover my depressed mood, I added, "I'm not the only one who's being quiet. I haven't heard anything from the birthday boy lately." I touched my dad's shoulder from behind the driver's seat.

Dad was turning forty-five and I knew he didn't want to make a big deal out of it. But I knew his mother would go all out. Grandmother told us she was planning a huge surprise party for my father that year.

"I'm doing fine up here," Dad said. "I'm just thinking about how good God has been to me. I'm so blessed!"

What he said made me realize I didn't have to dwell on my mistakes. I just needed to ask God how I could redeem myself. If I had to lose Foster in order to learn my lesson, then it was a sacrifice I was willing to make. I should have known that if I took my eyes off the Lord, I would fall.

Heavenly Father, I prayed, *show me how I can mend myself. I want to quit stumbling. Please give me a clean heart.*

"Laurel," my father suggested, "why don't you sing something for your old dad?"

I knew right away what I wanted to sing, so I started right in. I poured out a praise song that asked the Lord to give me a clean heart so I might serve Him. When I sang that I was not worthy of all God's blessings, the lyrics echoed the cry of my broken heart.

I belted out the last note with so much strength, I woke up Luke. "Are we there yet?" he asked, rubbing his eyes.

"Not yet," Mom answered.

While everyone in the car laughed, I realized that my brother's comment was symbolic of where I was in my Christian walk. I wasn't "there yet," but at least I was seeking a clean heart. The important thing was that I was going forward, and one day I would be with Jesus.

I thanked God for loving me through my disobedience and showing me that with His strength I could overcome.

"Surprise!" people yelled all through my grandparents' home as my dad walked through the front door.

I was thrilled to see my family, especially my cousins Reba and Cassie. I wasn't really that close to Reba because she was two years older than I, so we didn't really talk that much. But after dinner Reba asked me to go with her to one of the empty bedrooms upstairs.

"Sure," I agreed and followed her up.

"How have you been, Laurel?" Reba asked, her voice filled with concern.

I didn't know how to answer her. "You've never really asked me about my personal life before," I blurted out.

"I know," she said. "God's been working with me on not focusing on myself so much anymore. Your mom told my mom that you have a new boyfriend, and she seemed to think he was pretty great. So," she said, getting comfortable on the bed, "tell me about him."

I sat on a chair beside the bed and opened up to my cousin about breaking up with Branson, getting together with Foster, and the previous night's events.

When I finished, she said, "I've been praying that you would get a new guy. I'm so glad you found someone better than Branson. But you've both got to continue your walks with Christ."

"I want to do that," I told her. "I'm just not sure how, now that I've messed up so badly."

"Just keep praying," she told me. "When you pray about your relationship, you'll be able to honor God in it."

I reached out and hugged her tight. "I know I made a mistake. Tell me, how can I correct it?"

"I don't know if you can," she said. "Are you truly sorry about it?"

"What do you mean?" I asked. "Of course I am."

"Are you sorry because you might lose this guy? Or are you sorry because you fell in your walk with Christ?"

Her words made me examine my heart. "Foster is really special," I said, "and I hate that I messed up. But even more, I hate the fact that after God was so good to me, I turned around and misused His gift."

"Why don't we pray right now?" Reba suggested. "God doesn't want you to worry. You just have to leave your relationship to Him."

After my cousin and I finished praying, I felt a lot better about my life and about my family. I went right downstairs and found my dad, and I gave him a great big kiss on the cheek.

There were a lot of uncertainties in my life, but one thing I was sure about. I had a great family and they meant the world to me.

———————————

On Christmas morning I woke up at the crack of dawn. I went into my grandmother's sunroom, got down on my knees, and spoke to God.

"Heavenly Father," I prayed aloud, "thanks for waking me up this morning. I know You sent Your Son to earth to save my soul and wash my sins away. I have practically ruined my relationship with Foster and probably ended our relationship with my selfishness. I was so consumed with fleshly desires that I didn't even consider what that moment would cost me. Foster McDowell means so much to me. If there is any way that You can soften his heart to forgive me, I would greatly appreciate it. I probably don't deserve another chance, but I sure want one. On this day when we celebrate the night that You sent Your Son to be born on this earth to save us from sin, let Your glory fill me. Come into my heart, Lord, and let Your glory fill this house."

I had started the day off the best way I possibly could. Thanking Him made me feel renewed and alive. This was the day the Lord had made. It was Christmas!

Breakfast was delicious and the conversation fascinating. We went around the table and spoke of our favorite holiday moments and what Christmas meant to each of us. I shared with my family that I felt baby Jesus in my heart. There was a calm inside me, even when things weren't really the way I wanted them to be. I knew I could look forward to the new year with hope.

As I talked about my renewing, tears flowed from my eyes. When I wiped them away, I noticed tears in my mom's and my grandmother's eyes too.

"Sometimes you get so full of things from the world that you don't realize how awesome God is," I said. "But He is so good!"

"I know what you mean," my dad said. "I guess that's why I do what I do for a living. Jesus Christ is the living truth and salvation. God has prepared a place for us in heaven that we can't even begin to imagine. I can't wait. I am so thankful that my children love the Lord." He looked at me with misty eyes. "Your life may not be the perfect Christian walk yet, Laurel, but just keep walking and keep trying. I'm mighty proud of you. You're a beautiful young woman, and any man should be proud to date you. I encourage you to keep thinking about Jesus. Let Him fill the void you may feel. He loves you more than anyone ever could. Even your mom. Even me."

After the presents had been opened, and lunch was gobbled up, and the leftovers were put away, and the dishes were all washed, the football games started on TV. While everyone watched, I slipped away to call my friends.

I called Meagan and she called Brittany on three-way. I told them all about my experience with Foster.

"He'll come around," Meagan said.

"I don't know," I said. "He was really disappointed."

We went on to talk about everything and nothing. Just as we were about to hang up, Brittany said, "Wait, Laurel, there's something else I want to talk to you about." She paused. "I haven't always been a good friend, but I really want to know how to become a better person. I raised my hand to become a Christian when I was a little kid, but now I want Him to control my life. I don't know what that means in terms of not doing things God doesn't like. How can the Lord give me what I need?"

"God wants you to seek Him," I said. "Study His Word. Get yourself into church."

"Will you help me do that?" she asked.

"Sure," I said gladly.

"Yeah, and help me too," Meagan added.

I laughed with my friends. "I'll help both you guys and myself," I told them. "We can start an accountability group."

"What's that?" Meagan asked.

"That's when you make a commitment to your friends to be sure they don't fall. And when they do, you make sure they're accountable so they don't do it again."

"I really need that," Brittany said.

"Me too," cried Meagan.

Night fell on a wonderful Christmas Day. Most of my family went caroling but I decided to stay inside. I curled up with a blanket and a cup of Russian tea. I envisioned Foster sitting next to me shaking his head in disappointment.

If only I had another chance, I said to myself.

The phone rang loudly.

"Hello?"

"Merry Christmas, Laurel Shadrach," Foster spoke sweetly into the phone.

My heart skipped a beat. "Are you calling to talk to Liam?"

He chuckled. "No, I talked to him earlier today. He called me. Gave me this number in case I wanted to talk to you."

"Foster, I'm so sorry about last night," I blurted out. "I ruined us."

"It's not just your fault. I share some of the responsibility." He paused. "We've got a lot to work through. We have to make sure God stays in it all."

"Does that mean you still want me to be your girl-friend?" I asked, barely breathing.

"Well, yeah," he said. "Of course. Why wouldn't I?"

My heart started beating again. We talked and laughed for over an hour. As I twirled the telephone cord around my finger, I looked at the star on the top of the Christmas tree and winked at it. It was my way of letting God know I was thankful for His special gift.

"Dating God's way isn't easy, is it?" I said to Foster.

"No," he admitted. "But I know God will show us how dating can be special without all the physical things. Christ can connect two souls when He is the common bond. Sin is real and it is in every human being. But when God sent His Son, sin was washed away."

I had another chance with Foster and I was not going to blow it. Together we would overcome the obstacles.

I had a lot to celebrate that Christmas. My ankle had completely healed. I was enjoying a wonderful visit with my family. My boyfriend still wanted to be my boyfriend. Most of all, I was celebrating the birthday of God's Son, who came to this earth to die on the cross for my sins.

Jesus loved me despite my faults. Realizing that was a great way of celebrating His birthday.

You may contact Stephanie Perry Moore at:
P. O. Box 81806
Conyers, GA 30013
dsssmoore@aol.com